A PLACE CALLED
SWEET SHRUB

A PLACE CALLED
SWEET SHRUB

Jane Roberts Wood

**Delacorte
Press**

Published by
Delacorte Press
Bantam Doubleday Dell Publishing Group, Inc.
666 Fifth Avenue
New York, New York 10103

Library of Congress Cataloging-in-Publication Data

Wood, Jane Roberts, 1929–
A place called Sweet Shrub / by Jane Roberts Wood.
p.   cm.
ISBN 0-385-30187-1
I. Title.
PS3573.05945P5   1990
813'.54—dc20   90-32497   CIP

Manufactured in the United States of America
Published simultaneously in Canada

November 1990

10   9   8   7   6   5   4

BVG

A Place Called Sweet Shrub is the second book of what is to be a trilogy. The trilogy is dedicated to my husband, Dub. Without his help and encouragement the books could not have been written.

FOR
MELINDA AND SUSAN
AND FOR
DAVID AND BARBARA

PART ONE

TIES THAT BIND

1

MATTRESSES TO BE aired and silver polished. Floors cleaned and waxed and windows that needed washing. Mama and Aunt Catherine had been in a stew for days. My brother George was coming home and bringing with him the Oklahoma girl he had married.

It takes Mama and Aunt Catherine days and days to get ready for company. The first of the week, we washed, starched, and ironed the curtains. Then we had Uncle Jerry take the downstairs rugs out and beat them while we cleaned and waxed the parlor and the dining room floors. But the next morning was lost—not a floor waxed, not a window washed.

And Jacqueline Balfour walked past our house!

She walked down our sidewalk, holding her head high, as if she were again on her way to the lectern to deliver the salutatory address for Bonham High. And it was the sight of Jacqueline that made me know I'd marry right away. I saw with startling clarity what Mama has been saying for years. Jacqueline is withering on the vine.

The town of Bonham has waited twenty-eight years for her to fulfill the promise that Mama says radiated from her when she made her salutatory speech in the Baptist church the night she graduated from Bonham High School. But long ago Mama gave up on Jacqueline. "Poor Jacqueline is withering right *on* the vine," Mama's been saying for as long as I can remember, never realizing the same thing might be said of Aunt

Catherine. But Aunt Catherine shows no signs of it, although she's quite different from Mama.

Mama can get herself into a state over anything. A cough ("It can go right into pneumonia," she says), lightning, white slavers, Germans, tramps, hydrophobia, scandal—anything!

This morning it was Mrs. Walker's unmade bed. Mama, with a list of cleaning supplies to pick up at the hardware store, had just left the house, had not been gone two minutes, when she came back, running up the steps and across the front porch.

"Lucy, Lucy! Come here quick! Catherine, where are you? Come in here!"

We hurried to the parlor where she sat in the rocking chair, collecting herself and fanning.

"Mama, what is it? What's the matter?" I cried, kneeling by her side.

"I'm afraid something awful has happened to Louise Walker," she said. "I know it has! Last night I had a terrible premonition about her."

Well.

Mama's premonitions are quite serious.

"Here, Carrie Belle, now drink this tea. It's mint. It will calm your nerves," Aunt Catherine said, handing her a glass of iced tea, smoothing a lock of hair from her face. "Now. What's the matter? Can you tell us what happened?"

"Oh, dear me. Well, I was running late, so I cut across Mrs. Walker's yard, and (you'll never believe this), I happened to glance in her bedroom window. And, oh Lord, that was when I saw it."

"What, Mama? What did you see?"

"Her bed! Mrs. Walker's bed *is still unmade*."

"And it's way after eight," Aunt Catherine said, looking at the clock. "Oh, Carrie, it does seem like something's wrong."

Now, although Mama gets hysterical about trouble, she does not run from it.

"We'll have to go down there," she said firmly, getting up from her rocker. "Oh, I knew something bad was going to happen to Louise. That was a terrible premonition I had about her last night. I'd better take this, just in case," she said, taking the poker from the fireplace, grasping it tightly, as the three of us started out the door.

I saw that Aunt Catherine had picked up the broom.

"I think I'll call Uncle Jerry to come with us," I said, running ahead and out to the garden, where I knew he'd be. "Uncle Jerry, we're afraid that something bad has happened to Mrs. Walker," I told him.

Bracing his back with his right hand, he slowly straightened up from the tomato plant he'd been staking.

"Well, now, miss. What makes you say that?"

"Mama walked by her house, and her bed's not been made."

"That is right uncommon," he said carefully. "Folks like Mrs. Walker and your mama, they generally makes they beds."

"You'd better come with us. No telling what we'll find down there."

"Reckon I'd better," he said.

We hurried, catching up with Mama and Aunt Catherine just before they reached the corner of Mrs. Walker's yard.

"Now, Mrs. Richards, Miss Catherine, ain't no call to get yourselves excited. May be nothing wrong," Uncle Jerry said as we reached the walk leading up to her front porch.

We stopped and, leaning forward, listened. Mrs. Walker's small gray cat walked, quietly as snow, toward us, and halfway down the front walk, lay quickly on its side and began to bathe a paw. Early roses, blooming on each side of the front walk, nodded vaguely in the cool of the morning. A blue jay hopped onto the lowest step and pecked loudly at a bug. The sky was a bright blue.

It began to dawn on me that we had become a spectacle. Again. Mama never seems to mind it, our being a spectacle, but I do.

Now Mama tiptoed up the sidewalk, with Aunt Catherine following close behind. "Uncle Jerry and I will wait out here," I whispered to her.

I was beginning to feel more and more foolish. Mama, her poker raised, ready to strike, was knocking on the door, calling, "Louise, oh, Louise," and Aunt Catherine was peering through the front parlor window. Then I heard a door open and close and footsteps coming down the hall.

Uncle Jerry looked down, solemnly studying his shoes, but not before I'd seen the smile that crossed his face. You're always doing this, I said silently to Mama. Embarrassing us!

The door opened and I heard Mrs. Walker say, "Why, Carrie Belle. And Catherine. Come in."

And, carefully leaning the poker and the broom against the wall, Mama enthusiastically declaring, "Oh, Louise, you gave us such a scare," followed by Aunt Catherine's "Well, we were just a little worried," in they went!

I sighed. "Come on, Uncle Jerry," I said. "Mrs. Walker's all right. Let's go on back home."

And it was then that I saw Jacqueline Balfour gliding toward us, her long, slender neck seeming barely able to support the wide-brimmed, rose-colored hat she wore; her small, slender feet encased in gray leather shoes, pointed and buttoned in the newest fashion; her violet garlanded skirt well above her ankles.

"Good morning, Lucy," she said, and the sweetness of her voice mocked her eyes, vague and abstracted, and her once gloriously red hair, now drying to a grayish brown. Then I saw the fine lines around her mouth and around her eyes and saw that even the leather handbag that she carried on her arm had the same fine lines, lines that made a crazy map across the leather. Drying. Everything about Jacqueline was cracked and drying. And it was then, right that minute, that I made up my mind. I'd be getting married soon.

And all that afternoon (the morning completely wasted), while Mama and Aunt Catherine scrubbed and waxed and polished, laughing at themselves one minute and worrying about Mrs. Walker the next, I knew it more strongly than ever.

"You mark my word, Catherine," Mama said at the supper table that night. "Something's the matter with Louise Walker. That unmade bed. It's an early sign."

"Well, it is odd," Aunt Catherine said. "Whoever heard of such a thing? Letting a bed air out in the house."

"Where would such an idea come from? Not making a bed because it needs to air out," said Mama.

"Air out from what?" Aunt Catherine said, lifting her eyebrows, laughing. "Mr. Walker's never in it!"

"Catherine! Hush now," Mama said, but she laughed right along with Aunt Catherine.

I knew why they laughed, and yet I didn't. But I thought a lot about getting married and getting into a bed with a man.

As soon as the dishes were done, I went up to my room, put on my gown, and went to bed. With the smell of roses and wild plum trees and honeysuckle coming through the open window and the breeze lifting the lace curtains from time to time and letting them fall back across my breasts, I thought about marriage, and I knew a man's hand on my breasts would feel as good as the lace curtains blowing back and forth. Then I thought about Jacqueline. I would never be like Jacqueline. She's fallen *off* the vine, I said silently to Mama. *I'm* the one that's withering.

2

SUNDAY AFTERNOON. Waking from a nap, always the most vulnerable time for me, I felt a twinge of dismay, a slight discontent. Here I was still in Bonham, had been here the past three years. And for what! Closing my eyes, I saw poor, befuddled Jacqueline again. But the cause of my discomfort was more than that. Christobel's letter had arrived yesterday, and the words in it were there, too, like sand in my shoe, rubbing a little, not enough to stop and shake out, but uncomfortably *there.*

Most days I was happy and contented. For, although Lillian was the beauty of the family (but so fat now with the baby she was carrying that she took almost every step hanging on to Edmund's arm), I was healthy and most would say pretty, if a little thin. And these past three years, I had been the savior of my family. Everybody in Bonham said so.

And I did have my prospects. There was Mr. Rather, who taught math in our high school and who could be quite funny. Just last Sunday when we were out for a drive, he got out of the buggy to open a gate, and suddenly there was his hat on the gate post. Then Mr. Rather pretended the hat was talking; and the two carried on such a funny conversation, the hat with an Irish accent, about *me,* Lucinda Eliza Richards, that I almost fell from the buggy, I laughed so hard.

And Mr. Mosley would marry me in a minute (Mama says I'd never want for anything as his wife), but the thought of watching four children pour molasses syrup on their biscuits every morning is more than I can bear. That is the reason I rarely accept an invitation from Mr. Mosley, though I am embarrassed to say such things about motherless children.

Then the letter came from Christobel, bringing with it the past. Christobel wrote to say her husband was dead, choked on a bite of steak (the Constables always ate well) at his own table, and her letter made me feel, for just a moment, a sense of loss as great as if I had opened my eyes and found both my arms severed.

Certainly, I felt the sadness of Christobel's loss. That long year in West Texas she had been friend, sister and, nursing me through pneumonia, mother to me. But feeling the sadness of her loss, I felt again my own. Losing a well-loved dog, a beloved fiancé, and a sister, losing them all that year in West Texas, although only the first is dead, had been almost too much to bear.

And even as the letter, however briefly, restored the past, it hinted of a future too lonely for contemplation. "Lucy, I never thought you'd be in Bonham three years!" Christobel had written. "You must plan for yourself some wonderful adventure. Without plans, dearest Lucy, the years can slip by, can leave one behind, adrift on the shore."

Christobel's words had stayed in my mind, made me wonder if I was already "adrift on the shore." It is true that I had come home again. But was I adrift, waiting for a future that might never come, just as Jacqueline Balfour, perhaps, had waited?

The town where I live is a small East Texas town. It is the place where I grew up and to which I had returned after teaching a year in West Texas. Oh, we were proud of our town. But Bonham, like most small towns, had these few (and Jacqueline was one), who were markedly different, and we accepted them because we knew them, pitied them. We accepted the habitual drunkenness of Old Man Tyler, who was as often as not passed out beneath the carriage or automobile upon which he worked, and who would, on occasion, grab a child's ankle, chortling gleefully, before releasing the child to run home terrified to his mother; and the consummate goodness of the rabbi (a saint's life is more suspect than most), who looked steadily out at the town through those dark, clever, brooding eyes. Even the dangerous goings-on of Dilsey Fisher, dangerous because it was whispered that as many Negroes as whites came into her house through the back door, were accepted. And the invisible deterioration of Jacqueline, who walked into the country every day, some said as far as ten miles, and then would stand waiting in the middle of the dusty road for someone, anyone, to happen by and bring her back into town —*that* filled us with pity. Oh, and our own Leslie. Our brilliant Leslie who had been graduated summa cum laude from Harvard, who had come back home and had never gone out again, who had *never gone out,* but instead, had had his groceries and his laundry delivered, and the books he used for his inventions and his patents delivered. Even Leslie, once our beautiful young boy (I have seen his picture), now oddly old, broomsticked with his ill-assorted clothes hanging on, his face pole-thin, his gray hair long and sparse. But he was still a sweet man and oh, so polite, always, said his cleaning woman; and, this from Mr. Mac who owned the corner grocery, when the ox was in the ditch, and he himself delivered the groceries, there Leslie might be, whistling and working on some invention, never glancing around, but even so always polite and our town's own genius. Certainly Leslie was one of ours. Our attitude toward those few who were markedly different had always been one of caring and acceptance, an acceptance that comes in a small town because we knew these special ones, had always known them.

But which of us would join them, willingly become one of them? The thought terrified me beyond all measure.

Well.

If I had learned anything at all since my return to Bonham, it was not to lie in bed brooding, especially with company coming.

Relieved to be fully awake, I shrugged off the past, put aside the future, dressed and went downstairs, tiptoeing so as not to disturb Aunt Catherine, who has not been well these past weeks. Then I made myself a glass of lemonade and sat in the front porch swing, hoping Maggie Owens, who was coming for supper and a heart-to-heart talk, would arrive before Mr. Mosley, who was coming to take us for a ride in the country.

I knew that Maggie wanted to talk about George, my brother. She has been crazy about him since the third grade, but there's no hope for Maggie there. George is happily married to an Oklahoma girl.

At church just this morning I told Maggie that George was bringing Inez home to Bonham for the first time.

"We're expecting them next Saturday," I said.

"Oh, Lucy," she said wistfully, "after such a long time, I can't believe George will be right here in Bonham again. I remember so well the night he left. He said—"

But whatever my brother had said to Maggie was lost, for just then Mr. Mosley had walked up.

"Miss Richards, I'd like to take you for a drive later on this afternoon. Would you be free?"

When Mr. Mosley is excited, his right eyebrow jumps, and that was happening now. I tried not to look at it.

"A ride would be nice, Mr. Mosley. But Maggie Owens is coming for supper tonight."

I loved Mr. Mosley's automobile, and sometimes I thought of how I'd look in it if it were mine, but here were his children, hanging on to his legs, peeping out at me around his coattails and Emily Anne, the baby, in his arms peeping through her fingers. All Mr. Mosley's children are shy.

"Why, I'd like to have Miss Owens's company too," he said, beaming at us, not seeing that Emily Anne had pulled his watch from his watchpocket and had a good bit of it in her mouth.

I looked at Maggie. She looked at me. "Well," we said together.

"Good," he said, and noticing the watch, "Now, Emily Anne, you can't chew on Daddy's watch." His voice was gentle, and I liked him for that.

"I'll call for you ladies around five," he said, tipping his hat and moving away slowly, the children clinging to his legs, his coattails, and now Emily Anne was crying and waving good-bye at the same time.

"Oh, Maggie, I'm so glad you're going with me," I told her. "With someone else along, Mr. Mosley's company can be quite pleasant."

"We'll come home early," she said. "And then we'll put our heads together and think of somebody else to wipe those noses, button up those shoes."

Sometimes Maggie had the strangest sense of humor. When she said that she bent over double laughing, but I didn't think it was funny. My family liked Mr. Mosley, and after all, it was up to me to give away a prospect.

That afternoon, when Mr. Mosley had carefully driven us out by the river, through the fairgrounds and past his big house in Russell Heights, he took his leave. Then after a light supper with Mama and Aunt Catherine,

Maggie and I were free, *finally,* to talk about George. Poor, poor Maggie, still in love with him.

We went upstairs to my room, and with me sitting on the bed and Maggie for the most part pacing restlessly about the room, we talked, or rather, Maggie talked and I listened. Looking smart as ever, she fiddled with her lemon-colored gloves and her sash, bright against the gray of her dress, as she tremulously raised question after question about George.

"When George and Inez arrive for their visit next week, should I come right over to see them?" and before I could answer this question, "Lucy, maybe it would be better if I arranged a solitary meeting with George. You could help me. After all, I *am* your best chum."

"Maggie, I just couldn't do that. You're my best chum, but Inez is my sister now."

"Well, what if I run into George? Sooner or later I'm bound to run into him. Whatever *will* I say to him? What do you suppose he'll say to me? What if I just said right out, 'George, I'll always love you.' Oh, Lucy, what would he say then?"

She put a hand over her heart and sat down in the window seat to recover from the thought of what he might say. I looked closely at Maggie, six months older than I, relieved that she showed no signs of withering.

"Maggie, there's more than one fish in the sea. One day you'll meet somebody you will love more than you ever loved George," I told her, hoping that the words were true.

But Maggie tossed her head and looked out the window. "Divorce is certainly a possibility in this day and age," she said.

"Not in our family," I said.

I dozed off as she talked on and on, about George, about Inez, about Inez and George, and woke to see her pushing the yellow gloves onto the fingers of her hands, hearing, "Lucy, spend the night with me tomorrow. We can talk all night."

"I will if I can, Maggie. But with all this company coming, there's a lot to do. Come on. I'll walk you half-way home," I told her sleepily, and I did. We parted, calling out good night, good night, calling out to each other past the magnolia blossoms, luminous against the blackness of the leaves.

"Till tomorrow," she called. "I'll see you tomorrow."

I decided that when I spent the night with her, I'd tell Maggie she'd just have to forget about George.

3

MAMA, HAVING RECOVERED from the crisis of Mrs. Walker's bed, and I, content with my decision to marry soon, threw ourselves into the excitement of getting the house ready for George and Inez. By Wednesday we had waxed and polished all the floors, washed the rest of the windows, aired the mattresses, had Uncle Jerry take the upstairs rugs out and beat them, and sent for the scavenger man to come and clean the privy. The curtains, clouds of white organdy, lay across the spare room bed, waiting to be hung.

"No, Lucy, the curtains go up last," Mama said as I started to hang them. "They're the finishing touch."

On Thursday I scrubbed all the porches. There's something about being outside in the early morning air with the smell of lye soap and vinegar water washing away the light coating of dust and the feel of cool sudsy water on my bare feet that I enjoy, although Mama doesn't like to see me do it. "Don't ever let a man see your feet," she warns. "He'll think less of you."

The day before George and Inez were to arrive, we were exhausted, but the house had never looked better, smelled sweeter. Now there was the food to prepare, the flowers to arrange, and the silver to polish, still so much to do that Mama closed the hardware store. We baked pies and a cake, shelled peas, snapped beans, and doubled our usual order for artificial ice. Then we hung the curtains and put flowers from Aunt Catherine's cut-flower garden in every room.

I'd never seen Mama and Aunt Catherine as excited. Oh, George and Inez had planned to come before. Every year for the last three years we had expected them. But that first year Inez's father had died, and the next year George couldn't get away and then Inez was sick. But now they were really coming home. And I was excited too. After all, it's not every day a girl meets her new sister.

On Saturday afternoon, about four, George and Inez arrived. Seeing George's tall, slender form as he stepped from behind the wheel of a sleek black Marmon, it seemed to all the women in his family that he was a prince returning. We have always doted on George.

Then I saw Inez. As tall as George, slender, her figure almost boyish, she stood in the large tonneau, waiting for his hand. When he helped her from the car, the jewels on the hand he took caught the sun, showering cascades of tiny lights revolving upon her pale white face, her sleekly coiffed black hair, her glorious green dress. We watched her stride quickly up the walk, her long, slim thighs moving underneath the silk.

Running lightly up the steps, she held her cheek, for a moment, next to Mama's. "Mother Richards," she said, her voice unexpectedly hoarse, "it's been such a long time, and it was such a short visit." Holding out her hand to me, "You must be Lucy," she said. Her voice was serious as she asked, "How did you manage to teach all those wild children in that far-off place? Where was it you taught? Estelline? Well, George says you're the only woman in Texas who could have tamed them." Then, leaning over, bringing her face almost level with Aunt Catherine's, she said, "Catherine, I hope we can get to know each other. Let's have long talks right here," giving the swing a gentle nudge with her hand.

How easily we became her slaves in those few minutes

and now I understood the wonder in their voices when the family spoke of her. Entranced by the exotic, we suddenly remembered George, or at least, remembered to welcome him home. All that evening we tried, and failed, not to watch her every move while she, making no pretense, watched us steadily with her dark, smoky eyes.

Now she led the way into the house. Pleased, I think, with our wide-eyed enjoyment of his bride, George said, grinning at us all, "I'll get the bags from the car. Mama, where have you put us? In my old room?"

"You'll be in my room," I said, running ahead of Inez up the stairs, glad I had consented to move into Katie's room for their visit. Of all the bedrooms mine has the best view, and in Inez's presence, George's room with its slanting roof and small windows seemed far too small.

"I'll be back in a few minutes to see if you need anything," I said, drawing the curtains to soften the glare of the late afternoon sun.

"Oh, Lucy, stay," Inez said. "Stay and tell me about Bonham, and about your friends."

Stripping the rings from her fingers, the bracelets from her arms, unmindful of her dress or of the carefully made bed, she plumped up the pillows and leaned back against the headboard.

"Oh, Lucy, I wanted to come back sooner, but we just couldn't seem to get away. George was so happy to be coming home, he sang all the way from Tulsa. He is real musical. Why, he could be a singing star."

It was clear as anything that Inez was smitten with my brother. When Maggie saw how it was with the two of them, she would realize she'd *have* to forget him.

Inez leaned forward. "Lucy, you're not still . . . put out, are you? About Katie and Bob? I felt so sorry for you when that happened, but George says any man who'd give you up doesn't deserve you."

I turned my face away. I hated pity, and after all this time it was shocking to hear his name, to hear a question asked right out about him. And my sister, Katie.

"I'd rather not talk about that," I said finally. But the question pierced my heart, and I couldn't still the voice inside my head that whispered *betrayed, betrayed*. And by my own *sister*!

Inez, turning her great black eyes on me, found another subject. "You know, George worked for Daddy," she said. "He found oil for him, and now he's found some for us." And hearing George's steps, she turned her head toward the door. "Thank you, dearest," she said, as he set the bags inside the door.

Why, she's older, I thought, seeing her face in repose, a face somehow . . . famished.

George gestured toward the bags. "Which ones do you need?" he asked, smiling happily at her, then at me.

"All of them. Every one, and George, you're just beaming," she teased. "Lucy, in the bosom of his family, is he always like this?"

"We love him," I said, not knowing how to tease about love.

"Well, I do too," she said.

George leaned over, cupped her chin, and kissed her. "You," he said and left the room.

"Lucy, I'm going to get more comfortable," Inez said, unbuttoning her dress, stepping out of it. Then she opened a small bag and took from it a dressing gown. When she slipped it on, the purples and greens and oranges, gaudy a moment earlier, were subdued by her glistening eyes and her hair, released and hanging in soft coils below her waist.

"I think I'll have a little nap now, and then freshen up

for dinner. Tell George to wake me up in plenty of time. And Lucy," she said as I stood in the open door, "I'm so glad to be here with my new family."

But without being waked, she came early to the kitchen. My sister, Lillian, had just walked in and I was slicing the potatoes when her husky "Mother Richards, may I help?" followed by the silken sound of her dress and the woodsy scent of her perfume filled the kitchen so that we, beset by her otherness, were distracted from our ordinary tasks. Even the tapping of her long fingernails against Mama's cut-glass bowl, as she arranged roses and grapes and bright leaf lettuce into a centerpiece unlike any we had seen before, made us pause as if to decipher some cabalistic message she was tapping out, sending only to her husband's family.

"Is that a centerpiece?" Lillian whispered, but Lillian knew as well as I that it was beautiful.

The talk at dinner was stranger still, the food not once mentioned, although we sipped the sherry George had brought and said we liked it. But we talked about oil wells and their new house in Tulsa and the war in Europe (Mama telling us she'd had a premonition that the Germans would come right across the ocean, move into our house, and make us their slaves), and we talked about the roads to New Orleans and Georgian silver.

At first, Lillian's countenance as she watched Inez was a mixture of disapproval and wonder. As the evening passed, however, her voice took on a husky note, and her laugh came more quickly. By the time we were in the parlor, Lillian, with a bright blue scarf thrown over her shoulders, had become, from the shoulders up, surprisingly exotic. Of course, from the shoulders down, she was just expecting, no getting around it.

But each of us in our own way watched Inez that night. In a sense she was pinned against the wall, held there by our imitations and by our insatiable curiosity, and by a night so warm that Aunt Catherine had to go to bed right after dinner, and Lillian, leaning heavily on Edmund's arm, soon after. Then, and I wasn't sure why, but one minute Inez was moving to the music that I played, swaying with the swing of her green silk dress and humming deep in her throat, "Come to me, my melancholy baby, cuddle up and don't be blue," and the next she was falling, her "George, George" pulling at our hearts as she fell into his arms and was swept up and carried off to bed. Mama looked straight at me, raising her eyebrows and shaking her head ever so slightly. And all at once, I felt like a child again, outside a world I wasn't sure I wanted to enter.

After we had all gone to bed for the night, I heard George come downstairs and, taking up his banjo, play the song Inez had hummed. "Come to me, my melancholy baby," he played, twisting the melody around the beat, "Cuddle up and don't be blue," varying it, but playing it over and over again. "All your fears are foolish fancy, maybe, but you know dear, that I'm in love with you," he played again and again, making the song sadder than any I had ever heard.

Inez was first downstairs next morning, down before Aunt Catherine. But soon after, Aunt Catherine must have taken her morning tea and joined Inez in the front porch swing, for their soft voices and low chuckles came up from the porch, over the dormers, and into my open windows. I dressed, went down, and sat on the front steps while they glided back and forth in the swing, Inez's slender foot now and then nudging it into movement.

"I've been married before," she said, looking at Aunt Catherine. "Twice," she added firmly. I think she did not hear my quick intake of breath, and Aunt Catherine merely nodded. Inez, satisfied by her response, added, "George doesn't mind."

Aunt Catherine smiled at her. "Honey, it's as clear as the sky is blue this morning that George loves you. Course it doesn't matter."

Aunt Catherine is like that. She accepts anything. If I told her I had murdered somebody, she would nod in just that way and, maybe, help me truss up the body.

At ten this morning, George and Inez left for an overnight shopping trip to Dallas (Dallas has more shops than Bonham), taking Mama with them. "I'd better stay here with Aunt Catherine," I told them, glad to be away for a little while from Inez's chatter and Mama's fretting.

Now the house was quiet, except for Aunt Catherine's coughing. I worried about her. She seemed weaker. When I had first come back to Bonham, she was able to work in her garden, but now she often sat shelling peas or mixing up a cake or, in the evenings, doing fragile, beautiful handwork. Her hands were never idle. She was still busy, but now more quietly so.

I thought about walking over to tell Maggie that divorce was certainly not out of the question, but I didn't.

Being in the house alone, except for Aunt Catherine, was relaxing. I thought it was nice that they were planning to stay overnight in Dallas.

4

SOON AFTER Mama and George and Inez left, I went down to fix something for dinner. Aunt Catherine called from her little room off the kitchen. Lying in her narrow bed, already she seemed quite ill. Pale. Eyes sunken.

When I answered her call, she sat up and, coughing, tried to speak. When she lay back, her handkerchief was sodden with blood. I had the strongest feeling that she was in mortal danger and that the enemy that threatened her life must be set upon. Must be fought off.

I took the handkerchief, and, trying to sound very calm, I said, "Aunt Catherine, it's hot in this room. I'm going to put you in the parlor where it's cool. You can see the garden there."

I hurried into the parlor to make her bed, fetching pillows and sheets from the linen chest.

"Now, Aunt Catherine, just lean on me," I said.

Already she seemed frail as a feather, her bony fingers clutching my arm. Slowly we made our way through the kitchen into the parlor where I'd made a bed on the sofa, softening it with worn cotton quilts and linen sheets and feather pillows.

All that morning I brought her little tisanes—herbal, lemon, bourbon. She would sip a little and then fall back into a spasm of coughing or a restless sleep.

"I'm going to call Dr. Grey," I told her in the early afternoon. By then she was covered with sweat. Her body glistened with it.

"No, Lucy, don't call the doctor. This will pass. I'll be better in the morning."

"All right," I told her. "But you just lie here quietly and I'll run to the pharmacy. Mr. Harkness will know what to send."

I flew to the pharmacy and ran all the way home.

"Mr. Harkness says this is just the ticket," I said as I gave her a tablespoon of Botanic Blood Balm. She gagged. More blood. Then, still perspiring, she fell into a deep sleep.

I tiptoed into the hall and called Dr. Grey. "Aunt Catherine is real sick. She's asleep right now. She didn't want me to call you, but I think you'd better come out."

"Is she in any pain?" he asked.

"She doesn't seem to be, but she's worn out from coughing. And there's blood."

"Sleep is the best thing for her. Let her sleep, Lucy. I'll stop by first thing in the morning to see her. But if she gets any worse, you call me. Hear?"

I said I would and I tiptoed back into the parlor and eased myself quietly into a chair, guarding her. She moaned, opened her eyes, and looked at me. Slowly she shook her head. Grieving. Grieving. Sadness deep in her eyes. Unbidden, the thought came: Why, she's grieving her own death.

I took her small hand in mine. "Oh, Aunt Catherine. You'll be all right. I'm going to take such good care of you. When you're strong again, we'll go to Colorado. You and I. Live on a hill. With the whippoorwill." Now I was crying.

She squeezed my hand and slept again. I slipped into her room and opened the medicine chest at the foot of her bed. As I stood there, looking at the jars and bottles and bandages, the chest seemed empty, its magic gone.

Aunt Catherine had always known just which potions to choose, which herbs to mix.

About five o'clock that afternoon she woke up. "Lucy, I'm feelin' better. There's some chicken broth in there. I could have a little of that."

Aunt Catherine was better. Such a feeling of relief swept over me. Aunt Catherine would live. Holding the tears back, I blinked. We had won.

I heated the broth and poured a glass of cool milk. Then I put the food on a silver tray and went out to get a flower from the garden. A hollyhock. Just as the screen door closed behind me, a guttural sound came from the parlor. Harsh. Subhuman.

I ran back into the parlor. Blood. Boiling out of her upraised mouth as she desperately tried to right herself. I put my hand behind her shoulders and held her upright, wiping away the blood that came pulsing out, each surge sending a fresh bolt of terror to my heart.

Pushing pillows behind her, I ran again to the telephone. "Miss Opal, get Dr. Grey quick. Hurry! Oh, please hurry."

Back to Aunt Catherine. The bleeding had slowed. Almost stopped. She was unconscious. Or dead. Under the streaks of blood, her face was whiter than any sheet. The rank smell of blood filled the room. But this *thing* lying so still was not Aunt Catherine! It was only a grotesque caricature of Aunt Catherine. All gentleness gone, her terrible struggle had left only this awful lewdness of gaping mouth and clumsy arms.

Then I was running, running away from the thing that lay on the sofa. "Somebody help me. Somebody please help me," I sobbed.

Dimly aware of Dr. Grey's car passing me on the way to our house, I kept on running, past houses, the stores, the church. Reaching the Owenses' pasture, I threw myself down in the open field and cried for a minute. But then I told myself, "Lucinda Richards, where is the starch in your backbone?" and I stood up and started back to the house.

Hurrying, then running again, I saw Dr. Grey's car parked in front. I walked up the porch steps and, through the windows, I watched him take his stethoscope from his pocket, lean over and listen to her chest. Straightening, he shook his head. Suddenly he wheeled and went into the kitchen. I ran around to the back door. When I came in, he was washing his hands in the kitchen sink.

"Is she . . . ?"

"She's alive, but just barely," he said. "There's not much I can do about tuberculosis, but I'll stay with her. Do what I can. I told her years ago she needed a drier climate, but she just refused to leave her family. Lucinda, make some coffee. We've got our work cut out for us this night."

Through all that long night, Dr. Grey and I watched. "I'm sorry I ran away," I told her silently, and "I've always loved you best," I said to her unconscious form.

I was there when she opened her eyes and looked up at me and then at Dr. Grey, astonishment at the catastrophe that had overtaken her plainly visible on her face.

"Now, Miss Catherine," Dr. Grey said kindly, "I'm going to give you something to help you sleep."

She looked crushed, lying there. Trampled. Her face was still streaked with blood, her hair matted with it.

"I'll sponge you off," I said to her.

"No. Let her be," Dr. Grey said. "We don't want the bleeding to start again. A bath can wait awhile."

He administered a sleeping potion and when her breathing was deeper, although still unsteady, he left me there to watch alone.

"I'll be back about nine. She'll sleep till then," he said.

At nine he returned, and as he listened to Aunt Catherine's breathing and felt her pulse, she woke, but only briefly.

"She's a little better," he said. "Her pulse is stronger. Breathing steady. When she wakes up again, bathe her and give her some broth. Nothing heavy. I'll stop in again this evening."

"I'm so ashamed, Dr. Grey. I ran away when she needed me."

"Somedays, I'd like to run away myself," he said. "But sorrow rides a swift horse. You can't run away from it."

And sitting there throughout that long day, watching her sleep, I heard his voice again and again: *Sorrow rides a swift horse. You can't run away from it!*

Mama and George and Inez came home the next afternoon. The minute Mama walked in the door, I felt like a child again, crying and blowing my nose.

Hearing the car, "Mama's here" I whispered to Aunt Catherine and flew to the door. "Aunt Catherine's sick," I told her. "She was so sick I had to call the doctor. She almost died."

"What—" The rest of her words were cut off by the sight of Aunt Catherine, pale and shattered, still there on the sofa in the parlor, her breath wobbly and uncertain, her cotton gown not masking her fragility.

I motioned Mama into the dining room.

"She almost died," I said again. "Oh, Mama, I'm glad you're here." Putting it all in Mama's lap. Relief. Blessed relief.

But Mama's voice was as unsure as Aunt Catherine's next breath. "George, what will we do? If she's worse, what should we do?" she sobbed.

But George was going up the stairs by Inez's side, leaving behind Inez's frightened "My God, George, that's contagious. That stuff is really contagious," leaving the words floating in the air.

Then Mama, still crying, said, "I bought you a new silk dress, Lucy. Inez picked it out for you. It's green with roses scattered across the silk. But, Lucy, it's not at all suitable for a . . . for a funeral."

"Mama, don't talk about funerals. Aunt Catherine's not going to die. We won't let her."

"Well, she could get better," Mama said, brightening almost immediately. "She had a spell like this when you were in West Texas, but we didn't tell you. We just didn't want to worry you."

"See? That's been three years, and she's been all right since. Maybe a little weaker's all."

"Lucy, I don't know what I'd do without you," Mama said, looking tired and drawn.

"Why, anyone can live a long time with consumption," I told her. "Years and years."

But I knew Aunt Catherine would never be all right again. And all the while I smoothed her bed and plumped up her pillows, I heard Dr. Grey's voice saying, *Sorrow rides a swift horse. You can't run away from it.*

5

IT MIGHT HAVE been Aunt Catherine's illness. Or perhaps it was our general fatigue. But whatever the reason, after that night Inez was family. At supper that night, we even talked about the food.

"Let's talk about something more interesting than food when George and Inez get here," I had cautioned Mama and Aunt Catherine before their arrival.

"Well, what then?" Mama asked crossly.

"Oh, the war, travel, poetry," I said, thinking of Josh Arnold, my dear friend from West Texas, when I said the last.

But this evening it was Inez who brought up the subject of food.

"These peaches are so sweet and good," she said. "Are they from your trees?"

"These came from my own little orchard," Lillian said, jumping right in, "and Edmund picked the blackberries."

Edmund beamed.

Since George and Inez's arrival, Lillian and Edmund had been taking their evening meals with us. Before that, Mama and I, because of Lillian's condition, had been taking their meals down to them.

"It's no trouble," Mama would assure Lillian each evening when we arrived with their entire supper. "We enjoy it, don't we, Lucy? It's easy to snap an extra handful of beans, slice another tomato, put on a bigger pot roast."

But now, since George and Inez's arrival, Lillian made

her way down the street each evening. Her stomach, billowing out in front like the sail of a ship, seemed to pull her along, and Edmund, at her elbow, helped her step off the curb, cross the streetcar tracks, held her elbow as he guided her the half block from their house to ours. In my opinion, ever since she lost her first baby, Lillian's been a little spoiled.

Tonight, Lillian's back giving her trouble, they got right up from the table and left, before a single dish was washed. I did the dishes and then joined the rest of the family in the parlor, except for Aunt Catherine, who had gone to bed early.

And that night, without Aunt Catherine's easy talk and Lillian's laughter (she can get tickled over nothing), and George saying he couldn't sing "When a Fellow's on the Level with a Girl That's on the Square"—a song with the easiest range in the world—because of a scratchy throat, Inez's steady drinking of her small glasses of sherry, one after the other, became obvious. Pretending not to watch, but watching, Mama and I avoided each other's eyes as we secretly took stock, counting the glasses of sherry and, later, averted our eyes from Inez's slow, stumbling progress up the stairs. Right after George and Inez went up, I decided to go to bed, too, unwilling or unable to share with Mama the raised eyebrow, the shoulder's shrug, the gesture that would have said "I know. Yes, I know."

"Good night, Mama," I said, kissing her cheek, knowing her eyes were lifted to the room above the parlor, George and Inez's room.

Then I went into Aunt Catherine's room to say good night, but her heavy breathing told me she was already asleep. I ran up the stairs, undressed, and got into Katie's bed. Forcing my body into stillness, I tried not to hear the murmurs, the laughter, a pillow's light thump as it fell to the floor, the swish of bedcover tossed aside, the rhythmic sounds of the bedsprings, the suppressed cries.

When the house was quiet again, I rose and tiptoed down the stairs, quietly opened the kitchen door, and sat on the back porch steps, the siltlike dirt beneath my bare feet a pleasant coolness.

Leaving Bonham was out of the question now. Aunt Catherine needed me. And so did Mama. "Lucy, I have almost too much to bear," she'd said sadly, only the night before. "Why, if I didn't have you, I don't know what I'd do." Choosing between Mr. Rather and Mr. Mosley, I'd marry and stay in Bonham forever. At least, I'd never be like Aunt Catherine, who until her illness had always been the first to rise and the last to go to bed, who lived in the smallest room, who, somehow, spent her days on the fringe of life. And when I thought of Aunt Catherine, of Jacqueline Balfour, of all those who live always on the outside, the idea of marriage to Mr. Rather or Mr. Mosley did not displease me.

Coming from somewhere—the magnolia, the corner of the house, (now it sounded as if it were underfoot), a cricket chirped. The moon was so bright I could see the freckles on my hands. The night was awash with moonlight. The leaves on the trees, the magnolia blossoms, each blade of grass around the worn bare circle enclosing my feet, each hair on my arm—all had been dipped in the moon's soft light. The breeze quickened, bringing with it the piercing, bitter smell of ragweed, and suddenly Josh Arnold's face was there before me. His voice was in my ears: *I love you, Lucy. I've loved you since "I was tangled in thy beauty's web, and snared by the ungloving of thy hand."* Josh Arnold loved poetry, especially Keats. I wondered where he was this very minute. Maybe on his way back to Tennessee. He thought we'd be at war soon. But he was wrong about that. President

Wilson had firmly declared our neutrality. I wondered what Josh Arnold would think of Mr. Rather. Of Lillian. Of Bonham. Next to Christobel, he had been my best friend in West Texas, but never more than that. It was Bob's touch I had hungered for, his voice I longed to hear. Betrayed by him and by my own sister; still, there were times when I longed for that which could never be.

Well. There *were* other fish in the sea, I told myself. I'd find somebody to love more than I ever loved Bob Sully. And Mama said love often followed marriage. Sometimes, Mama was right about things. I would marry, probably Mr. Rather, and live right here in Bonham.

But all the same, I knew I'd like to see Josh Arnold again. And Christobel. I thought about all the children I had taught that year in West Texas. I hoped they were happy. And still in school and learning. I thought about Mr. Sully, who had hired me, his kindness to me. I would not let myself think about Bob and Katie.

6

GEORGE AND INEZ stayed another week, although Inez was plainly uneasy about Aunt Catherine's condition. And now I understood certain household precautions— Aunt Catherine's separate dishes, the care she took to drink pure cream and to have lots of fresh butter, her "Now, Lucy," as she turned away from some spontaneous gesture of affection on my part, precautions I had never noticed.

She was weak as a kitten and Dr. Grey's report each morning was always the same: "She's holding her own. I expect she'll begin to improve in a day or two." I'd never known Aunt Catherine to be cross, but now she fretted about her garden, about the piano being out of tune, about Mrs. Walker not coming to visit her. Most of all, she worried about putting a damper on George's visit. It was this that convinced me we should go ahead with the party we had planned for George and Inez.

"We're having a party," I told him, "for you and Inez."

His face lit up. Oh, George has the sweetest smile, and just then, with a lock of blond hair falling over his forehead and his bright blue eyes, he looked like he was about sixteen. He put his arm around my waist and whirled me across the parlor rug.

"We won't tell Mama, but what we'll have is a dance," he said, laughing.

Now, the Richardses have always loved a party, and a dance more than anything. And although we had never had one at our house, we are all good dancers. There's nothing like it to lift one's spirits. I went right to the phone and invited Maggie Owens first. Then I rang up Mr. Rather and asked him to come.

"Mr. Rather, bring Mr. Porterfield along," I said. I had not met Mr. Porterfield, the new Latin teacher, but I hoped he could dance. "We'll be dancing," I said.

"Really!" Mr. Rather said, knowing Mama, while not opposed to dances, had never allowed one in our house.

Determined to have plenty of partners, I hesitated only a minute before ringing up Mr. Mosley. He's smooth as silk doing the waltz and the two-step, although he sits out the fox trot.

"Why Lucinda, I'd be delighted," he said. "And I'd like to have a little supper party for your brother and his wife. Would you all be free some evening?"

I was sorry I'd asked him. Mr. Mosley complicates things.

"They're leaving a few days early," I said, crossing my fingers. "So they don't have a free evening. But they're looking forward to meeting you."

I invited George's friends and mine, and the young married crowd that Lillian and Edmund run with. George found Uncle Jerry in the garden and told him we'd be needing a piano player.

Uncle Jerry shook his head. "Now, Mr. George, your mama won't like it," he said.

"Well, I know Mama, and she just might enjoy a dance," he said, grinning. "Besides, she told me the other day her preacher's gone to Galveston."

Uncle Jerry looked doubtful.

"You get us a piano player, and whether Mama lets him play or not he gets a fiver."

Uncle Jerry said he'd get his nephew.

The day of the party, Inez hung Japanese lanterns in the garden, and I went down to the hardware store so

Mama could come home and bake the cakes. And Aunt
Catherine perked up.

Dr. Grey stopped by. "You're better this morning, Catherine Richards," he said. "You can sit up a little while
tonight." We made her a bed on the settle bench in the
dining room so she could watch the activity.

I was planning to wear the green dress Mama had
brought from Dallas, but Inez said, "Wear it another
time. Tonight wear my blue chiffon. The blue is perfect
for you, and I want to do your hair a new way."

I tried on her dress, a soft blue chiffon with bugle
beads and deep ruffles in the skirt. "Goodness," I said,
whirling around in it. "I'll have to be careful in this. You
can see my knees."

"For the Lord's sake, Lucy, don't worry about that!
What's knees?" Inez said.

That night when the party began, I thought everything was going to be just perfect. When a fox trot
started, Mr. Rather would step right up before Mr. Mosley had time to take me to my seat. I was dancing every
dance and having a wonderful time. Well, except for
when Maggie arrived.

We had talked a dozen times that day, about how she
would do her hair, what she would wear, whether she
should come with someone, about what she would say to
George. But when she came it was hard. Coming up the
walk, she was smiling and holding her head high, but
the minute she saw George, she wilted. Her smile was
forced as she took Inez's hand, her movements stiff
when she turned to George.

"Maggie," I wanted to say to her, "where is the starch
in your backbone?" She looked like a Maggie ten years
older than she had looked a minute earlier coming up
the walk. I pushed Mr. Rather away. "Go dance with

Maggie," I told him. And he did. A little later, I said,
"George, say *something* to Maggie! Dance with her!"

"Oh, Maggie's all right," he said, whirling Inez onto
the middle of the parlor floor.

His answer seemed heartless to me, almost cruel, but
Mama thinks George is perfect. Certainly, he is the only
one who could have gotten away with a dance at our
house. After a while I saw that even Mama, sitting on
the sofa tapping her foot, was enjoying herself, and
Maggie was dancing almost every dance with Mr.
Porterfield, clearly the best dancer there. I forgot about
Maggie and began to enjoy myself once again. But then
stepping into the dining room a little later, I heard the
news that ruined the party.

"George, dear, can't you and Inez come back in a few
weeks?" Mama said as she wiped a smudge of icing off
George's chin. "This is the first time she'll be home—"
and the sudden burst of laughter from the parlor
drowned out the rest. But then I heard "private railway
car," and I knew what Mama was talking about. *They*
were coming home. With little Annabel and in their own
railway car, they'd be arriving in splendor. And Mama
hadn't even told me!

I had never been so mad. I wondered if Aunt Catherine
knew. And Lillian. Did she know? Did everybody know
but me?

I wheeled around, went into the parlor, and walked up
to Mr. Porterfield. "Mr. Porterfield," I said firmly, "can
you do the Kitchy Koo?"

He was surprised, but he hesitated only a minute.
Then he raised his eyebrows and grinned. "Sure," he
said.

I turned to Will at the piano. "Play 'Ballin' the Jack,' "
I told him. And we slid right into it. The movements I
had imagined in the privacy of my bedroom were there

waiting, and Mr. Porterfield added others. Mr. Mosley frowned and looked away; Mr. Rather grinned and looked down. When Mama came into the parlor she said, "Lucy!" but I pretended not to hear. She should have told me Katie was coming home. And in the middle of the Kitchy Koo I decided to get engaged before they arrived.

7

GEORGE AND INEZ left the next day. I helped him take the bags out to the automobile.

"Wait a minute, Lucy," George said as I turned to go back into the house. "You told me once to get away from Bonham. Now I'm telling you. Lucy, this loving, sweet family of ours will nibble away at your life, bit by bit, until you won't have any left. You *have* to get away."

"I can't leave Aunt Catherine right now. And Mama needs me at the store. Besides all that, Lillian's baby will be here soon, and, oh, George, what's one more year?" I didn't tell him I had decided to get married right away.

I no longer felt angry, only sad. When Aunt Catherine had said good-bye to George her brown eyes were full of unshed tears. Words that could not be said hung in the air as George sat on her bed, patted her hand, teased her about being lazy. Mama, too, hated to see George go. She had a dozen questions to ask him about the store. Both Mama and Aunt Catherine look to him for advice, although mine is just as good. Or better.

But with their visit over and done with, I felt some relief mixed with the sadness. Soon after the car turned the corner, I stopped thinking about Inez and her little glasses of sherry. By the next day I could tell myself that we had exaggerated the extent of her drinking.

Now I told Mama I would open the store this morning.

"Well, thank you, Lucy," she said, and it crossed my mind that neither of us wanted to talk about what had happened the night before. I knew that even Aunt Catherine in her mild way disapproved of my dance, although she would never have called it vulgar, as Lillian had.

As I walked by her house on the way to the store, I saw Lillian, leaning on the porch railing, looking as if the slightest breeze would topple her over into the flower bed below.

"I was surprised at you last night, Lucy," she called. "Where did you learn to do *that* dance?"

Her remark was so uncalled for that I decided not to answer. Then she said, "Where're you off to so early this morning?"

Her tone was sharp, the emphasis on *you*.

"I'm going down to open the store," I said then, feeling really mean, "but Mama will be down in a minute to make up your bed and wash your dishes."

By then I was turning the corner and I couldn't hear her response.

When I had first come home from Estelline, I found that Mama had not changed one thing about the hardware store since Papa died. Not one thing! Visitors, mostly the Methodist ladies, would stop in a minute to visit and cool off, but Mama had almost no customers. The first time I had gone down to help out, only two wandered in. Ban Ray Berry wanted to buy a hoe handle.

"Mr. Berry, Richards' Hardware doesn't carry handles," Mama had said. "But we have plenty of hoes."

After he left empty-handed, I said, "Mama, nowadays people don't make their own handles. Why don't you order some?"

She said, "Your papa never found it necessary."

A little later Mrs. Weatherbee came in to buy a preserving kettle and Mama said she had sold her last one. I was dumbfounded. I asked her why she had not ordered more, and she said she didn't intend to order another thing until the business improved.

We seemed to have quantities of items people in Bonham no longer wanted to buy, and none that people still needed. Spittoons, no longer in fashion, lined an entire shelf. Dozens of wedges, froes, mauls, gluts, and adzes crowded the aisles, gathering dust and cobwebs, because people no longer build their own homes, barns, outhouses. But Richards' Hardware had long ago sold out of churns, walking canes, brooms. "Brooms," I said to Mama. "You mean we don't even have a broom to sell!"

"Lucinda, watch your tone of voice when you speak to me," Mama said sternly.

"I'm sorry, Mama," I said, and still more humbly, "Mama, I do want to help you. Could I go over the books?"

But there were no books; no accounting of monies spent or taken in, of items ordered, sold, or unsold. There was only a money drawer filled with receipts, check stubs, and scrawled notes.

Then I got the idea (it just came to me!) that turned the business around. I wrote to Mr. Elliot in Estelline and explained that in Bonham spittoons were no longer fashionable (in style the East is always a little ahead of the West), and I sold twenty-seven spittoons to Elliot's Hardware Store in Estelline at a reduced rate, letting them have the whole batch for eleven dollars and eighty cents, plus shipping charges. With the cash, I bought two churns, half a dozen brooms, a dozen mops, and a dozen hoe handles.

Then Uncle Jerry and I cleaned the store from top to bottom, and as a finishing touch, Maggie Owens and I made a most attractive window display. We painted three cardboard walls like those of a modern, bright-colored kitchen. Then we put a small breakfast table, two chairs, and a rag rug in the middle, the whole scene designed to show off the blue enamelware I had persuaded Mama to order. The enamelware didn't sell (some said it didn't look clean), but we took a dozen orders for the rag rugs that a lady in Lone Oak began to make for us and still does. I've heard that people drive all the way from Paris to see our window displays. Maggie always helps me with these.

Today I hurried down to feed Lillian's canary, a part of our newest display. Everybody had had a fit about this one, a porch scene using some of our own painted wicker furniture, featuring huge urns with beautiful green ferns in them. For this display we had borrowed Lillian's canary, which Edmund had bought her when she wanted a cat (Edmund is allergic to cats), and with the white wicker furniture and the green ferns and the little yellow canary singing its heart out, everybody who walked by stopped to admire it. On Saturday mornings Maggie and I, to add reality, sometimes sit in the display and drink lemonade.

This morning I unlocked the door, fed and watered the canary (a sweet little thing and sleepy this morning), changed the paper in the cage, and dusted off the counters. Then I totaled the week's receipts and got out the new catalogues for ordering, all the while in the back of my mind thinking, *I am going to get married.* But then, right on the heels of this thought, came others. I had only two quilts and a pair of pillow cases in my hope chest. And Mama always says that when poverty comes in the door, love goes out the window. From this standpoint, Mr. Mosley would be better. But then, Mr. Rather was a better dancer. And he did not have three children. I thought about Mr. Porterfield and the dimple in his chin. I knew he could dance. I wondered if he rode. Sadly, I knew that no one would ever look as handsome on a horse as Bob had looked on his beautiful Surprise. Well, there were other fish in the sea. I'd forget about Bob Sully. Whatever he once seemed to be was false. He had betrayed me, and the worst betrayal was that suffered at the hand of a loved one. But I had long since recovered. Whatever he once was to me, he was now just a brother-in-law.

And it was a blessing I had come back to Bonham. Mama couldn't manage the store by herself. And what would Aunt Catherine do without me? I couldn't leave them now, no matter what George said. I would stay where I was needed, and I'd marry and live happily ever after.

But underneath was this other thing I knew and would not think about. *They* were coming to Bonham. The man to whom I had been engaged, and Katie, the sister who had betrayed me.

It wasn't that I still grieved. Or hated. That had long since passed. But to *see* them together. To *hear* their "Hello, Lucy." And what would be in their eyes? Pity? Disregard? Imagining all this was a knife in my heart.

I was glad when a customer came in. It was Mr. Walker, and he almost always bought something.

"Well, I see you're selling a new item this morning, Lucy."

"Oh, you mean the fern containers. Aren't they nice? And they're big enough so you won't have to replant the ferns for several years."

"I don't mean the fern pots," he said, and the twinkle in his eyes should have warned me, "I mean the dead bird!"

His booming laugh followed me as I ran to the window display and, yes, there it was, on the floor of the white wicker cage. Lillian's canary. Dead. I took it from the window, wrapped it in a newspaper. "Oh, Mr. Walker, this is the worst time for this to happen," I cried. "You just don't know"—and now I was putting it in a match-box—"how my sister loved this bird. What will we do? Oh, we can't tell her. She's expecting right away! Mama will just about die."

I thought about crying, but Mr. Walker couldn't seem to stop laughing at his own jokes that he continued to make about dead canaries being a little cheaper than the other kind and was Richards' Hardware suggesting canary for Sunday dinner in Bonham along with fried chicken. He kept on until I had to laugh too. His laugh is just like Josh Arnold's. Contagious.

Mama came in just then, and at first she was horrified, not at the bird's death, but at the thought of telling Lillian, but then, what with Mr. Walker putting his hat on and taking it off and telling her his bird jokes and wiping the tears of laughter from his eyes, she soon joined in the merriment.

"We'll just not tell her," Mama said, when she was able to stop laughing. "When that baby comes, one little bird won't matter to Lillian one way or the other." After Mr. Walker had left, she said, "Lucy, I never did think bringing that canary down here was such a good idea. Young lady, sometimes, you get ahead of yourself!"

But I didn't want to talk about the canary. "Mama," I said, "I want to know when they're coming."

Her eyes opened wide. "Who?"

"Bob and Katie."

She sighed. "It's not settled yet, but they'll probably be here in about a month. Lucy, I was going to tell you."

"You shouldn't have said they could come."

"Lucy, Katie is my daughter too. She'll always be welcome in my house."

Well. I had no answer for that.

After a minute, I said, "I'll go on home."

"I made a cream soup this morning, Lucy. Maybe you can think of something to go with it. If anyone can get Catherine to eat, you can."

I was about a block down the street when I heard Mama calling. Turning, I saw she waved a letter in the air.

"Lucy, I almost forgot. Mr. Benson brought this letter over right after you left. It came Special Delivery."

My heart skipped a beat! The handwriting—the flourishes, the big loops, the squared-off capital letters—was Josh Arnold's. The letter was postmarked Boston. I couldn't wait to read it!

8

SLIPPING THE LETTER into my pocket, feeling its sharp
edges with my fingers, I hurried home. I had kept all of
Mr. Arnold's letters, thirty-five of them. His letters made
me wonder about, oh, about poetry and the war and
whether I would vote for Sam Rayburn (I decided I
would), if women could vote. That first year his letters
had come from Estelline. Then, from Tennessee, he
wrote: "I discovered that without your presence West
Texas has lost its appeal. I will not be going back there.
This next year I am going to manage the farm for
Mama. And I'll be reading law here in Nashville. I believe I'd make a good lawyer." This last year Mr. Arnold
had traveled some. His letters were full of that and his
law studies, but always, like a huge backdrop looming
over his every observation, was the tragedy of the war in
Europe. "War is no longer romantic, if it ever was, nor
are its warriors chivalrous, if they ever were," he had
written from New York City. And from Virginia: "England is losing an entire generation of young men in the
trenches—from shells and shellshock, from gas, from in-
fectious wounds, from pneumonia. And with this great
and terrible loss, she is losing her very soul."

I read this letter again and again, but in the quiet of a
Bonham winter, nothing about the war seemed real.

Now as I ran up the porch steps and opened the screen
door, "Lucy, is that you?" came Aunt Catherine's voice.

"Yes, and I'll bet you're hungry," I told her, knowing

that if I fixed our dinner first, I could read my letter unhurriedly and in private.

I thought Aunt Catherine was looking better, the circles under her eyes not so pronounced, the frown on her forehead not as deep. She came and sat at the kitchen table, watching while I sliced tomatoes and dropped two roasting ears into a pan of boiling salted water. For dessert I opened a jar of peaches and poured heavy cream sweetened with sugar and flavored with brandy over them. Over dinner I entertained her with Mr. Walker's humor over the loss of Lillian's canary. She shook her head. "I don't know how we'll ever tell her," she said, but she was smiling.

She insisted on drying the dishes, and looking down at her thin, gray hair twisted into a bun on top of her head, seeing her frail shoulders, her trembling hands, I knew that Mama was right. If anyone could help Aunt Catherine get her health back, I could.

Opening the back door, I threw the dishwater on the lilac bush, and Aunt Catherine folded and laid the cup towel across the dishpan to dry. I did not mention the letter in my pocket, nor did she, with her usual tact, say anything of it to me, although she must have known that Mr. Benson had delivered it.

"It's my nap time, Lucy," she said. "And you might lie down awhile too. A young girl needs her beauty rest."

Before I was out of the kitchen I had opened the letter. "I'm coming to Texas," Mr. Arnold began. "It's been three years, long enough for a man to be without the woman he loves."

Well.

I turned the letter facedown, unsure of whether I wanted to read more. I went out and sat in the front porch swing. I looked at that part again and read a little more: "I'll arrive on the twentieth of June." Now I

stopped the swing, and counted the days until then. Today was Friday, the sixth. He'd be arriving in about two
weeks. Company just leaving, and more coming. Mama
would have a fit. I read still more: "It happens that I'll be
thirty-one on that day." Now, why was he telling me
this? Now his handwriting was very large and round:
"When I leave Bonham, I am taking you with me. So tell
your mama and your aunt Catherine. Tell your friend,
Maggie Owens. Tell the whole damn world that you will
be leaving Bonham with me."

Just like Josh Arnold, I thought, setting the swing into
fast, quick motion. Not a word about marriage, although
of course he meant it. All in all, a ridiculous letter. Mr.
Arnold and I had never been more than friends. At times
I couldn't even remember what he looked like. But even
if I loved him (and I didn't), there was no way in the
world I would ever leave Bonham. Why, I'd marry Mr.
Mosley first. Then it occurred to me that Josh Arnold
didn't even know me now. I had been a girl, eighteen,
when he left me that night on the Texas prairie. Now I
was a woman grown.

Well, thank goodness, he wasn't the only fish in the
sea. And Mama needn't worry about my being an old
maid either. Just the other night she had hinted that
being an old maid was a fate worse than death, and Aunt
Catherine had said, rather sharply, too, "Carrie Belle,
there are worse things." Mama did not answer her, but I
could tell she didn't think so.

I decided I'd walk over to Maggie's after my nap and
tell her Josh Arnold was coming. I thought I just might
give him to Maggie. Josh loved poetry, and if Maggie
hurried, she'd have time to memorize a poem or two before he arrived.

9

MAGGIE WASN'T HOME. "She's gone for a ride with Mr. Porterfield," her mother told me, all smiles. I could see that Mrs. Owens was happy Maggie had a beau, someone to help her forget about George.

When she invited me in for a glass of lemonade, I said I couldn't stay, but I asked her to be sure to tell Maggie that a friend, Josh Arnold, was coming. I also mentioned that he was fond of poetry. Then I borrowed Mrs. Owens's newest pattern book and decided to walk down and relieve Mama at the hardware store. She'd be glad of the chance to go home early.

With the warmer weather, I sold three ice picks, an ice box, and an ice-cream freezer right away. After that, nobody much came in.

Looking through Mrs. Owens's pattern book, I decided to plan my trousseau. Right off I found just the dress to be married in, a slender-skirted dress with two pleated ruffles right at the bottom. In the picture the dress was made in a black pussy-willow taffeta with pantalettes of black Val lace. But made up in a cream-colored taffeta and worn with the new Paris pumps, so stylish now, it would make an elegant wedding dress.

Since I would be staying in Bonham anyway, there was no great hurry about getting married, although I planned to be engaged before Bob and Katie came.

Now there was another possibility. The store was doing so much better that I could get a real job in Bonham. When I had first come home, I had planned to teach. But when I realized we were about to lose the family business, I knew that was out of the question. Mama needed me at the store. But there was never money for a salary, not even for her.

One of the best parts about teaching in West Texas had been having my own money. I had bought a car, and presents for my family. A new hat. Material for a Christmas dress. Without asking anybody! And I had loved teaching, but a woman teacher could not marry, even in Bonham. Or wear bright colors. Or dance. I longed for the freedom men had. They could go anywhere. Do anything.

I looked at the "Want Ads" in the newspaper. Somebody wanted a German girl for general housework and cooking. "Must know how to milk," the ad said. That let me out on two counts. "Finishers on high-class dresses" were needed and "Ladies needed to sell tailored corsets." Several ads began, "Refined widow in need of work." Most said "would keep house for elderly or ill lady," but one said, "Refined widow: Would keep house for gentleman in Dallas." I wondered about *her*! Reading the ads made it seem like the best thing to do was marry.

A garden catalogue on Mama's desk pictured tall crepe myrtles, which bloomed in season all over Bonham. The crepe myrtle was pretty but nothing like the streams of golden and scarlet wildflowers that sprang up on the West Texas prairie after an early rain. Oh, the beauty of it! But there had been violence there too.

A man dead. Decapitated. I had seen it. And there was Mrs. Monday, dead now of cold and starvation, who had loved her boy more than anything. Jinks Mayfield, with her wide grin and freckles, would be eleven now. And Oda Ray and Ida Fay would be nine. I wondered if they thought of me. I hoped they hadn't forgotten.

It was a brutal country, but oddly, living there, I had

never felt so alive. Thinking of it now, I experienced a stirring of unrest so pronounced that it had no name.

The thought of Katie and Bob coming home was a bitter one. What could I find to say to them? What could they say to me?

"Why did you marry her?" I longed to ask Bob. "How could you?" And to Katie, "How could you do this to your own sister? Why?"

But, of course, I knew why. Carrying a baby, Katie had had to marry.

The kitchen talk in Bonham was that Olive Ann Lippencott's baby would be coming along about July. The whole town knew she was expecting, knew her daddy kept her up in the attic, sending Mattie, their colored girl, up with a tray three times a day. And everybody pretending that Olive was visiting cousins in Georgia.

Just last Sunday, Maggie and I visited Mr. Rather's church (he sang a beautiful solo), and I was right behind and clearly heard Brother Simns say to Mr. Lippencott, "Now, when will Olive be coming home?"

"Oh, she'll likely be home about the middle of July," Mr. Lippencott had said, squeezing his wife's arm so hard his knuckles showed white.

"Well, Mrs. Lippencott, you'll be mighty glad to see her. I know you've missed her."

Mrs. Lippencott didn't answer. Tight-lipped, she turned away and hurried down the steps.

Olive Ann is the third girl in as many years from Brother Simns's Sunday school class to have to go visiting cousins during the school year. If it had been anybody but Brother Simns, I would have called his questions prying.

Well, everybody knew that Dr. Grey would be called one day soon (or one night), the baby delivered, and then Olive Ann would "come home." Pretty soon after that

Mrs. Lippencott would return from visiting relatives with a new baby and a story about a young mother dead of childbed fever or a hemorrhage.

Oh, I knew *why* Katie had married, had reached out with those soft, plump hands and those soft gray eyes and persuaded Bob to betray me.

But what I didn't know was how I could live in the same house with her during the days of their visit.

I was glad Josh Arnold was coming. He knew everything, was the only one who did, and having him there, a friend, would be a great comfort.

10

NOW I WAS the one fussed over, smiled at, doted on. Before it had been George, the only man in the family, or Katie, because she was the baby, or Lillian, losing two babies and with a third on the way. But now, with Bob and Katie coming home, the family doted on me.

Telling Mama that more company was coming was easy because of it. "Why, what's one more, for goodness sakes! Lucy, I think it's nice that Mr. Arnold is coming all this way to see you," she said, clearing the table. "Why, we've got all this room. Now, let's see. Katie and her husband will be in Katie's old room (you don't need to be always giving up your room), and if Mr. Arnold's still visiting when they come, we'll put him in George's room."

And Aunt Catherine chimed in with, "Lucy, you're looking a little peaked. I want you to be getting a little extra rest this next week."

This was enough to set Mama off. "Catherine, I've noticed that too," she said, cupping my chin in her hand, looking into my face. "Lucy does need some extra rest. I won't need her at the store this week. And I've asked Queenie to come every day while the company's here, and told her to bring Jeremiah to help too. They might as well start tomorrow. That way Lucy can get all the rest she needs."

I was enjoying the attention, basking in it, and with so much talk about my looking unwell, even beginning to wonder if I might not be just a little sick. Or something.

Still, having Queenie come every day! And Jeremiah! "Mama, we can't afford that!" I said.

Mama sat, slowly rocking and fanning herself. I could tell by the way she rocked she was satisfied with her arrangements.

"You know that old set of porch furniture that's been sitting in the store for three years. Don't know why we ever bought unpainted wicker. Well, Queenie wants that for Jeremiah. They came in the store the other day and saw it. Jeremiah said he'd work it off."

"But Queenie doesn't even *have* a porch," Aunt Catherine said.

"She wants the furniture for Jeremiah's room. Jeremiah said that's exactly what he wants. He's going to hang the porch swing in his bedroom. Said it would help him study."

Silently we sat, the three of us, thinking about Queenie and Jeremiah, and Jeremiah studying in a swing in his bedroom. I had never seen a swing in a bedroom, but now I could see one in mine. It was big enough. I thought I'd like a swing in my bedroom.

Jeremiah was a foundling. Queenie had found him one crisp fall day when she was out in the Roseborough woods, picking up pecans. There he was, tied to a grapevine, just a toddler, not able to talk and getting cold. She had looked and called and waited for someone to come back for him, waited until almost dark, and then she had brought him home and raised him in the kitchens where she worked.

It had been in all the papers, but nobody ever claimed Jeremiah. Still, nobody could have loved him more than Queenie. Why, Queenie thought there was nothing in the world but Jeremiah.

With his school out, he'd be coming with Queenie tomorrow, and while she rolled out the crusts for lemon pies or polished the silver or set the rolls to rise, she'd be talking to him in that soft, almost crooning way she had.

"Now, Jeremiah, get me the eggs out of the ice box, and tell Mr. Layton we be needing ten cents' worth more ice, and then you go right on out there and work with Uncle Jerry in the garden. It take three of us getting ready for all the company we expecting. You hear?"

"Queenie can't stand it when Jeremiah be out of her sight," Uncle Jerry chuckled, watching the two of them together.

I wondered what would come of it, how it would end, because the truth was that with every day that passed it was clearer and clearer that Jeremiah was a white boy, and people were beginning to talk. "That boy's white," and "It just ain't right. Him living with the colored," and "Something ought to be done about it," Bonham was saying, and what had, at first, been only whispered about, was now heard openly. And the truth was that Jeremiah *was* white. I hoped Queenie never heard the talk.

Well. I had enough to think about without worrying over Jeremiah. I was just glad Queenie was coming, glad to be the pampered one in the family.

This morning, I even looked forward to going down to Lillian's. Her "Good morning, Lucy" had been so sweet the last few days, and yesterday she had told me I looked like an illustration in the latest *Delineator*.

These past months Mama and I have waited every morning until Edmund leaves the house. ("I'm not one to interfere in my children's marriages," Mama says.) He gets fatter every day, right along with Lillian, but he manages to look quite jaunty walking to the bank, wearing his straw bowler and carrying his cane. Just as soon as he is out of sight, one of us goes down. Sometimes both of us.

Yesterday morning, Mama cleared the breakfast

dishes while I swept the floor. As Lillian moved to get a cup towel, Mama said, "No, Lillian, you just sit right down! Lucy and I will do these dishes in no time, won't we, honey?"

"Yes, ma'am," I said, thinking that a *little* exercise might be good for Lillian.

When we finished the dishes, we mopped the kitchen, filled the reservoir in the stove, and swept off the front porch. Then Mama made a pot of tea, and I cut the coconut cake Aunt Catherine had sent down the night before. By the time we were having our tea, it was almost time for Mama to open up the store.

Hurriedly Mama told Lillian about our arrangements. "Starting tomorrow, Queenie's coming," she said. "I want Lucy to get some rest before Mr. Arnold arrives. Why, she's just about worn herself out, what with the store and Aunt Catherine and—"

"And me?" Lillian said crossly.

"That too," Mama said firmly.

Lillian and I looked at Mama. Mama hardly ever speaks up to Lillian. Still I *was* beginning to wonder if I might be coming down with something.

"Mama, I'm going to run on home," I said. "There are a few things I need to do this morning."

"Now, you do that, and Lucinda, you make time to sit down awhile this afternoon. You could work on those pillow cases I've started for your hope chest," Mama said, hugging me tightly.

When I walked into the house, I found Aunt Catherine resting in her room. With the house quiet, I went up to my room, turned down the spread, and lay down to read awhile. But with first one idea and then another going through my head, I couldn't concentrate. I longed to talk to Christobel. In West Texas, a visit with her had always cleared my mind. I decided to write her a letter.

"Dear Christobel," I wrote. "So much is happening here. Where can I begin? Well, the first thing is that Katie and Bob are coming to Bonham. They'll arrive in less than a month. And the next thing is that Josh Arnold, whom I have not seen for three years, is coming on the twentieth. I hardly know how I feel. About any of it.

"Christobel, I've been home now for three years. And I'm not sure I should have come back at all. Here, too often, I feel like a little girl again, and in West Texas I felt wise and sure, as if I could conquer the world.

"And yet, I am so needed here. Without me Mama would be sure to lose the hardware store, and Aunt Catherine is suffering from consumption. If you have a remedy for it, tell me what it is. She is quite ill. That is the main thing that keeps me here.

"Aunt Catherine depends on me. I am the only one who knows what will tempt her appetite. Just three weeks ago, she had such a spell, terrible and heartrending, and it was only my thinking to chill peaches and serve them with cream in a pretty bowl that began to restore her appetite. Not a day goes by that she doesn't say, 'Lucy, I don't know what I'd do without you.' Mama says it, too, and, sometimes, even Lillian.

"But the thing is that here I feel closed in, and I long for something more. Christobel, is it marriage for which I long? And does love sometimes *follow* marriage?

"I have prospects here in Bonham, two of them, and I am quite fond of them both. One, Mr. Rather, wants a wife, a house, and children. The other, Mr. Mosley, only wants a wife, as he has the other two. What would you say to me if you and I, right this minute, were walking along the rim of the canyon, enjoying one of those wonderful West Texas sunsets? What would you tell me to do?"

I signed the letter and put it out for Mr. Benson. Writing it made me feel better, almost lighthearted. Suddenly I was no longer tired.

I decided to go out into the garden to help Uncle Jerry pick the early sweet peas. Aunt Catherine loved them, and Queenie could cook some for dinner tomorrow.

11

IT WAS FRIDAY. Josh would arrive in a week, but there was not the household flurry which usually preceded guests. Mama was thinking about other things. "Besides," she said, "men don't notice dust." Aunt Catherine and I smiled at each other. There was never any dust to be noticed in our house.

We were at supper, a light meal of grits and ham and biscuits, which Queenie had prepared before she left. Throughout the meal Mama had been unusually quiet. Now she turned her head away from us and smoothed her hair into place. She cleared her throat. "Lucy, I'd like another piece of ham," she said. Then, "The Weatherbees asked me to milk their cow while they're vacationing in Galveston."

Aunt Catherine chuckled. "I can't imagine their asking us, Carrie. We've never kept a cow. But maybe Dr. Grey knows somebody who could do the milking. How long will they be gone?"

"I said I would," Mama said, and pushing back her chair, she began to clear the table.

Aunt Catherine, frowning, lowered her head, rubbed her forehead with her fingers. "Carrie Belle," she said gently, "you've never milked a cow."

"Well, I'm about the only one in Bonham who hasn't! It's time I learned. Besides, any fool can milk."

"I tried it once, and I couldn't," Aunt Catherine said. "The cow wouldn't let down her milk."

Silently the three of us contemplated the mysterious

and whimsical mind of a cow. It was beginning to seem like a crisis.

"Uncle Jerry can milk the cow," I said, wondering why Mama had not thought of it.

"His arthritis won't let him," Mama called from the kitchen. "Now, with all that company coming, we can use the milk. Come on, Lucy. Bessie's waiting!"

Mama came back into the dining room, took the pins out of her hair and retwisted it into a tighter bun. "Lucy," she said, "comb your hair and take off your apron before we go up to the Weatherbees'. No telling who we'll see."

I groaned. That was exactly what I was afraid of. I'd die if Mr. Mosley saw me milking. Or Mr. Rather.

"Lucy, there's no disgrace in honest work," Mama said, reading my mind.

Mama hurried ahead. Apparently, she had forgotten all about the state of my health. "Come on, Lucy. Hurry up. This may take a while."

I hurried to catch up with her. "Why did the Weatherbees ask us to milk their cow?"

"Lucy, I don't know."

"Well, don't they know we can buy all the milk we need?"

"Lucy, everybody knows that Mr. Lawson waters the milk he sells. Now, Bessie's milk will be fresh and good. Besides, our funds are low, and we'll have to be mighty careful until our ship comes in."

By now we had reached the Weatherbees', and we hurried around the big, rambling house, its wood beginning to show through the white paint, passed the flower and the vegetable gardens, and opened the gate into the cow lot. There was Bessie in her stall, waiting to be fed and milked.

"Well, hello, Bessie," I said.

Bessie moaned softly. Her eyes were liquid. Her flanks soft as sunshine. I liked her.

While Mama put some hay in Bessie's stall, I rubbed her neck. We watched as Bessie began to eat, slowly, peacefully. I had never seen a sweeter cow. Mama put the bucket under her. We looked at each other. "I'll do it," I said, bending over to begin. Bessie's tail swatted my cheek. I jumped back. Stupid cow, I thought.

Mama said, "I'll hold her tail."

I leaned over to begin again. I squeezed one of Bessie's teats. A few drops of milk hit the bucket. Feeling quite pleased, I squatted down and began to use both hands. Bessie kicked. The bucket went over, spilling the milk into the dirt.

"Gosh durn it!" I yelled.

"Young lady, watch your language!"

Mama and I looked at each other. We began again. I held the bucket with one hand and milked with the other while Mama held the tail. Milking was clearly a three-person job. Tomorrow we'd have to bring Aunt Catherine along to hold the tail. After a while we had a quart of good, foamy milk. But that was all. The Weatherbees had promised there would be a gallon, at least. But, evidently, Bessie had decided not to let down any more.

The next morning we milked again; and that evening. In a few days I was getting better at it, but Bessie seemed to be getting worse. Wednesday I told Mama I'd have to skip a time or two because Josh would be arriving on Friday, and I needed an entire day to get ready. It wasn't every day a friend came all the way from Tennessee to see me, and I wanted to look my best.

12

THURSDAY MORNING I awakened to the sound of rain falling lightly on the roof, running into the gutters and down the gutter spout into the already half-filled rain barrel. There'd be rainwater aplenty for washing my hair and for bathing. I'd empty the barrel first thing so as to let it fill with fresh rainwater. Stretching, I savored the thought that I had a whole day for myself. And to get ready for Josh Arnold.

I would be in the swing when he arrived, wearing white and with a white rose in my hair. Or maybe a red one would be better. I'd ask Maggie what she thought.

This morning I'd press my petticoats and my dress. Then I'd give myself a cornmeal facial and put some lemon juice on my freckles. I should have been doing *that* for weeks, but today would help a little. Tomorrow, when Josh arrived, I'd be all ready. And composed. I wanted him to see me as I was, a woman now, and grown.

Now I stretched myself fully awake, and to let in the fresh smell of rain, opened my windows a crack. Then, barefooted, I padded downstairs and ran out to the privy. Along the back fence the hollyhocks rose, slender and tall in the falling rain, their blooms, intermittent bursts of pink and red and white, embroidering their green stems. When the sun came out the bees would be there, nuzzling the blossoms, drawing from each its sweetness.

Coming out of the privy, I saw that the rain had turned into a gentle mist, but more clouds, dark and heavy, were rolling in. A hard rain was coming, a spring rain that would cool things and be gone. I was almost in the kitchen when I remembered the rain barrel. I turned and hurried down the steps and around to the front corner of the house where the rain barrel stood. My hair hung, damply wet, down my back, and my wrapper, wet too, felt uncomfortably close.

I tipped the rain barrel over, dropping it onto its side. Watching the clear water form a pool around my feet, the blades of grass around the pool's edges swaying to and fro with the water, I leaned over to right the rain barrel. As I pulled the barrel up, my right foot slipped, and down I went into the mud, pulling the rain barrel with me.

A laugh, loud as thunder, broke through the rain.

Josh! It was Josh Arnold! "Lucy, what in the world are you doing out here in the mud, fighting with a rain barrel?"

In one sweeping motion he lifted me to my feet and, chuckling all the while, righted the rain barrel. His eyes were greener than I remembered. His hair, made so by the rain and by the overcast skies, black as coal.

"You were supposed to come tomorrow," I said, pulling my wrapper out, away from my body.

"When I got to Texarkana, Bonham seemed so close I decided to drive on in. Lucy, oh girl, let me look at you."

His voice was husky. Drawing me to him, he held me in his arms so that I caught the remembered scent of wild horsemint. Gently, I pushed him away.

"Josh Arnold, I'm a mess! Look at your coat. I've got you all muddy."

"Who cares?" he said, moving to take me in his arms again.

I put out my hands, taking his. Once again I'd have to define what we were to each other.

"Mr. Arnold, I'm glad you came. A friend is always welcome here."

"Mr. Arnold, is it? Lucinda, I've come a long way to see you, and I'll not answer to any name but Josh."

And with that he grasped my shoulders, drew me to him, and kissed me. That was unhurried too. He kissed me as if we had all the time in the world, and as his lips touched mine, I heard the rain quicken and my heartbeat too, and I let myself be carried away by the kiss, the rain, the scent of horsemint. Then, unbidden, thoughts of Katie and Olive Ann came into my mind. So this is how it happens, I thought, girls getting swept away. Into trouble. Turning my head, twisting out of his arms, I stepped back.

"Josh, no!" I said.

Josh, his head tilted, pushed his hair out of his eyes. He smiled. "Well, at least it's 'Josh' now. Come on. You'd better get out of those wet things."

Turning, he opened the door for me, and I led him up the steps, across the porch, and through the parlor, the dining room, and into the kitchen.

"Wait here, Josh," I whispered. "I'll be right back."

Before I'd finished dressing, the smell of coffee wafted up the stairs to me. Slipping into a flower-sprigged dimity, combing my hair, I thought about how I must have looked when Josh arrived. Out in the rain in my wrapper, with my hair straggling down my back, struggling with the barrel. Falling. If it had been anyone but Josh, seeing all this, I'd have died.

Now I dabbed on a little rose water and hurried downstairs. "Josh, I must have looked so funny . . ." I began.

"Funny. Wonderful. Your hair's longer, and out there, all tumbled around your shoulders and your, What was that you were wearing? Your whatever it was following every line of your body, you looked, wonderful. Beautiful." Then, grinning, "But that was the first time I ever saw a fight between a girl and a rain barrel."

"And I lost," I said, and then we were both laughing. After a while, weak with laughter, I was leaning on the table and Josh was laughing that rollicking laugh of his, his head thrown back, his arm flung over the open door of the dining room.

"Lucy, Lucy," came Mama's voice. "What in the world is going on down there? Who's down there?" And Aunt Catherine was opening her bedroom door, her face all squinched up with sleep, asking, "Lucy, whatever in the world?" Then Josh, wiping his eyes, was saying, "Lucy, tell the ladies that breakfast will be ready in about half an hour, and show me where the pots and pans are. I'm cooking a Tennessee breakfast this morning."

My answer to Mama, calling up the stairs, "Mr. Arnold is here, Mama. A day early," was answered by silence (Mama wouldn't approve of a guest's arriving a day early), then by Aunt Catherine's, "I'll be in to meet Mr. Arnold in a few minutes."

And then we were all there at the table, and I could see how much Mama and Aunt Catherine enjoyed having a man in the house again, however puzzled they were by his cooking breakfast (after all, no man had ever cooked breakfast or anything else in our house before). But he beguiled them all the same, and I had forgotten that Josh could do this. And I had forgotten how pleasant his Tennessee accent was as he told stories about the roads between Texas and Tennessee and the people he had met on these roads.

"A summer trip is really nice in an automobile," he was saying now. "Why, an automobile in motion is nothing less than a cooling plant. I'd advise anyone to travel in the summer. Then, the automobile owner has his summer resort with him every time he drives a car. And my little Maxwell just jinned along. Made the trip just fine. And, too, the car's light enough so that pushing it out of the mud's no trouble, when it comes to that."

He told us about the position he had accepted for the coming fall. "I'm going to be the school principal in a place called Sweet Shrub," he said. "It's in Arkansas, not too far down the river from Memphis."

"Sweet Shrub," I said. "That's an unusual name. Our towns are named after heroes of the Alamo or early settlers. Or sometimes cities in Europe."

"They tell me there is a plant that grows there called Sweet Shrub. And in the spring the plant smells so good that the school children pick the buds from the plant and put them in their pockets and in their lunch boxes, sometimes behind their ears, so that a wonderfully spicy fragrance is everywhere—in the schoolrooms, on the playground, in their houses."

I could see it. The girls in their starched pinafores, the boys in their pants and shirts, their faces all scrubbed, their eyes bright—marching into the classroom in the lemon sunlight of early morning, bringing with them the scent of the pastures where they played.

Aunt Catherine, too, was charmed by the story. "I wonder if the plant would grow here?" she asked. "I'll certainly inquire about a cutting."

"Miss Richards, I'll send you a cutting just as soon as I can find one. You can count on it. People who've been everywhere say that in the spring that little town is especially pretty."

"Why, I'm sure Sweet Shrub is nice," Mama said. "But Mr. Arnold, did you know that Bonham won the *Holland* magazine award for being the prettiest city of its size in the United States?"

"Hearing that, I'm even more delighted that I came to pay Bonham *and* Lucinda a visit," Josh said. Then he

remarked about Aunt Catherine's cut-flower garden,
saying it reminded him of English gardens his grandmother had told him about.

"Why, Mr. Arnold, you're exactly right about that,"
Aunt Catherine said, beaming. "My flower garden's pat-
terned after my mother's in Penzance, England."

"Penzance. That's right on the southern tip of England, isn't it?" Josh said. "I've heard that's also one of
the most beautiful spots in the world."

Then Josh turned to Mama, asking questions about
our hardware store, telling her he had stopped in a hardware store in Little Rock and another one in Texarkana.
Now, he told her, he was looking forward to seeing the
Richards' store right here in Bonham.

Aunt Catherine hurried about, bringing Josh more
coffee, telling him we had no objection to a gentleman's
smoking in the house on a rainy day, and saying that
since the rain seemed to have stopped, she'd like to show
him through her garden. And Mama too! Mama was won
over too.

"Mr. Arnold, I think I'll open the hardware store a little early this morning," she said. "You might like to walk
down with me. Lucy, I don't think Lillian really needs
me today, do you?"

Well! This was the first time that Mama had entertained the idea that Lillian didn't need her every minute
of every day.

But then Josh overstepped his welcome. Bringing in a
second serving of hot biscuits, I offered one to Josh. He
took it and then, clear as anything and right in front of
the family, he said, "Thank you, sweetheart."

Aunt Catherine smiled faintly. Mama stared at Josh,
then at me, raising her eyebrows. I hurried into the
kitchen to refill the preserve dish. Now Mama would be

asking all kinds of tiresome questions. About Josh. About Josh and me. There would be no end to it.

I refilled the bowl with apricot preserves and went back into the dining room. Frowning down at Josh, I offered him some preserves. He did not look up, but he shook a spoonful onto his plate and replaced the spoon. Then, as I turned away, he took my free hand, brought it to his lips, and kissed it!

"Thank you, Lucy," he said, smiling up at me.

The summer shower that had fallen outside the dining room windows might as well have been sleet, so cold did the mood of the room become. Mama looked sharply at Josh, and Aunt Catherine raised her eyebrows. I took some salt from the saltcellar and shook a spoon of it over the preserves on my plate before I knew what I was doing.

Buttering his biscuit, heaping preserves on the biscuit, Josh smiled at Aunt Catherine. "Miss Richards, looks like the sun's coming out. You suppose we could take a peek at your garden now?"

But before Aunt Catherine could answer, here was Queenie, almost as tall as Josh, bigger all over, coming in the back door. Her smile broad, her teeth white as the apron she was tying round her waist, she strode across the kitchen floor and into the dining room.

"Good morning, Miss Catherine. Mrs. Richards," she said, her voice deep and cool as well water. "And here's Lucinda, looking pretty as a morning glory. All down here, getting an early start on the day?"

"Queenie, this is Mr. Arnold, a friend from West Texas," I said.

Josh held out his hand, and Queenie, startled, wiped her hands on her apron before taking his, out of habit I suppose, since she hadn't been in the kitchen long enough to begin her breadmaking. Then Josh said,

"How are you, Queenie?" as if he really wanted to know, and a frown crossed Queenie's face as if she might tell him about her troubles. But the moment passed and she smiled and said she was fine.

"Where's Jeremiah?" I asked, Mama and Aunt Catherine not yet recovered enough from Josh's familiarities to hold up their ends of the conversation.

"He in the garden, helping Uncle Jerry," Queenie said. "I reckon we gonna have some sweet corn today. Maybe some early peas too."

"Mr. Arnold, if you'd like to see the garden, I think we could walk out there now, before the sun's well up. Be too hot and steamy then," Aunt Catherine said, easing her chair back from the table.

Knowing all the questions that waited behind Mama's anxious expression, I said, "I believe I'll go with you."

Aunt Catherine's herb garden lay just outside the house, protected from the weather's harshness by her room and the screened-in back porch. Josh, clearly enjoying himself, watched Aunt Catherine walk through it, pinching off mint leaves to put in his hand, rolling a sprig of parsley in hers, tamping down the soil around a clump of rosemary. This morning the sun's warmth on the wet leaves brought out the smell of chervil, parsley, thyme, and rosemary, and blended them in the early morning air.

Then we went through the vegetable garden. Hands in his pockets, Josh strolled along, now and then stopping to examine a tomato or peel the leaves from the tip of an ear of corn or thump a melon. ("Not near ready yet," he said.) The two of them talked about fertilizing and corn blight, about the best way to get rid of tomato bugs and corn earworms.

When we reached the pea patch, Jeremiah was there,

trying to find enough early peas for a light mess for dinner.

"Morning, Miss Richards, Miss Lucy," he said, standing, his movements lithe and graceful.

"Why, Jeremiah, you're almost as tall as your mama," I told him, surprised I hadn't noticed it before.

He smiled. Then his eyes caught the light from the morning sun, and I saw that they were the same color as his hair, brown with flecks of auburn in them.

"Is Queenie your mama?" Josh asked.

Jeremiah and I laughed at the disbelief in his voice.

"Yessir," Jeremiah said. "The only one I remembers."

"Jeremiah's a foundling," Aunt Catherine said gently. "And Queenie says that every day since she found him, he has made her life sweeter."

"A white boy and a colored mother," Josh said, smiling at Jeremiah.

And there it was. Out.

Nobody said a word. We were all too surprised! Of course we knew Jeremiah was white, but hearing it said like that, right out, we stood there, not looking at each other, thinking about it.

Finally, Jeremiah, looking embarrassed, said softly, "I reckon so, but ain't nothing to be done about it."

"What does Queenie"—Josh carefully corrected himself—"what does your *mama* say about it?"

"She don't know it," Jeremiah said, frowning. "And she got too much on her right now to hear it."

"Son, she knows it. You can be sure she knows it."

And with that, Josh strolled off to the cut-flower garden, looking at the primroses that were just about to open, as casually as if he had not just dropped a bomb right in the middle of the pea patch.

13

OH, THE DAY went quickly after that. Josh told Mama that it would be too much of an imposition to stay with us and that he had already made reservations at the Alexander Hotel. Promising to be back in time for supper, he took himself off to the hotel to settle in. I steeled myself to answer Mama's questions.

"Mama, I promise you that Josh Arnold is no more than a friend to me, a good friend," I told her on the way to Lillian's. "If he were more than that, I would certainly tell you." Then, doing up Lillian's breakfast dishes, "Marrying Josh Arnold has never crossed my mind. He's just a friend, no more than that." And on the way to the store, "Mama, I'm going for a drive with Mr. Rather tomorrow evening. I may very well say 'yes' to him on the drive." But then, dusting the preserving jars at the store, I lost my temper completely. (Oh, Mama can drive you to it!) "I'll tell you one thing," I shouted, "I had rather marry Josh Arnold than Mr. Mosley. And Mama, it just may be that you're going to have *another* old maid on your hands!" A mean thing to say about Aunt Catherine, and I was sorry as soon as I'd said it.

Mama knows when she's gone too far. She dropped her duster, hurried over, and put her arms around me.

"Lucy, it's just that Mr. Arnold seems so . . . oh, Mr. Arnold is so . . . Lucy, he's unsettled! Oh, don't you see that he's like a whirlwind! Coming here a day early and telling Jeremiah he's white (Yes, Aunt Catherine told me about that!), and well, he's just too unsettled is all!"

"Mama, Mr. Arnold is a friend who's come all this way
to see me. And he'll be gone in two or three days. Now,
I'm asking you to make him welcome while he's here.
Mama, I hope you remember that when I was in West
Texas, Mr. Arnold was real nice to me, nicer in every
way than my own sister, who'll be right here in this very
room just next week."

I hated to remind Mama about Katie because, more
than anything, she grieved that we could never again be
sisters, but I knew it would persuade her.

"Course we'll make him welcome," she said now, "and
when have we ever been anything but hospitable to a
guest? In fact, why don't you ring up the hotel right now
and ask him if he'd like to walk over here. He said he
wanted to see the store."

When I rang the hotel, Mr. Green said Mr. Josh Arnold
from Tennessee had just stepped out. I left Mama's message, and after I had totaled the week's receipts and ordered a dozen hoes, as many files, and two mowers, I
went home to help Queenie with dinner.

Turning the street corner onto our block, I saw Josh in
front of Lillian's house. And Queenie with him. I started
to call out, but something between them—Queenie's outstretched hands, the intensity of Josh's bearing—something conspiratorial, *significant,* kept me from it.

Queenie saw me first, her hands falling helplessly to
her sides, and then Josh turned toward me, but almost as
if he hadn't seen me, he turned back again to Queenie.

Walking slowly toward them, I heard Josh say, "And it
might die down, Queenie. But it's bad. Bad for you and
the boy."

Queenie shook her head slowly. "Can't do nothing
'bout it, Mr. Arnold, but just keep on keeping on."

"Well, I'll do what I can," and he smiled at her like she
was an old friend. Josh makes friends like that. Fast.

Then Josh looked at me and smiled; his eyes danced. "Lucy," he said, and even Queenie had to smile at the laughter in his voice, "the hotel's making up a basket for us. And you and I are going to drive to the country and have us a picnic."

"Josh, you drove all night long. Aren't you tired?"

"Yes, I am. But"—and this right in front of Queenie—"I've come over seven hundred miles to see you, Lucy Richards, and that's what I plan to do. Right now."

"But I've got to see about Aunt Catherine's dinner."

"Queenie here can do that, can't you, Queenie?"

"Yes, sir. Sure can. Now, you run along. Don't fret about Miss Catherine. Me and Miss Catherine gonna do just fine."

"You ever see a prettier day for a picnic, Queenie? You ever see a prettier girl?"

Well!

With the sun shining and the breeze light and cool, it *was* a glorious day, a day to step out into. All at once, I felt like a picnic more than anything else in the world.

"Queenie, you tell Mama not to worry. We'll be home in plenty of time for supper."

Almost running, Josh and I hurried back to the Alexander to pick up the picnic basket and his car. And in a few minutes we were out of Bonham, speeding along the Honey Grove Road.

The wind blew my hair around my face, into my eyes. Sweeping it up on top of my head, I thought, Josh is right. The car in motion *is* a cooling plant. Settling back to enjoy the ride, I asked, "Josh, where are we going? Do you know?"

"No, but we'll just drive until we find a good place to picnic. Must be plenty of places around here like that."

I could have shown him one or two, but not in the direction we were headed. After a mile or two, he turned north, onto a country lane. On one side was a field of cotton, the tender green plants just up, and on the other a pasture, mostly of buffalo and Johnson grass, and some distance ahead of us, in a wide semicircle, the woods rose thick and green. We drove toward the center of the encircling woods and now the cotton field on the left gave way to tall grass and on the other side the grass grew even taller. Feeling the wind in my face, bringing with it the deep-down smells of hay freshly cut, and wild grasses, and plowed earth, I felt suddenly almost giddy with happiness.

Josh drove more slowly now, carefully skirting an occasional rock or rough place in the road. I put my hand out the window into the rush of air, lightly brushing the feathery tips of the grass, so tall that it seemed to envelop the automobile, as in front of us—and this just as we reached the woods—the road fell away and gradually disappeared in an ocean of grass. We've reached the end of the road, I thought—but no, Josh turned to the left, and finding the road again he followed the tree line until we came to an opening into the woods, and there we turned onto an almost imperceptible trail, which fell gradually at first and then more sharply. Now the landscape was ragged, the woods growing thicker, and the smell of wood sorrel and moist earth and honeysuckle was heavier.

And, there! Josh had to brake sharply, for right across the road ran a stream, running swiftly, almost hidden on the right by bramble bushes and vines, but on the left, it ran free and clear.

"Josh, let's go wading!" I said, turning toward him, but seeing the look on his face, of excitement maybe, I turned away.

"That's my girl," Josh said, switching off the car motor. Then it was all so quiet, so *suddenly* quiet that, stilled by the quiet, we listened and heard the call of a mockingbird and in the distance the scabrous cry of a crow and from nearby the steady murmur of water going across the road.

Then as I moved to get out of the car, "Wait a minute, Lucy. Let's drive across first," Josh said.

We drove through the shallow stream and up onto a small green incline and stopped. Now we could go no farther, for just ahead lay woods too thick even to see into.

I got out of the car and turned to run back down to the stream, and then, conscious that Josh was not following, I turned around to see that he was spreading a blanket on the grass.

"Aren't you coming?" I called, a little uneasy about the blanket.

"You go ahead," he said. "I'm going to rest a minute."

Running down the hill, kicking off my shoes, taking off my stockings, I waded into the stream. I thought of Mama, could hear her saying, "Lucy, don't ever let a man see your bare feet. He'll think less of you."

What a goose Mama is, I thought, enjoying the surge of water against my ankles. I glanced up the hill toward Josh's automobile. No sign of him. Upstream, the bushes hung low over the water, and on that side of the road the water was deeper, or was this even a road? I could not be sure, for looking at the water on one side and then on the other, it seemed to be more of a dam than a road. Seeing the darkness of the water underneath the bushes, I thought that anything might lurk there, and as if on cue a snake doctor appeared and hovered over the darkest place.

Hitching up my dress, I waded downstream. Here the water ran clear and smooth, along each side patches of wood violets and forget-me-nots; a cluster of wild lilies at the base of an oak tree. And all at once, a swarm of tiny yellow butterflies appeared, flickering close to the water, now covering the grass with a blanket of yellow, then rising, moving haphazardly upstream—a sight so beautiful it took my breath away.

And Josh was missing all this! I turned, and splashing back to the road, ran up the hill.

"Josh, come on!" I called. "There are a million yellow butterflies down here. You've never seen so many."

But when I reached the Maxwell, I saw that Josh, sprawled comfortably across the blanket, was sleeping soundly. I stood looking down at him. His trip has finally caught up with him, I thought. He lay on his back, one hand under his head, the other outstretched. Mr. Rather's better-looking, I thought, but even asleep, Josh looked *active.* He was dark, as dark as Jeremiah. Swarthy, Mama would say. Mama didn't like swarthy men. In her eyes a man had to look like George, blond and blue-eyed, to be handsome. Mama thought that West Texas had just about ruined my complexion. "Lucy, that shade of yellow just brings out your freckles," she'd say, or "Lucy, don't even think about pink until your skin returns to normal."

Feeling thirsty, I tiptoed over to the picnic hamper to get a drink of water. Exploring the basket, I saw that Mr. Green had packed ham and turkey sandwiches. Oranges too. The oranges must have cost a pretty penny. I peeled one and ate it. The cookies looked like Aunt Catherine's peanut butter cookies, but they weren't. These were almond flavored. I ate two, and after that, decided to eat half a sandwich. Opening my mouth to take a bite, I saw that Josh's eyes were open. He chuckled.

"It's good I woke up," he said. "Wouldn't be any left."

"Here," I said, leaning forward, holding out a sandwich to him. Taking my hand instead of the sandwich, he pulled me to him, down across his chest, and with one arm around my shoulders and the other on the back of my head, he slowly forced my lips on his. And feeling the sun on my back and the warmth of his chest beneath my breasts, I opened my mouth to his.

Then he kissed my eyes, my lips, but before his lips could reach the hollow of my neck, I sat up, stood up.

"Josh, I am not, *will not be* like Katie. Please! Can't we just be friends?"

Josh stood and walked over to his automobile. He sat down on the running board, rolled a cigarette, and lit it.

"Lucy, you know I love you."

"If we can't be friends, just friends, we can't be anything," I said, repeating the words that had become almost a litany between us in West Texas.

Josh stood up, threw his cigarette down, and stepped on it. Kicking the blanket out of the way, he walked over and took me by the shoulders.

"Lucy, I've tried to forget you, tried for three years. Three years!" And slowly, his hands still on my shoulders, he said the words I'd heard so long before: " 'Time's sea hath been five years at its slow ebb/ Long hours have to and fro let creep the sand/ Since I was tangled in thy beauty's web.' "

"Josh, I have missed Keats! Oh, I've missed that. I've missed all that, you know. I do want to be your friend."

"Lucy, we're more than that now," Josh said, putting his finger under my chin, and then, just as I thought he would kiss me again, he stepped back. "Well, I've waited three years. I'll wait a few more weeks," he said cheerfully, unwrapping a ham sandwich.

I *was* glad Josh had come. I told him why. "Nobody around here cares about poetry or even reading. All anybody talks about is Olive Ann's baby and Jeremiah being white and—"

"Lucy, I want to talk to you about that sometime," Josh said, "about Jeremiah. Queenie's afraid something terrible is going to happen."

"Everybody says something bad's about to happen."

"Like what?"

"I don't know, but everybody's worried about it. And last Sunday, Mr. Rather said that Brother Simns's sermon was on Ham. And he said that foreign ideas have come to Bonham, and he said that lies were sweeping in from up north and from Germany. He said one lie that had taken hold here in Bonham right before our eyes was that white and colored could live together as family. Everybody knows he meant Queenie."

Josh frowned. "I suppose they could take Jeremiah away from her. How old is that boy, anyway?"

"Queenie's not sure. She thinks he's about twelve."

"A mighty big twelve. With that beard and a voice already changed, I'd say he's closer to fourteen or fifteen."

"Is that what you and Queenie were talking about?" I asked. "About Jeremiah's age?"

"No. Last night Jeremiah decided to tell Queenie what I said about his being white. Just now Queenie told me she had known it for years. She said it was a relief to find out that Jeremiah knew it, too, because now, maybe, they could worry over it together. Then she told me about this new trouble."

I knew about some of Queenie's troubles. About the trouble she had with the collection man when her rent was late, about how every year she tried to save enough to buy Jeremiah a coat and then along came her burial insurance and took it. Queenie's funds were always low. And Queenie didn't have a ship out.

"What trouble is it?" I asked Josh.

"Last Saturday some fool threw a rock with a piece of

paper wrapped around it through her window. It said, 'Don't let the sun set on you in Bonham.' "

"Who would do such a thing? Everybody likes Queenie."

"Some coward," Josh said. "But the sun set and nothing happened. So Queenie's not taking it too seriously. And it's likely she'll hear no more about it. But she's trying to keep Jeremiah close to home these days. I wonder if a visit with Brother Simns would help. Maybe he could be persuaded to pour a little oil on troubled waters."

"Josh, there's Dr. Grey. We could talk to him."

"Who's Dr. Grey?"

"He's our family doctor, but since Papa died, we call on him for everything."

I knew that Dr. Grey would help Queenie. She had worked for Mrs. Grey for years. And Josh would talk to Brother Simns. Suddenly I felt happy again. Glad to be having a picnic in the sunshine, happy to have Josh here in Bonham. I told him about the butterflies.

"Maybe they're migrating," he said. "There is a butterfly, the monarch, which migrates thousands of miles. Sometimes, especially when I'm driving, I think of that small creature with its fragile wings, making its long and dangerous journey through canyons and mountain passes, being swept off course by currents of wind and rain, and yet somehow it makes its way. It's a mighty thing. There's an old word, 'wondrous,' that describes it. It's a wondrous journey."

Josh's voice was filled with energy and excitement.

"Josh, I love it when you talk like that," I said. "Why, you could be a southern orator." Impulsively I leaned over and kissed him on the mouth, but before he could do a thing about it, I was up and repacking the basket and folding the blanket.

"Josh, we have to go. Mama hates for anybody to be late for supper. Besides, we're eating early tonight. Lillian's invited us down for cake and lemonade."

I didn't tell Josh that Aunt Catherine had made the cake for Lillian or that I'd promised to come early and squeeze the lemons. "Now, Lucy, plan to go down there a little early so you can help your sister," Mama had said the night before. "She wants to do her share of entertaining."

When we got home, there was Maggie, on the front porch, all dressed up, and with *Poems by Mr. Longfellow* on her lap; Maggie who has not opened a book of poetry since high school, with a book of poems on her lap.

I introduced Maggie to Josh. Then Mama popped her head out the door, and I could tell she was in a state, in spite of her "Good afternoon, Mr. Arnold. You all have a nice picnic?"

"Lucy," she said, "Maggie's having supper with us, and if you'll just come set the table for me, I'm sure Maggie will entertain our guest."

Wide-eyed, Maggie looked up at Josh. I hadn't noticed it before, but Maggie's eyes look a lot like Bessie's, right after we've thrown her some hay. Maggie moved over a little, patting the swing's cushion beside her.

"Lucy says you like poetry," she said.

"Some poetry," Josh said. Knowing Mr. Longfellow was not a favorite of his, I smiled at Maggie. "However," Josh said, "I'm going to run over to the hotel to change before supper. Miss Owens, if you'd like to come along, I'd be glad to have your company."

Mama opened the door and came all the way out on the porch. "Well, that's a nice idea, Mr. Arnold. Maggie can wait in the lobby for you," she said.

Mama didn't need to tell Maggie that. Course she'd wait in the lobby, but on the way over and back, she'd be flirting too. Well, I certainly didn't care. Even before Josh arrived, I had halfway decided to give him to Maggie.

"Lucy," Mama said, before they were out of sight, "you might want to run upstairs and make yourself a little more presentable. And why are you carrying your stockings?"

"Mama, for goodness sakes! I went wading while Josh took a nap."

"Lucy, don't you think that's a little unseemly? But, then, you are a grown girl. Now, please hurry back down. Queenie left early today, and I can't do everything by myself."

I changed into my white lawn dress, brushed my hair back, hurriedly tied it with a blue ribbon. I *was* late and there was a lot to do.

"Lucy, if you'll set the table, be sure to put some flowers on it, and watch those beans," Mama said. "Don't let anything burn. I'll run milk Bessie right quick."

"Mama, we can do that after supper."

"No, we can't, Lucy. After supper we're going down to Lillian's. Now, it's all planned. And your sister's counting on it."

But Mama stayed on in the kitchen, to add a little more butter to the peas, to stir up a pan of cornbread, to peel the tomatoes, so that when Josh and Maggie returned, she was just slipping out the back door, calling, "Now, don't let anything burn, Lucy. Be sure to check on the cornbread."

Watching her hurry off, her head thrust forward over her slightly stooped shoulders, why, she looks almost . . . *old,* I thought. Mama, who has never been sick or tired or anything but *indomitable,* will be old someday.

Then Maggie's "Lucy, we're back! We're here!" reminded me I had no time for gloomy thoughts. I went to meet them, taking them into the parlor with its comfortable old horsehair sofa and armchairs and its smell of roses and silver polish and, when Aunt Catherine came in through the kitchen, the odor of roast and onions cooking wafting into the room on little drifts and eddies of air.

"Good evening, Catherine," Josh said, calling her Catherine! And he stood and took her hand, led her over to sit by him on the old black sofa, and it was Aunt Catherine now who flirted with Josh, leaning toward him, a rosy flush coming to her cheeks, her eyes sparkling, her lips parted softly in an easy smile. And the years just fell away from her!

"Josh, we don't keep strong spirits in the house, but we do have a little wine," she told him. "Lucy, bring Josh a glass of that wine Maggie's mother sent down when I had that last spell." Then surprisingly, she said, "Lucy, just bring us *all* a glass. We'll be having fresh, cold milk with our supper, most of it Bessie's, though we did have to buy a little yesterday. I do hate to buy milk from Mr. Lawson."

"It's watered," I told Josh, answering the question in his eyes. "Mr. Lawson rinses out the milk container and pours it back, water and all. I've seen him do it."

"Lucy, while you get the wine, I'll just get the butter on the table and pour the milk," Aunt Catherine said. "Then we'll be all ready when your mama gets back."

Coming back in with the wine, I noticed that Maggie and Josh seemed to agree on everything.

"Mr. Arnold, you're absolutely right," she was saying now. "The children need to be in school. They must be taken out of the cotton fields. But, not changing the subject, Mr. Arnold" (course she was doing exactly that), "have you seen *The Birth of a Nation*? It's wonderful.

Why, that poor girl! I was worried to death about her. It seemed so real."

"Well, I'd like to see it," Aunt Catherine said, coming back into the parlor, "but I don't want to drive all the way to Dallas to see a moving picture."

"Josh thinks we're going to be drawn into the war," I said, introducing a subject Maggie couldn't comment on because she didn't know a thing about it.

"Americans won't forget the *Lusitania,*" Josh said. "The Kaiser's apology won't bring back one hundred and twenty-eight Americans who were lost on that ship. It's a long fuse, but it will lead to an explosion one of these days."

"Seriously," Maggie said, resting her hand gently on Josh's arm, "do you really think the Kaiser has a withered arm? Isn't that the saddest thing?"

"We've all heard it," Aunt Catherine said, encouraging Maggie. "And you know he had to be resuscitated at birth."

Josh looked at me. His eyes said, clear as anything, you are right. Nobody wants to talk about the war.

It was then we heard Mama! She hit the back door running, trotted through the kitchen and, pointing to the milk on the dining room table, hollered, "Don't take a swallow of it." She held the receiver of the wall phone with one hand and furiously rang up Miss Opal with the other.

"Carrie Belle, what's the matter?" Aunt Catherine asked, half rising from her chair.

"Bessie's gone mad!"

Mama's hair, falling loose from its bun, straggled down one side of her face and, on the same side, her apron had come untied, and it sagged well below her dress. In front of our eyes, Mama was falling apart.

"Mama, what happened?" I cried.

Ignoring me, she spoke into the telephone. "Opal, get Dr. Grey. Yes, I know it's his suppertime, but this is an emergency!"

I glanced toward Josh. On his face was a look of startled surprise. He had sprung to his feet when Mama ran in, but now he slowly resumed his seat.

"Oh, Lord, did anybody drink any of this milk?" Mama asked, taking in all of us with an extravagant sweep of her arm, before turning back to the telephone.

Josh stood up again and walked into the dining room. He looked carefully at the milk on the table. Maggie took my hand nervously and, still squeezing it, edged toward the front door. Clearly, Maggie was about to run. Josh came back into the parlor and sat down again.

"Dr. Grey, thank God, you're home. Bessie's got hydrophobia!" Mama shouted. Then, "Oh, my, *yes* I'm sure," she said.

Josh leaned forward and placed a hand carefully on each knee. "I never heard of a hydrophobic cow. But Lucy and I know how frightening a hydrophobic dog is," he said.

Fleetingly, I thought of poor H.H., remembered his growling under the house, his lunge toward Josh and me. Josh had known instantly that he was mad.

Mama was too busy answering Dr. Grey's questions to hear Josh. "Yes, I'm sure. She's running wild, foaming at the mouth. Dr. Grey, it's a wonder I got out of there alive."

"Josh, do something," I said.

Josh gave no indication that he had heard me. Clearly, all his attention was focused on Mama, who, intent on her conversation with Dr. Grey, grasped the telephone receiver so tightly that her knuckles were white.

"Yes. Why, yes. Bessie's in the Weatherbees' cow lot," Mama was saying now.

"I guess a cow could have hydrophobia," Josh said
slowly.

"Anything could!" Maggie agreed fervently.

"I'm awful glad we had that wine," Aunt Catherine
said. "Good wine kills germs."

"Oh, thank you, Dr. Grey. But tell him to hurry!"
Mama hung up the phone and, leaning against the wall,
turned to us. "Oh, what would we do without that man?
Now, don't you all worry. Everything's going to be all
right," she said reassuringly. "Dr. Grey's sending Leroy
over here to see about it. Now, Leroy's slow, but he *is*
dependable."

Holding her right side, leaning forward slightly,
Mama made her way to the rocking chair. "Well, I've
never been so frightened," she said.

Josh was looking at Mama as carefully as he had, a
minute earlier, examined the milk on the table.

Aunt Catherine handed Mama a glass of wine. "You
remember that Nailling boy, Carrie Belle," she said.

"Oh, Catherine, who could forget it? Why those last
days, they had to tie him up to keep him from biting his
own mother."

"How awful," Maggie said.

Josh nodded. "Then you've had a recent scare," he
said.

"Well, when did that happen to that poor boy, Catherine?" Mama asked.

"I know exactly when it was, Carrie Belle. And how
could you forget? It was the year George was born."

"George? Your brother?" Josh asked, turning to me.

"But Mama, George is twenty-eight," I said. A mad
cow was beginning to sound more and more doubtful.
"Oh, Mama, are you *sure* Bessie has hydrophobia?" I
said.

Josh stood up again and, pushing his hair back from

his forehead, walked toward the front door. "Lucy, show me where the cow lot is," he said briskly, "and I'll just walk down there, take a look at Bessie, and. . . ."

The explosion that stopped him in midsentence rattled the windowpanes.

"Good God, what was that?" he said, rushing out the front door, Maggie and I right behind him.

"Girls, come back inside. This very minute," Mama said, but she, too, was out on the porch.

"It came from up there," Lillian called, leaning over her porch railing to point toward the Weatherbees'.

She's bound to topple over one of these days, I thought, my head spinning.

Mrs. Walker came trotting down the walk, her breasts bouncing. To the left. To the right. Coming together. Clearly, Mrs. Walker had not taken the time to dress properly.

"You all hear that," she called breathlessly. "What on earth was it?"

"Must have been a car. Backfiring," Josh said. "But it sure did sound like a gunshot."

At that moment, Leroy Perkins, carrying a rifle, came round the corner of the Weatherbees' house. "Miz Richards," he called when he was within hailing distance, "you don't have to worry no more about yore cow. I jist shot her."

"Mr. Perkins," Mama said, "that wasn't my cow."

That brought Leroy up short. "What?" he said.

"I was taking care of that cow for the Weatherbees," Mama said stiffly.

Leroy, as if frozen to the ground, stood staring at Mama. "Whew," he said, finally.

"Lillian, you go on back inside," Mama called. "All this excitement might be too much for you," she added, looking reproachfully at Leroy.

Josh, overtaken by a spell of coughing, walked down the steps and out to his car. Kicking the tires, coughing still, he walked around it. When he took his handkerchief from his pocket and wiped his forehead, I knew it was a spell of laughing, not coughing, that had overtaken him.

"Oh, Mama, how could you?" I said to her. "There may not have been one thing wrong with Bessie, and you've gone and got her shot! And what in the world are we going to tell the Weatherbees when they come home from Galveston?"

"Lucy, watch your tone of voice," Mama said sternly. "Now, you just remember who you're speaking to!"

14

IN SPITE OF BESSIE, we went right on down to Lillian's, Mama acting as if getting poor Bessie shot was no more than swatting a mosquito. But we didn't stay long. Lillian, tired and listless, brightened only when I introduced Josh to her. Right after that the talk turned to her canary, long dead though she didn't know it.

"Mama, I think Happy's been in the window display long enough," she said. "I'd like to have him at home now. It would cheer me up."

Speechless, I stared at Lillian. Mama, taking a deep breath, leaned forward, I think, to confess. "Lillian," she began, but then Edmund, not even knowing Happy was dead, saved the day!

"Now, sweetheart," he said, putting his hands on either side of her face, "Happy would just be one more thing for you to take care of right now. And you do too much as it is."

Well, another thing Edmund didn't know was that Mama and I did all Lillian's housework and most of her cooking.

"Edmund's right, Lillian," Mama said. "You need to conserve your strength."

"Well, I do seem to get tired lately."

Lillian's saying the word *tired* was all Mama needed. She hurried us out of the house, telling me to "Come on, Lucy," even as I was picking up glasses and dessert plates to take to the kitchen.

"I'll be down tomorrow, Lillian," I called. Looking

back, I saw that Lillian's form, as she leaned way out over the porch railing to wave good-bye, looked so unbalanced it was frightening.

"Lillian," I called, "you really are going to fall right over into your rose bushes one of these days."

At this, her laugh, so loud and clear, rang through the night, lifting all our spirits, and a rush of love for her swept over me. What would we do without her, I wondered. Who else but Lillian would we fuss over? And, oh, I was glad Dr. Grey would be there when her time came. And Mama.

Afterward, Josh and I walked Maggie home, and when we got back all the upstairs lights were off. We sat on the front porch, now and then giving the swing a lazy push, watching the lights along the block go off one by one.

"It's been a very long day," I said now, rubbing the back of my neck, setting the swing into an easy glide.

"An eventful day," Josh said, chuckling. Then, slipping his hand under mine, rubbing my neck, my shoulders, he said, "I like your mother, Lucy. She's a brave woman. Running this house, the hardware business. Taking care of your sister and your aunt. And she's exciting too."

I had never thought of Mama as exciting, and yet, I supposed she was, in a way.

"Mama's always doing that," I said, yawning, "getting everybody all excited. Embarrassing the family."

I put my head back, found Josh's shoulder beneath it.

"Oh, I'd love to be here when the Weatherbees come home all prepared to thank Mrs. Richards for taking care of their cow," Josh laughed.

"By tomorrow that story will be all over town. I'm just sure Dr. Grey thought the cow was Mama's when he sent Leroy over."

"You reckon he had any idea Leroy would just haul off and shoot Bessie?"

"I doubt it. I imagine Dr. Grey was as stunned as we were when he heard it, and I suppose Leroy's told him by now," I said, smiling at the idea.

"Bessie may just have been chewing her cud," Josh said. "Cows do that. And it does look like foam. With the milking schedule off, she was probably uncomfortable."

The breeze quickened, rustling the leaves of the oaks. The limbs on the old magnolia swayed slightly.

"Josh, do you suppose—" I began, but whatever I started to say was lost, for Josh was kissing me, at first tentatively, and then urgently. And I was kissing him back, answering his urgency with my own and then surprised at the sudden warmth, almost painful, that flooded my stomach, I felt that with each kiss I was drawing all the sweetness in the world from Josh's lips. A feeling at once natural and urgent swept over me so that I put my arms around his neck, pulling him closer, ever closer, yielding up my whole being to his ardor.

"Lucy, girl," he said, "are you sure you want this now?"

The words brought me back to my senses. Slowly, I sat up in the swing, took my arms from around his neck.

"Josh, I'm not that kind of a girl," I said. Then, trying to speak with dignity, I told Josh, "You'd better go," buttoning the topmost button of my blouse, straightening my skirt.

Josh took my head firmly in his hands. "All right, Lucy," he said, and he kissed me on the forehead, a quick kiss, an uncle's kiss.

Ignoring the porch steps, he jumped over them to the ground and, whistling, walking briskly, he disappeared down the front walk into the darkness, and I knew the words to the tune he whistled. "Let me call you sweetheart," he whistled, "I'm in love with you," and, slamming his car door, "let me hear you whisper that you love me too."

I heard him whistling just before he started his car, imagined that I could hear it as he drove away, and humming the tune under my breath, I was soon undressed and in bed, pretending the pillow under my head was Josh's shoulder.

15

BUT IN THE CLEAR light of day, it was all so different. In the first place, Mama knew. Somehow she knew what had happened between Josh and me the night before. And Aunt Catherine, looking down, pushing her preserves around on her plate with the tines of her fork, knew it too. Breakfast was no sooner done with than Mama said, "Lucy, come upstairs. I want to talk to you."

My heart sank. I knew what Mama wanted to talk to me about, and I didn't want to hear it. We had had talks like this twice before.

I went into my bedroom and sat down in the window seat. Mama, her arms crossed, her chin thrust forward, stood just inside the door.

"Lucy," she said, looking over my head, "I know you've heard all the talk about Olive Ann. Now, I want you to think about that poor girl. Think about the disgrace for poor Mrs. Lippencott. For that whole family." Gathering conviction with each word, Mama put her hands on her hips and looked right at me. "Think about that poor little baby about to come into the world under a cloud, *a cloud it can never live down.*"

Oh, I wish I did not have such a temper, for suddenly I was shouting. "And what about Katie? What about her cloud? What about that?"

I could have bitten off my tongue as soon as I'd said it. "Mama, I'm sorry," I said immediately.

"Words said can never be unsaid," Mama answered, taking her handkerchief from her pocket, wiping the tears from her eyes. "But your sister *is* married. She's not under a cloud. Now, Lucy, I'm going to say this once and I never intend to say it again: Don't ever," and her tone was ominous, *"let the gate down.* If you do," she continued, "someone will come along and"—now she clapped her hands together—*"put it up!"*

The thought was terrible. The gate down. Someone, a stranger maybe, putting it up. Our family in disgrace. And added to that, with the bright morning sun shining through the lace curtains in my room, I was almost sure I didn't want to marry Josh. Oh, I liked his kisses. But kissing was a far cry from marriage to a man who would take me away from Aunt Catherine—whose very life rested in my hands—and Mama. Each day she was kept from the poorhouse only because *I* ordered the brooms and preserving kettles that people bought. *And* he'd take me away from Bonham, a place I knew and loved above all others.

"Mama, you don't have to worry," I said. "Josh will be leaving in a day or two, and besides, I'm going out with Mr. Rather tonight. Who knows? I may say 'yes' to him then."

The words were no sooner out of my mouth than Josh was there on the front porch, calling, "Lucy, Lucy, where are you, girl?"

Mama came all the way into my room. "Lucy, what in the world is Mr. Arnold doing over here so early in the morning?"

"I don't know," I said. Leaning out the window, I called down, "Josh, I'll be down in a minute. I'm talking to Mama right now."

His footsteps across the porch followed by the *wisp, wisp* of the swing told us he had settled down to wait. Mama came over and sat down by me on the window seat.

"Lucy, your daddy once said to me, 'Carrie Belle, you can always depend on Lucy. Of all our children she's the one you can depend on.' And I have. I *have* always depended on you, and I just couldn't stand it if something . . . something terrible happened to you."

Turning her head away, her shoulders bent forward, crying softly, Mama seemed so wounded. And vulnerable. The hopelessness of her crying was heartbreaking.

"Now, Mama, please don't cry. Don't. Nothing's going to happen to me. I promise. And I would never leave you and Aunt Catherine. Or Lillian either. I know how much you need me."

"I know you wouldn't. It's just that sometimes, well, it's all too much." Now Mama sat up straight, dabbed at her eyes, pushed her handkerchief back into her sleeve. "Lucy, I want to say one more thing before we go down. It's natural to marry. Have your own life. Your own family. I want that for you. I am *not* a selfish mother."

"I know you're not," I said, hugging her. "Now, enough of all this. You'd think we were having a funeral. Now, turn around here and let me do up your hair. Why is it that this side always comes undone?"

"Thank you, Lucy. Lucy, honey, I'm the one's been crying, but your eyes are red. Now, you splash a little cold water on your face, and I'll go tell Mr. Arnold you'll be down in a minute."

Knowing Mama would be polite but distant with Josh, I hurried to get downstairs. But a few minutes later, coming into the kitchen, I was surprised at the happy smile on Mama's face, the warmth of her chatter.

"Lucy, sit right down and have a cup of tea with Josh (calling him Josh!), and have one of these cookies. They just came from the oven."

"Good morning, Lucy," Josh said, sounding every bit as cheerful as Mama.

I sat down and took a cookie, still warm, from the plate. Mama poured me a cup of tea.

"Lucy, Josh just told me he's checking out of the Alexander Hotel this morning," Mama said brightly.

I looked at Josh. He gazed past me, contentedly watching Uncle Jerry at work in the vegetable garden.

"Oh?" I said, wondering at the sudden tightness around my heart. "Josh, you didn't say a word about that last night."

"I just decided this morning, and you know, I'm going to miss Mr. Green's company. He's a man ahead of his time, and I enjoy visiting with him."

Not a word about missing me. Last night had meant nothing to him. Or he had forgotten. But I remembered. I remembered his hands on the small of my back, the rustling of the magnolia leaves, the sweetness of his kisses.

"I'll drop by later on today," he said, smiling at Mama, then at me.

"I'm going for a drive with Mr. Rather this afternoon," I said stiffly.

"I hope I get to meet this Mr. Rather. Folks speak highly of him," Josh said cheerfully. Pushing his chair back from the table, he said, "I'll be going along, then. I have to get my things together, and I told Mr. Green I'd be settling up with him around noon. And Mrs. Richards, will you tell Catherine those cookies were the best I ever ate?"

I did not look up as he left the room, but Mama went with him to the door. "I'll drop by later this afternoon," I heard Josh tell her cheerfully.

"Now, you do that, Mr. Arnold," Mama said, and a minute later was back in the kitchen.

"Lucy, where are your manners? Not walking company to the door? And where in the world is Queenie this morning? If she's going to be this late getting here, she might as well not come."

"Oh, Mama," I said, "Queenie will be here. Now, you go on to the store and don't worry about Queenie. I'll straighten the house, and then I'm going to work in the garden awhile."

I spent most of the morning working alongside Uncle Jerry, pulling weeds, picking beans, finding the little green worms and pulling them off the tomato plants. Trying not to think about Josh Arnold, I worked furiously, so furiously that it was late in the morning before I noticed that Uncle Jerry had not said one word all morning long.

"Uncle Jerry, you're mighty quiet," I said. "Is something the matter?"

Uncle Jerry put his hands, one over the other, on top of the hoe, rested his chin on his hands, and looked mournfully off into the distance.

"Something mighty bad done happened down to Queenie's last night."

"What? What happened?"

"A fire. Plumb burnt up Queenie's back steps. Near 'bout ruint her kitchen."

"Oh, Uncle Jerry! Why didn't you tell me this sooner? Did somebody start the fire?"

"Sure seem like it."

"I'm going down there right now," I said. "Now, don't you worry Aunt Catherine with all this. If she asks just say I've gone to Pig Branch, and I'll be back as soon as I can."

Running, walking fast, breaking into a run again as soon as I caught my breath, I hurried toward Queenie's. The houses on either side became more and more sparse until those on the right gave way to the Big Pasture, leaving only the Wilkinses' house and, a little farther on, Old Man Tyler's on the left side of the road.

In the distance I saw Jacqueline Balfour walking, who knows where, in the heat. As I caught up with her, I turned away so as not to see again the vagueness of her eyes, the fine lines on her face, but her "Good afternoon, Lucinda" drew my eyes to her face and I saw that the lines there, caked as they were with face powder and perspiration and dust, were more deeply etched than before.

Speaking to her, looking quickly past her, I saw the Wilkinses' house (everybody says they're white trash), which had always looked deserted, and looked deserted still, even as I watched a baby tumble off the porch and saw a slatternly woman, in answer to its cry, step off the porch, right the baby, dust off its diaper, and then stand idly watching as I hurried on.

The only shade in the Wilkinses' yard was a dusty fig tree upon which Mr. Wilkins hung his medicine bottles —the blue that Parsons's Day and Night Ointment came in, the green Lydia Pinkham's Vegetable Compound bottles and the brown Botanic Blood Balm bottles—hung on the ends of the branches to ward off sickness.

And it is true that the Wilkinses were never sick. Dr. Grey said that for two cents he'd have a bottle tree in his yard, because he had never been called to the Wilkinses' house for sickness, had never treated a one of them, except for worms, since he'd been practicing medicine in Bonham.

Today even the bottle tree looked dull and hot, its bottles shaded by the wide fig leaves and covered with a fine overlay of dust. And now, right at the edge of Pig Branch, I saw Old Man Tyler's shack, the last house in the white section of Bonham. Old Man Tyler lay on his back, the upper part of his body hidden by the automobile upon which he worked. Today he was repairing (or sleeping under) Mrs. Cudgie Lace's car, a Columbia electric, the only one of its kind in Bonham. Knowing his habit of grabbing at passing ankles, I made a wide path around the outstretched legs.

Now the road became fainter, dustier, no more than a wide footpath falling away into a slough, the weeds on either side, rank and sour, forecasting dilapidation. And coming up from the slough I saw Queenie's yard, shaded by a locust tree on the right and a dusty bois d'arc on the left, shade-filled but for the thin, hot sunlight that filtered onto the bare earth and fell in narrow patches on the shrunken planking of the whitewashed cabin.

Before I reached the corner of the house, I smelled the musty, dank ashes of the fire.

"Queenie, oh, Queenie," I called, going around the side of the house, past the dust-covered zinnias, the pale roses blooming out from the almost leafless bushes.

From behind the house came the harsh sound of wood being ripped away from wood. And it seemed to me that everything—the whitewashed planking, the undernourished roses, the bare swept yard, even the shrieking sounds of wood—all fought vainly against the despair that threatened to engulf Queenie's house.

Queenie, in answer to my call, rounded the corner of her house. "Look here, Miss Lucy, what some fool's gone and did," she said grimly. "Near about burnt down my house."

"When did this happen? Where were you?"

"Sleeping, but could be I heard something. Must have! All of a sudden, I be wide awake. Then I see this light, a flickering. Took a minute but then it comes to me, oh, Lord Jesus! A fire! And I hollared for Jeremiah, and him and me, we got it out before it caught hold good."

We stood watching Jeremiah pry the last of the steps away from the house. He did not look up.

"Jeremiah, this is terrible. Who could have done this?"

Without answering, Jeremiah, his manner sullen and intractable, turned to drag the charred remnants of the steps away.

Queenie answered for him. "Wilkins trash," she said.

"Queenie, are you sure? Do you know this for sure?"

"I know it," she said.

"Did you see them?"

"Didn't need to."

"You'd better come on back to the house with me. Both of you."

"Miss Lucy, all I got in the world, I got right here, in this house. I can't leave it."

"Aren't you afraid?"

"He ain't fixin' to bother nobody in the daytime. Tonight, well, we got all day to see about tonight."

"Queenie, I'm going to tell Dr. Grey about this right now."

"Mr. Arnold. He the one to tell."

"Well, Mr. Arnold's leaving today. But Queenie, don't you worry. Something's going to be done about this. I'll be back as soon as I can."

I had reached the bottom of the slough when I heard the sound of running behind me. Jeremiah. I waited for him to catch up.

"Miss Lucy, you got a gun I can borry?"

"Jeremiah, no! We don't even keep a gun and the last thing Queenie needs is for you to get yourself in trouble with one. Now, you just forget about that!"

We stood for a minute, looking at each other. Then he lifted his chin and curled his hands into tight fists. "I say this to you, Miss Lucy," he said softly, "and to anybody. I don't ever aim to be white!" Then he turned and walked away, leaving me shaken more by what he had said than by his request for a gun.

Hurrying to Dr. Grey's, I longed for Papa. Papa would have known what to do. Or George. George could have done something. But thank goodness for Dr. Grey. After all, Queenie had worked for Mrs. Grey, had worked several years for her. And there was Mr. Rather. I had forgotten about Mr. Rather. He would help Queenie.

July is too hot for hurrying. By the time I reached Old Man Tyler's again, my blouse was soaked with perspiration. I decided to call Dr. Grey when I got home, but then, no, I thought, since his office was almost on my way home, I'd stop in and see him.

Dr. Grey was out at his farm helping one of his mares in trouble foaling, but Mrs. Grey said she'd tell him. I started down the steps and she called, "Lucy, just a minute."

I turned and went back up the steps, stepped inside, and waited while she closed the door.

"Lucy, I want to tell you something about that boy of Queenie's. And I want you to tell your mother this. If I were you all, I'd watch out for him."

Trying to make sense of the words I heard, I wondered about Mrs. Grey's eyes, what color they might once have been. Gray to match her name? Blue? Now almost as whitewashed as the planking on Queenie's cabin, who could tell? And even as she spoke, the moles on her face, two on her nose and one, slightly off center, in the middle of her forehead, became more and more noticeable, making it hard for me to concentrate. "Brother Simns stopped by here this morning," she said. "He said Jeremiah's been walking that little Wilkins girl home. Done it two or three times."

"What?" I said, trying to sort it all out. Both the Wilkins girl and Jeremiah were white, but in Bonham Jeremiah had the reputation of being colored, and a colored boy didn't walk a white girl home, or anywhere else.

". . . and maybe you ought to go."

"What?" I said now, trying to catch up with what Mrs. Grey had just said. "Where?"

"To church Sunday. Brother Simns is preaching about it. He's taking Acts 17, verse 26, as his text. And it says right there, anybody can read it, that the Lord has *'determined the bounds of their habitation.'*"

"Oh. Well, that's not our church," I said. Then I turned and fled.

At the corner of Ash and Pecan Street, Josh, waving cheerfully, passed me in his car. The suitcases tied on the back told me he was ready to leave. This seemed the final straw, Josh saying he loved me and then leaving when I needed him.

I hurried home and fixed Aunt Catherine's lunch. Then I took Uncle Jerry's out to the grape arbor.

Too restless to sit still, I waited for Mr. Rather, waited for Dr. Grey's call. And I worked, doing all the things that Queenie had so recently done for us. I tidied up the kitchen, dusted the parlor, and swept the front porch. A bundle of clothes, starched and sprinkled for ironing, was on the work table in the kitchen. This was the task I disliked most, but I could iron a few pieces before I bathed and dressed for Mr. Rather. However, after I had scorched a blouse and had had to resprinkle a skirt to get the wrinkles out that I had pressed in, I put the iron away.

Now I'd have time for a leisurely bath. This was better. I filled the tub with water, added a cup of vinegar to soften it, and sat in the tub until the water had cooled completely. Then, choosing the coolest dress I had, a thin yellow cotton, I let it fall over my head. Still I had some time, and feeling confused and a little reckless over the conversation with Mrs. Grey, I lay down on my bed, fluffing up the pillows, carelessly throwing aside the spread. I knew what Mama would say about Jeremiah and the Wilkins girl. And about Queenie's house. "Now, Lucy, you stay out of it!" she'd say. "Remember that I'm a widow, alone in the world, and you're a young girl. And with Aunt Catherine sick, somebody else will just have to help Queenie."

The ringing of the telephone and a knock on the door came at the same time. Running downstairs, I answered the phone. It was Dr. Grey. "Just a minute," I said, and went to the door. Mr. Rather's a little early, I thought, but here was Josh in the swing, his arms stretched along either side.

"Just a minute, Josh," I said. "Dr. Grey is on the telephone." Then back to the telephone. "Dr. Grey, somebody tried to burn down Queenie's house last night," I told him.

"Lucinda, Mrs. Grey just told me about that. And I am right sorry to hear it."

"Dr. Grey, what are we going to do?"

"Do?" he said, as if the answer were the simplest thing in the world. "Why, Lucinda, you just tell Queenie and Jeremiah that this business of walking the Wilkins girl home has to stop."

His voice was slow and gentle, the sound of it was reason itself. I wondered why I had made it all so complicated.

"Well, all right, Dr. Grey. Thank you." But still I held the receiver, vaguely dissatisfied, waiting.

It was as if Dr. Grey felt the waiting, for after a minute he said, "Lucinda, I'd talk to Queenie myself, but she and Mrs. Grey had a little misunderstanding. In view of that, I think you'd better talk to her. You or Mrs. Richards. Tell her this walking's got to stop."

I went out again to where Josh waited. He smiled and stood up. Then he sat back down and stretched his arms out on either side of the swing.

"Lucy," he said, grinning, "I want you to remember that this is *our* swing. Don't you be sitting in it with Mr. Rather."

"When are you leaving?" I asked, wondering at the vast chasm that separated us: his lighthearted humor on one side, my responsibilities on the other.

"Leaving? Why, Lucy, I'm not leaving. I don't intend to leave you again. In fact, I'm all settled in at Mrs. Lace's. Mr. Green told me she ran the best boarding house in Bonham. He said he sometimes slips over there himself to eat with Mrs. Lace," Josh said, chuckling.

"I thought you were leaving," I said, dumbfounded.

"Lucy, maybe you better read that last letter I wrote you again."

I didn't need to read it again. I knew what Josh had written, but I couldn't think about it now.

"Josh, you've got to talk to Queenie," I said. "And Jeremiah."

Then I told him all about Queenie's porch steps, and about Queenie's saying it was Mr. Wilkins who started the fire, and about Mrs. Grey's telling me that Jeremiah had been walking the Wilkins girl home, and about Jeremiah asking for a gun. And, finally, I told him what Dr. Grey had just said.

"What in tarnation does that mean?" His voice was incredulous. "You mean to say that Dr. Grey thinks you ought to just sit still while some idiot burns down Queenie's house? Why, burning a house down in the middle of the night is arson. Besides that, Queenie works for the Richards family. And it's up to you, not white trash, to correct her *and* her son, if they need correcting. Well, sweetheart, don't you worry one bit about it. I'll take care of Munger Wilkins. Folks like that are easily taken care of. It's the Brother Simnses of the world who are hard."

Hearing Josh say it, I knew that Queenie's problem with Munger Wilkins was just about over. Sitting there by Josh in the swing, I knew that he would take care of it. For the first time since I'd heard about the fire, I felt easy about Queenie.

16

"JOSH, WHAT WILL you say to Mr. Wilkins?" I asked, the words no sooner out than Mr. Rather's buggy, black and shiny as patent leather, came into view. We watched Mr. Rather tip his hat to Lillian, who appeared on her porch and then, just as quickly, disappeared into her house. (Lillian thought she was too far along now to appear out in public.) When Mr. Rather reached our house, he ground-tied the small bay mare and walked briskly up the steps.

Josh stood to shake hands with him, but not before Mr. Rather had seen his arm stretched along the back of the swing, his hand resting lightly on my shoulder. I introduced the two of them to each other.

"Someone set fire to Queenie's house last night," I said, jumping right in to take Mr. Rather's mind off Josh.

"I heard that. Bill Porterfield told me about it. He got it from Mrs. Grey."

"Isn't that the most cowardly thing you ever heard of?"

"Well, yes, but . . ." Mr. Rather shifted his weight from his left to his right foot.

"But what?" I said.

"Mrs. Grey said Queenie's boy has been walking Munger Wilkins's girl home."

I couldn't believe my ears. It was as if he thought those words made the fire *understandable*.

"Son, setting a house on fire is a criminal act," Josh said.

Now I stared at Josh. *Had* he called Mr. Rather "son"? I couldn't be sure. Josh went right on with what he was saying.

"And, more importantly, Queenie is the Richardses' maid, and it's up to them to speak to her, if it's needed, about anything Jeremiah may or may not do."

I couldn't take my eyes off Josh. He was right about the fire, but Queenie wasn't *our* maid. She had worked, at one time or another, for a good many families in Bonham. Queenie wasn't really anybody's maid. And, too, there was Jeremiah's color to think about. Somehow, when he walked the Wilkins girl home it didn't matter that he was really white. Did that somehow mean that color didn't matter in Bonham? And yet, I knew that it did. I'd have to sort this whole thing out.

I looked at Mr. Rather, standing pigeon-toed, twisting the brim of his hat in his hands. I wondered what he was thinking. Josh, leaning against the front porch post, his hands in his pockets, made Mr. Rather look uneasy. And young.

Taking pity on Mr. Rather, I said, "I'm ready to go." And turning to Josh, "Mama will be home soon, and Aunt Catherine will be up from her nap, if you'd like to wait."

But Josh wasn't listening. "Lucy, this man, this Munger Wilkins, where does he live?" he asked abruptly.

"Just this side of Old Man Tyler's," I told him, describing the house. "They've got a bottle tree in front."

"A bottle tree? You mean a bottle tree to ward off evil spirits?"

"Mr. Wilkins has medicine bottles on his tree. He says it wards off sickness. Josh, are you going down there to talk to him about Queenie?"

"I might stop in. I was planning to do a little squirrel hunting down that way."

I wasn't sure I wanted Josh to do anything at all about the fire at Queenie's. But Josh could usually persuade a person to think a different way. I had seen him do it. Josh and I would talk it over later, decide together what to do.

The three of us left at the same time, although Josh waited to start his automobile until we had turned the corner so as not to startle the mare. And the little mare, Daisy was her name, was the best part of the buggy ride. She stepped out smartly and eagerly as, again, we drove to the Big Pasture, but my heart wasn't in it. When Mr. Rather put his hat on the gate post this time, it seemed a childish, silly thing, and I could not focus on his talk for wondering what Josh might be saying to Mr. Wilkins.

Finally, I gave up and asked Mr. Rather to take me home, saying Aunt Catherine needed me there. Hurriedly, I thanked him for the buggy ride and went right into the kitchen to start supper.

A few minutes later Mama got home and came immediately to the kitchen. "Lucy, did you know that Mr. Arnold has taken a room at Mrs. Lace's?" she said sternly. "He's not leaving."

"He told me that this afternoon."

"And did you know that he went down to the Wilkinses' and shot all the bottles out of their bottle tree? Everybody in town's heard about it by now."

My heart sank. "Oh, my goodness! Who told you?"

"Mr. Walker stopped by to tell me all about it just as I was closing up. He was so tickled over the whole thing, he had to sit down in the window display to recover."

I could certainly imagine that! Mr. Walker laughing, his face red and getting redder, the tears rolling down his cheeks, pulling out his handkerchief and putting it back, and all the while laughing, laughing.

"Well, Lucy, when Mr. Walker finally stopped laughing, he said Josh Arnold was shooting at a squirrel up in Mr. Wilkins's bottle tree. He kept missing the squirrel, but he broke a dozen bottles. And after that, with his rifle in plain view, he drove Queenie to Mr. Mac's grocery store and back home again. Now, Lucy, to do that he had to drive right past the Wilkinses' house. Twice. And then, Lucy, listen to this: after he took Queenie home, he drove up to the Wilkinses', walked up the steps, knocked on the door, introduced himself, and then he told Munger Wilkins he was counting on him, on Munger, to see that no further harm came to the Richardses' maid, her boy, or her house."

Putting her hand over her heart, she shook her head. "Lucy, I'm sending Uncle Jerry over to Mrs. Lace's boarding house (I don't know why on earth she doesn't have a telephone put in, but I guess it's the money), with a message to Mr. Arnold. I'm asking him to stop by our house. And then I'm going to tell him as politely as I know how to stay out of our affairs."

But when Mama, still grumbling about Mrs. Lace not having a telephone, went out back to Uncle Jerry's shed, she found him on his way to Pig Branch. "No, you go ahead," she told him. "You can take this note over to Mr. Arnold just as well in the morning."

And that night Josh came with his own invitation. I had already gone to bed when I heard his car. Mama answered the door, and I went over and sat in the window seat where I could hear every word.

"Why, Mr. Arnold," I heard Mama say, with such formality Josh must have known she was displeased with him, "Lucy has already retired for the night."

"Mrs. Richards, I apologize for the lateness of the hour, but driving by I saw your lights and decided to stop by. I'd like to have your company at dinner on Friday. Yours and Lucy's *and* Miss Catherine's, if she's feeling well enough. Could you join me for dinner at the Alexander Hotel?"

Mama loved to dress and go to the Alexander for dinner more than anything. When Papa was alive, they had dinner there, regularly, three or four times a year. Of course, since Papa's death, this was a luxury we could no longer afford. And now, hearing the energy, the enthusiasm in Josh's voice, I knew what her answer would be.

"Why, Mr. Arnold—"

"Mrs. Richards, call me Josh."

"Thank you, Josh. I can't answer for the others, but I, why yes, I'd enjoy that."

"Good. That's settled then. I'll stop by again tomorrow to see if Lucy and Miss Catherine can join us."

I could imagine him tipping his hat, turning to leave. Then I heard Mama say, "Oh, Josh," and the sound of his footsteps coming back up the steps.

"Yes, ma'am?"

"Josh, a widow, even in a town the size of Bonham, has to live a more circumspect, a more careful life than others. And I have to think of my children. Nothing is more precious to me than my four children."

Now Josh would be nodding sympathetically. Josh was a good listener.

"Now, about this business with Queenie and Jeremiah. I've known Queenie for years. She helps us out when we need her. Queenie says she can make more helping out than working for one family. In fact, that's the reason she quit working for Mrs. Grey. She asked Mrs. Grey for a raise! Now, I can see both sides of that. Queenie worked for the Greys for years, hardly ever missing a day, but Mrs. Grey was awful good to Queenie, giving her buttermilk and bacon grease. And clothes, perfectly good clothes. And when Jeremiah had measles and whooping cough at the same time, Dr. Grey went to

Pig Branch twice (once in the middle of the night) to doctor him. Well, when Mrs. Grey said no indeed about the raise, Queenie went back to filling in."

"Queenie strikes me as a mighty good cook," Josh said.

"Oh, she is. And I like Queenie. But Josh, I can't afford to get mixed up in Queenie's troubles. Why, the thought of what might come of all this sends cold chills down my spine."

The silence lasted so long I thought that Josh might have somehow slipped silently away. But then I heard him ask, "Are you afraid?" His voice was gentle.

"Oh, yes, I am. And in spite of what Lucy says (Lucy doesn't know enough to be afraid), it *is* a man's world, Mr. Arnold. And here we are, three women in a house without men. We just cannot afford to get mixed up in Queenie's problems."

"Mrs. Richards, I promise you that Queenie won't have any more trouble with Wilkins. He's mean, but he's a coward. And like most cowards, he listened carefully when he noticed I had a gun. In fact, he told me he never intended to go near Queenie's house again, all the while denying he had ever been near it."

"Well, we'll just have to wait and see about that. But it's not just Mr. Wilkins."

"It's that preacher, too, isn't it?" Josh said. "One of these days, I'd like to hear his reasons for preaching that Jeremiah can't live with the only mother he's ever known."

My heart sank. Josh had always used words to persuade and now he had used a gun. Whatever Josh might do about Brother Simns, I hoped it would not be as violent as shooting bottles in a bottle tree.

The next few days I tried to avoid Mama and her questions about Josh, but finally I said, "If you want to know anything about Josh Arnold, why don't you ask him yourself."

And then a letter came from George saying Inez was not at all well, and that took Mama's mind off Josh and his intentions toward me.

On Friday, Mama closed the store early so that we wouldn't have to hurry getting dressed. I planned to wear the dress Mama had brought me from Dallas, and Mama was wearing her gray silk, old but freshened by a new lace collar. That afternoon I got out all my clothes and did up my hair before I bathed. Then I dried off slowly and patted on the rose water Mama had chilled in the icebox. Trying not to perspire, I put on everything but my dress and sat in the window seat, waiting for Josh. When I saw his car turn the corner, I slipped my dress over my head and went downstairs.

Mama was there before me. Waiting. Sitting tall in her chair, holding her head high, her ankles crossed gracefully, she looked composed. And pretty! I had forgotten how pretty Mama was.

"Mama, you look beautiful," I told her.

"Thank you, Lucy, but remember, pretty is as pretty does," she said.

Josh was surprised, too, at how nice Mama looked. For a minute he just stood there, in the doorway, looking at us. Then, "I can tell you that I'm going to be the envy of every man at the Alexander tonight," he said, "but what about Miss Catherine? I was looking forward to her company too."

"Catherine asked me to tell you that—" but here was Aunt Catherine herself, looking pale and tired, but smiling.

"Josh, I am sorry," she said, "but I've somehow caught this cold. Silly, to catch a cold in the summer, isn't it? Perhaps you'd ask me another time."

"As soon as you feel up to it," Josh said, gallantly offering her his arm, carefully settling her onto the sofa, telling her how sorry he was she wouldn't be joining us.

As we drove to the Alexander that evening, I enjoyed watching Josh with Mama, teasing her about Bonham, about Bessie (her laugh was a little restrained at that), about Tennessee's being prettier than Texas. It's too bad I'm not married and settled here in Bonham, I thought. Then Mama could give herself over completely to the enjoyment of Josh's company, for it was clear she did enjoy Josh.

Mr. Green, clearly delighted to see Josh again, led us to a white damask-covered table in front of a window curtained by green palms brought from Galveston, and directly beneath an ornate electric-lighted chandelier. Seeing Mr. Bowden, the owner of the electric plant, at a nearby table, I thought, it's no wonder he eats here. With all the electric fixtures the Alexander has, Mr. Green is probably his best customer.

After Mama and I were seated, the men, still standing, went on talking. This was the chance Mama had waited for.

"Lucy, everybody thinks well of Mr. Arnold. But how long does he plan to be in Bonham?"

"Not now, Mama," I said. "Let's not talk about that now."

"I just don't want you to lead him on, make him think there's some future for him here."

Looking up at Josh and Mr. Green, smiling at them, I ignored Mama. She could pick the worst times to discuss a subject, but it was easy to pretend she wasn't saying a word. Mama could talk without moving her lips. She should have been a ventriloquist.

"Hush now, Mama," I said again.

I looked around the room. Maggie's parents were

there, at a table just inside the door. I wondered if Maggie was out with Mr. Porterfield.

Mrs. Lace, Josh's landlady, and her sister, Miss Barbara, were at the table next to the Owenses. As befitted her name, she wore a high-necked blouse, one so lacy that her camisole, lacy too, showed through. As she turned her head to signal the waiter, a pearl comb in her luxurious black hair (everybody said it was dyed) caught the light.

Years before, Mrs. Lace had left town and come home with a new name, saying she was a widow. But there was never any evidence of it. And she was never seen in mourning.

Now she nodded, rather formally, toward our table, but the smile and wink she gave Josh when she saw him was anything but formal. I wondered how old Mrs. Lace was. Not as old as Mama, certainly, but older than Lillian. Sitting there with her sister, she looked comfortable. Cheerful. Looking at her made me want to put my elbows on the table.

But then, oh my Lord! there were the Weatherbees, just getting up from their table and beginning to make their way over to ours, stopping first to speak to Mr. Bowden.

"Mama!" I gasped. "The Weatherbees!"

"I see them," she said, sending a quick smile their way. "I didn't know they were back from Galveston. I wonder if they've heard about Bessie," she added, through perfectly still lips.

Josh had just taken his place at the table, and seeing them coming toward us, he winked at me and grinned, his eyes dancing. Clearly, Josh was all set to enjoy what was coming.

Mama, sounding as glad to see them as if they had been new customers, said, "Why I.B. and Kitty, I didn't know you were back."

"As a matter of fact, we just drove in. And I said to Kitty, 'Since the stove is cold, we'll let it rest one more day, and we'll eat our supper out. Then, on the way home, we'll stop by Mrs. Richards's and thank them for milking Bessie.' Didn't I say that, Kitty?"

"He did. He certainly did," Mrs. Weatherbee said proudly.

"We were glad to do it," Mama said lightly. "Why, that's what neighbors are for. But"—and here she paused, closing her eyes—"I thank God nothing terrible came of it."

Mr. Weatherbee frowned. "How's that?" he asked, as if he hadn't quite heard what Mama had said.

"Well, we were all so worried about Lillian," she said. "You know," lowering her voice, "she's—"

"Oh, I know," Mrs. Weatherbee said fervently, so quickly that Mama didn't have to say more.

Mr. Weatherbee cleared his throat. "Well," he said, folding his hands in front of his belt buckle. With the subject of Lillian in the conversation, he obviously didn't know what question to ask. The Weatherbees waited politely while Mama took a sip of water.

"I barely got out of the cow lot with my life," she continued.

"Goodness!" Mrs. Weatherbee said.

"Dr. Grey's hired hand had to shoot Bessie," Mama said, sounding regretful and relieved at the same time.

Mr. Weatherbee's jaw dropped. "Well, what got into her?" he said, after a minute. "Bessie'd hardly flick her tail at a fly. She's been that gentle."

Mama shook her head, her expression now a combination of puzzlement and despair over Bessie. "Hydrophobia," she said.

Mr. Green, who had been standing over by the Galveston palms, walked right into the middle of the conversation. "Loco weed," he said. "I think she got into some loco weed."

"Could have been that," Josh conceded.

"Well, I'm sure sorry," Mr. Weatherbee said, scratching his head. "I'd never have asked you folks to milk Bessie if I'd had an idea in the world a thing like that would happen."

Now Mrs. Lace was out of her chair and coming over. "Hello, there," she said brightly. "Barbara and I were just talking about the cow Leroy Perkins shot, and my sister and I think it was . . ." she hesitated, looked at our still-empty plate, "you folks haven't been served yet so I'll say it, we think it was . . . *worms*."

Josh nodded. "That can sure give a dog a fit."

Apparently Mr. Weatherbee still hadn't heard a diagnosis that satisfied him. "Maybe it was just a mean streak," he said. "Come to think of it, Bessie was dehorned. And I've heard a dehorned cow'll sometimes take a notion that she's a he-cow. Well, Mrs. Richards, I'm real sorry it happened."

Josh bit his lip, took his handkerchief from his pocket, wiped his forehead, put the handkerchief back in his pocket. I knew he was enjoying the conversation. He saw that I watched him and winked again.

Now Mr. Bowden, on his way out, limped over. (Mama says his arthritis is caused by sleeping on all the money he keeps under his mattress.) He leaned on my chair and Mama's, gathering himself to speak. "It was most likely a bee," he said. "Probably stung that cow on the nose. I've seen it happen to cows *and* horses."

"You know, I bet that was it," Mr. Weatherbee said. "Yessir, Mr. Bowden, I bet you just hit the nail on the head."

Satisfied, Mr. Bowden hobbled off and Mrs. Lace rejoined her sister. After a minute Mr. Green went back to his post by the Galveston palms, and then the Weatherbees, offering apologies and firmly rejecting Mama's offer to replace the cow, left too.

Relieved, I smiled at Josh. "I'm hungry," I said.

Josh and I ordered steak and Mama, sighing that oysters were not in season ("I do wish July had an 'r' in it," she said), settled on pork roast. Just as our supper came, the Roses—Miss Opal, Miss Pearl, and their brother, Mr. Dennis Rose—came in.

Nodding toward them Mama said, "Josh, see the girl in the plum-colored dress? Well, when you ring up the operator, that's who you get. That's Opal. When the Roses bought the telephone exchange, she became a famous person. Everybody knows her. People stop Opal on the street and ask her to talk to see if she sounds in real life like she does on the telephone."

Josh's obvious interest encouraged me to tell him the other interesting fact about the Roses. "The Roses don't marry," I said. It was common knowledge, but at this Josh threw back his head and laughed so that everyone in the dining room turned and looked at us.

"Well, they're not a marrying family," I said, blushing.

Josh, still chuckling, said, "Well, somebody's marrying somebody."

This evening Josh knew almost as many of those dining at the Alexander as we did. And Mama enjoyed that too. Professor Bucinni, who teaches at Carlton College, stopped at our table to speak to us, saying it was a damn shame, "excuse me, ladies," about Queenie's house.

"Mr. Arnold," he said, "this situation, about Queenie and that boy she's raised, presents a problem to the citizens of Bonham. People just don't know what the answer is. And since they don't, it seems logical to me that they should stay out of it."

"You're right, Professor Bucinni," Josh said. "But they

don't seem to be staying out of it. Now, according to this preacher, this Brother Simns, Jeremiah is white. And yet, Simns doesn't think he should be walking the Wilkins girl home." Josh, warming to his subject, spoke without regard to Mrs. Lace and her sister (and others at nearby tables), who were obviously interested in the conversation at ours. "But," he continued, "Jeremiah talks like the colored and he lives in Pig Branch. So what makes a person colored? Is it the way he talks? The part of town in which he lives? The color of his skin?"

Professor Bucinni laughed. "Mr. Arnold, I don't think it's the last. Here. Look at my hands. Are this colored woman's hands darker? I doubt it."

"In Shakespeare's time it didn't seem to matter," Josh said.

"Perhaps, in some ways, the Elizabethans were luckier than we are," said Professor Bucinni, smiling at Mama and me. "But I've interrupted your supper with these ladies too long. I'm sorry. But such a subject interests me."

Shrugging her shoulders, Mama whispered, "Crazy talk," her whisper making its way around the salt and pepper shakers, over the iced tea glasses and into my ears.

After Professor Bucinni left, Josh, sensing Mama's impatience with the conversation, engaged her in a light, bantering conversation. But all the while he listened to Mama, and spoke to those who stopped by our table, he was aware of every gesture I made, every smile, every sigh. Even my unspoken words, it seemed to me, were heard by Josh as he asked a waiter to move an electric fan which had been placed too close, asked another to bring more lemon for my iced tea, winked at me over Mama's insistence that Bonham had more to offer than Dallas.

"Just wait until the chautauqua gets here," Mama said. "Last year they had a German prisoner, a British hero, and a quartet of college girls that sang and danced at the same time. And lots more. I can't remember all they did have on the program."

"Mrs. Richards, I've never seen a chautauqua program. I imagine it's changed since Emerson's time."

Josh is an interesting man, I thought, but then, suddenly, for no reason, a longing for all that my life might have been swept over me. It should have been Bob here with me at the Alexander, I thought, not Josh. I should have been the one coming home with a handsome husband and a baby. Filled with despair, I saw all those times ahead when I would remember Bob and be overcome at that which could never be. At this thought, a cold chill went down my spine.

"Lucy," Josh said, "what is it?"

"Nothing," I answered. "Somebody just walked over my grave."

"Don't say that, Lucy!" he commanded, and rising, pulling out my chair (forgetting all about Mama), he said, "Come on, sweetheart, I'm going to take you home."

17

THE NEXT MORNING Josh asked me to marry him. For the
last time. I was just out the door on my way to the hardware store when he came round the corner of Mrs. Walker's house. "Wait a minute, Lucy!" he called. "Can't you
wait just a durn minute for a man who wants to marry
you?"

Of course I waited, shushing him the whole time, but
by the time he reached Aunt Catherine's garden the
whole neighborhood could hear him. "Lucy, this is the
last time I ever intend to ask you!" he called out to me.

Even if Mama and Aunt Catherine had not heard him,
I was sure Mrs. Walker had. And she'd tell her Sunday
school class.

I ran to meet him, put my hand over his mouth. "Shh,"
I said. "Everybody in town can hear you."

Chuckling, he put his hands on my shoulders, drawing
me close. Then his eyes, greener than anything in Bonham, narrowed and he raised his right eyebrow. "Lucy,
I'm asking you. *Will you marry me?*"

As I started to say . . . something, he waved it aside.
"No, don't give me an answer now. Just think about coming with me to Sweet Shrub. Next year that's where we'd
be, with the lakes and the dogwood blooming in the
spring, and the children coming into the classrooms
with buds from the sweet shrub plant in their pockets.
During the day I'd be working at the school and nights
I'd be reading law."

That's what Josh would be doing, but "What would I do there?" I asked.

"Why, Lucy, you'd be my helpmate," he said. "You know married ladies can't teach."

Of course I knew that. Still . . . "Josh, you have no idea of all my responsibilities in Bonham. My family needs me here and besides—"

Josh's quick kiss silenced me, but my mind would not be still. The man I married would have to live right here in Bonham. And, besides, where was there a place for love in Josh's plan? I had never said I loved Josh, not even to myself, and love wasn't something to put in a suitcase along with your best dresses and silk stockings. The love I knew was right here in Bonham with my family and my own bedroom with the curtains blowing in the summer breeze and the smell of Aunt Catherine's garden and the monument to the Confederate soldier and Jacqueline Balfour's walks into the country.

After the kiss, Josh walked over to the porch railing and, spreading his arms out on either side, he looked across the street toward the vacant lot and over the tops of the trees growing on it. "Lucy, right now, all I'm asking is your promise to think about it. We could marry about the middle of August and take a little honeymoon trip, maybe to Hot Springs. And then we'd go to Sweet Shrub and settle in before school starts. Will you just think about it? That's all I'm asking."

Thinking about it seemed easy enough. And polite. And I did enjoy Josh's kisses.

"I'll think about it, Josh, but . . ."

"No 'buts,' " he said. "Now, come on. I'll walk you to the store."

When we reached the store, he took the key from my hand and unlocked the door. "At noon I'll stop by to drive you home. It's getting too hot for you to walk," he said,

and he went off down the street, whistling, "You Made
Me Love You (I Didn't Want to Do It)."

During the next days, Josh came to seem like my best
friend; no, he was more than a friend. Certainly, to
Mama and Aunt Catherine he became a member of the
family. They called on him for everything!

He ran errands for them and repaired windows that
wouldn't stay up and doors that wouldn't close properly.
He rewired the chandelier in the dining room so that it
was as bright as day when we turned on the light, and he
moved the furniture around in the parlor when Mama
bought a gentleman's chair. And he entertained us, taking Mama and Aunt Catherine for rides in the country,
and he went frog gigging with Edmund out on Lake St.
Claire. He took me roller skating, and we played lawn
tennis with Maggie and Bill Porterfield. And almost every morning he walked me to the store and in the heat of
the day he drove me home.

Mama relaxed a little about money, even when she
had to spend a little of her principal. She told Queenie
and Jeremiah we'd be needing them every day because
she wanted to get the house and the garden in apple-pie
order. "And, Jeremiah, that way you can work off the
furniture in no time," she told him. Of course, I knew,
without its being mentioned, that all this flurry was because of Katie and Bob's approaching visit. Bob had
never been to Bonham and Mama wanted to make a
good impression.

Usually, Jeremiah worked with Uncle Jerry in the garden, but now Mama had him paint the porches and re-
pair the brick walk going out to the privy. Sometimes, if
we needed him there, he would walk with me to the
hardware store. And these walks had a quiet intensity
about them. Jeremiah, his arms and hands only a shade
darker than mine, walked along by my side, saying little,

but when he spoke, the tightness in his voice made my throat hurt.

That next week, the first week in July, it was so hot that we tripled our order of artificial ice. In the afternoons we made big pitchers of lemonade, and sometimes right after supper we'd make a freezer of vanilla or peach ice cream. Then, when the sun set, Lillian and Edmund would walk down (Lillian could hardly breathe with the heat), and Josh would be there. Maggie and Mr. Porterfield might drop by, and when Mr. Walker was in town, both the Walkers would come. Then we'd bring more chairs out on the porch and have ice cream. After that, the men would pitch horseshoes, the *plink, chuff, chuff* of their hits and misses punctuating the long twilight hours. Or we'd sing. Mama has perfect pitch and she'd start us off on "Just a Song at Twilight" or "Danny Boy." Then Mr. Walker (always off key), would begin "That Old Girl of Mine" or "It's a Long, Long Way to Tipperary." We sang the catchier tunes, too, tunes like "When You Wore a Tulip and I Wore a Big Red Rose," and "By the Beautiful Sea."

But just as often, Josh and I would go to the Queen Theatré (we saw *A Fool There Was* and *The Goose Girl* in the same week), and then the Pathé news made the war seem terrifyingly close. Seeing the British soldiers disembark at Gallipoli I thought how *familiar* they looked. Why, it could as well have been Mr. Mac's delivery boy or Leroy Perkins or the young man at the *Bonham Daily Favorite* newsstand smiling and walking jauntily down the gangplank as those young British soldiers. I hoped that we'd soon be watching their victorious return to England. But Josh was pessimistic about the war.

"It will be months and months, maybe years, before the war ends," he said. "And America is bound to be drawn into it. We can't stay out of it for long."

But the war. What could I do about the war? Here in Bonham, as the time grew nearer for Bob and Katie's visit, I waged my own war, trying to forget West Texas and those nights when Bob's arms were around me and I had thought they always would be there.

Then, almost without my noticing, Mr. Rather and Mr. Mosley gradually dropped out as suitors. When Mr. Rather stopped by to see me, Josh, who was often there, would engage him in lively conversation. He advised him about his teaching. "Son, from what you tell me I think you need to ask *more* of your students," I heard him say to Mr. Rather one day. And they had long talks about the war, Josh explaining why the British losses at Gallipoli should never have happened, could have been prevented. And all one Saturday afternoon they worked on Mr. Rather's buggy, replacing a broken spring. Oh, Mr. Rather continued to visit, but now he only stopped by when Josh's motorcar was there.

Mr. Mosley did not give up so easily. He'd come to see me and sit in the swing or one of the parlor chairs and stay all afternoon, standing if I stood, sitting if I sat, smiling when I smiled. But one day, somehow, there we were, the three of us, at the skating rink, Mr. Mosley and Josh and me, Mr. Mosley protesting that he didn't know how to skate and Josh (skating backward, his hands clasped loosely behind him), telling him that if he would just let go of the railing he would be able to skate fine. "It's a *mind* sport," Josh, gliding by, called out to him. "Just tell yourself you can skate and you can!"

Mr. Mosley should never have listened. Taking a deep breath, he pushed himself away from the railing, and he managed to stay on his feet until he reached the center of the rink. Then he fell, crawled to his feet, balanced there for a second, and fell again! He got up again. And fell. And each time he fell, he became more grimly determined to get up again.

"The fool, he's going to break something for sure," Josh muttered.

"Josh, go help him!" I cried. "And let's just quit all this and go home."

We did. And that was the last time Mr. Mosley called.

But it was a long time before I thought much about Mr. Mosley, for right after that Brother Simns came to the house to talk to Mama. We had just finished dinner, and Josh had gone to hear Sam Rayburn, our congressman, who was speaking at Honey Grove. Mama and I were in the front porch swing when Brother Simns drove up.

"Wonder why he's coming to see us?" she said, through perfectly still lips. She took her handkerchief from her sleeve (how often had I heard, "Lucy, a handkerchief is the mark of a lady"), and stood to greet him.

Smiling at us, nodding, Brother Simns stepped down from his motorcar and with his hat in his hand and his Bible under his arm, hurried up the steps. He's come to ask us to attend his revival was my first thought, and then, this can be a pleasant visit if he doesn't call Mama "Sister." Opening the door, I was just glad that Josh was not there.

I took his hat, and Mama asked him to sit down. "Lucy, bring Mr. Simns (Mama, being raised Methodist, was not comfortable calling him 'brother') a glass of lemonade and tell Catherine we have company," she said.

Knowing Mama wanted Aunt Catherine's moral support, I did that first, and then I fixed a tray of lemonade and cookies. By the time I got back, they were already talking about Queenie and Jeremiah.

"Mrs. Richards, *I* believe, and a good many of the folks

in my congregation believe," Brother Simns was saying, "that something has to be done about your maid and that young man."

His voice was dry, monotonously reedy, barren. I wondered how he could exhort his congregation to any purpose. And some words, it seems to me, don't deserve a reply. I hoped Mama wouldn't answer.

"Lemonade?" I asked, handing Mama and Brother Simns a glass. I had never noticed before, but his mouth was *full of teeth,* more than the usual number. He could barely smile around them.

"Well, I don't know what could be done," Mama said, clasping and unclasping her hands. "And I don't even know what *should* be done."

Anybody would agree with that, I thought. "Brother Simns, sometimes isn't it the hardest thing in the world to *know* what's right? To be sure?" I said to him.

"Why, no, Sister Richards," he said. "It's the easiest thing in the world to know what's right. All you have to do is to open your Bible, open it on any page, and the answer is there. Well, here, let me show you how you can always find the answer to any question," Brother Simns said, pushing his coat sleeves up, waving the Bible through the air. "Let's just look at Acts," he said, quickly turning the pages to Acts (I had thought he was just going to let the Bible fall open), and he smiled at Mama and at Aunt Catherine, who was just coming into the room. Then he closed his eyes and lifted his chin.

"Sit down, Catherine," Mama said. "Mr. Simns is going to show us a trick."

He opened his eyes. "Well, it's not a *trick,* Mrs. Richards. It's faith."

"Oh," said Mama.

"Listen," he said, "are you listening?" I was. " 'And hath of one blood all nations of men for to dwell on all

the face of the earth and' "—now his voice was stern—
" 'hath determined the times before appointed, and the
bounds of their habitation.' "

With the last words, his voice had become triumphant.
Smilingly, he snapped the Bible closed. "Well, ladies?"
he said.

Mama looked down into her lap, rolling a loose thread
from her dress into a tiny ball. Aunt Catherine picked up
her embroidery, studying it as if she did not know where
to begin. I cleared my throat. "Brother Simns, what you
just read sounds like we're all meant to live here. Like a
family."

"Miss Richards, we are. But not *together*. Now, you
just heard," he explained, gently tapping his Bible, "that
the Lord has determined the bounds of their habitation.
That means that the white people live in one place and
the colored live in another."

I thought about running upstairs to get my Bible.
"But—" I said.

"Lucy, perhaps Mr. Simns would like another glass of
lemonade," Mama said briskly, reminding me that
Brother Simns was a guest.

As I moved toward the pitcher, Aunt Catherine said,
"Lucy, honey, you might answer the door first. I believe
Mr. Arnold just drove up."

And then Josh was in the parlor, making it seem
smaller than it had a minute earlier, smiling at all of us,
but his raised eyebrows said clearly, "What's he doing
here?" when I introduced him to Brother Simns.

Brother Simns smiled briefly at Josh and waved him
to a chair. "Ha, ha," Brother Simns said, coughing out a
laugh, "we were just having a Bible lesson," he said.

Josh cocked his head to the side, crossed his legs, and
nodded. "Go right ahead," he said.

"Now, the main answer to this Queenie question is to

be found in Genesis. Now, we're all familiar with the
story of Noah and Ham."

Nobody said anything. I had thought they were two
different stories.

"Aren't we?" he asked. As I was *somewhat* familiar
with it, I nodded. "Now, in verse twenty-five it is written
that Canaan would always be a servant. Now, kuh-*learly*
the Lord means that if that young man goes on living
with Queenie, then Queenie *will be his servant.*"

Mama's mouth fell open and Aunt Catherine took a
deep breath. The idea made my head swim. Then Josh
threw his head back and laughed. Still laughing, he got
up, walked over to Brother Simns, and put his hand on
his shoulder.

"If you'd just stay around here a day or two, Brother
Simns, you'd know that could never happen." Josh's
smile was so benevolent that I thought he might be getting ready to call Brother Simns "son."

"Why, Brother Simns, the scripture that that boy
knows, and knows bone deep, is 'Honor thy father and
mother.' And if you saw them together, you would know
that he does honor the only mother he's ever known."

Mr. Simns pulled his lips together over his teeth. "But
it's not meant that they *live* together. Going against the
Bible can be dangerous," he said.

"What about Philemon and the slave?" Josh said.
"Didn't Paul ask Philemon to forgive his runaway slave,
not to punish him? Doesn't this suggest that it's the mas-
ter of a servant who is responsible for the servant?
Seems to me that it's up to the Richards family to talk to
Queenie about Jeremiah, if anyone needs to talk to her."

"Mr. Arnold, you are twisting the meaning of the Good
Book," Brother Simns said.

"Maybe we both are," Josh said kindly. "But Brother
Simns, I'm depending on you, and so are these ladies, to

see that nobody interferes with their cook. Or with their cook's boy."

"Doing the Lord's will is never interference," Brother Simns said. "Well, good afternoon, ladies," and, tucking his Bible under his arm, he walked to the door so fast I barely got there in time to open it for him.

When the door closed behind him, Aunt Catherine said wonderingly, "You know, Brother Simns sounded just a little *mean*."

"Josh, I wish you hadn't laughed," Mama said.

"Mrs. Richards, you're absolutely right. But Simns's conclusion was just plain funny. Can you imagine Queenie working for Jeremiah?"

Shaking her head, Mama smiled at the idea.

Josh leaned forward, clasping his hands between his knees. "Since Simns is taking that position, it will be hard to convince some folks to let Queenie and Jeremiah alone. And as Professor Bucinni said, it is a problem in logic. Maybe it would be best if they left town."

"Where would they go?" I asked.

"Well, there is a third choice, maybe the best. Jeremiah could cross over."

"You mean, live as a white?"

"After all, we're pretty sure that he is white," Josh said. "And as a white boy, he would have a better chance in life. He could certainly get a better education."

"Let's ask them what they want to do," I said. "Queenie probably doesn't want to leave town. And I'll bet she doesn't want to give up Jeremiah either. And Jeremiah said he never intended to be white. He told me that."

"Well, we could do that. We *should* do that, now that you mention it. Mrs. Richards, you have a brilliant daughter. When Queenie comes tomorrow, you can ask her. And you can talk to Jeremiah about it."

"Mama, let Josh talk to Queenie. She tells him things she would never tell us."

"Why, that's a good idea, Lucy, if Mr. Arnold's willing."

"Be glad to," Josh said. "I'll talk to her one day this week."

With that we dismissed the "Queenie question," as Brother Simns had called it. Bob and Katie would soon be arriving, and each of us, in our own way, began to get ready for their visit. And getting ready, we forgot about Queenie and her boy.

18

A FEW DAYS before Bob and Katie were to arrive, the weather changed so that the days were a little cooler and the nights just about perfect. And Bob would be here soon, walking up the porch steps, sitting at our table, going to bed in our house. I could not stop thinking about him.

I remembered the sweetness of his expression when he had fastened the pearls, luminous in his hand, around my neck. "Wear these today," he had said, "and the day we marry." I felt again the terrible anxiety of the night he had eloped with Katie. And I had never suspected! All that long night I had waited, never once thinking they might be on their way to Oklahoma.

Now Josh asked, "Lucy, why are you so quiet?" but he did not insist on an answer. Perhaps he knew I thought about Bob.

Then the weather turned hot again. Underneath the pewter-colored sky, the grass turned yellow and died. Enervated by the heat, Josh and I turned to quieter diversions. We played cards and we read to each other. He read Byron and Keats to me, sometimes reciting long passages from memory, and I read parts of *Vanity Fair,* the novel I was reading, to him. And he helped me translate a passage from Virgil, my first. "Lucy, you have a good mind," he said.

At night when the house was quiet, we'd sit in the swing and he'd tell me about Tennessee and his life there. And he'd kiss me, whispering, "I love you, Lucy.

You know I love you," his voice a soft vibration, like music, in my ear.

And then it was the weekend, and Mama insisted on meeting Bob and Katie in Sherman, for they would not be coming, after all, in the Sully's railroad car. "On the train all those hours. Why, that baby will be exhausted," Mama said, so Josh and Mama left early to drive to Sherman to meet them.

Aunt Catherine and I bustled around, clearing the table, doing the dishes, running a mop over the floor. "Everything we do now will help Queenie when she comes," Aunt Catherine said. "She has an awful lot to do today."

She cut sprigs of pale pink crepe myrtle from the bush in the backyard. "For the baby," she said, arranging them in a small yellow pitcher. Then, smiling, her cheeks flushed, she crossed her arms and leaned against the dining room door. "I just can't believe that Katie's coming home today and bringing a baby with her," she said. "Lucy, there's nothing sweeter in this world than a baby."

"You said that right, Miss Catherine," Queenie, just coming in the back door, answered. "Why, the day I found Jeremiah, he made the whole world sweet."

I had not thought that everybody would be so glad Katie was coming home.

"What about now, Queenie? With all the trouble you've been having over Jeremiah?" I asked crossly.

"World's still sweeter," she answered reasonably.

Aunt Catherine laughed softly.

"You look like you feel real good, Aunt Catherine," I told her. "Like you've had a good long rest."

"That baby's gonna rest us all," Queenie said, "*and* wear us out! Now, you all go on 'bout your rat killing and let me get things ready for that baby *and for your sister*."

I didn't need to be reminded about my sister. "I'm going to eat dinner with Maggie," I told them, the thought just occurring to me. "I won't be home until late this evening."

But I didn't go to Maggie's. Instead, I cleaned the store from top to bottom. I washed the windows on the inside, leaving the outside for Jeremiah. Then I wrapped a rag around the broom and swept the spider webs and dust from the ceilings and corners of the store. After that, I dusted all the shelves and swept the floor. Then I rang up Miss Opal. "It's Lucinda Richards, Miss Opal. Ring number twelve, please?"

"I hear your sister's coming today," Miss Opal said. "I'll bet you're excited."

"Well, I've never seen the baby."

"Goodness! Gracious! Aren't you tickled? I would be."

"I hope they're not all out in the garden where they can't hear the telephone," I said, to remind her to get back on the job.

"Well, we'll just see, but if they are I'll ring up Mrs. Walker. She can run down there and tell them to go inside and pick up the receiver."

But Queenie answered right away and said she'd send Jeremiah down to do the windows.

Waiting for him, I decided to run over the floor with a dust mop. Then I heard someone whistling "You Made Me Love You," and I knew it was Josh. They're home early, I thought. But it was Jeremiah, coming into the store.

"Jeremiah, I want you to wash the windows on the outside, but first, sweep the sidewalk. Will you?"

"Yes, ma'am. Sure will," he said.

I stood in the doorway watching him. "You're mighty happy this morning, Jeremiah."

"Yes'um. I am."

I waited, and in a minute he stopped sweeping and smiled, a wide, disarming smile. "I've been thinking about next year. About something I just might do," he said. "Been talking to Mr. Arnold about it."

His head high, the broom in his hand held as lightly as a fishing pole, Jeremiah looked so *alive.* Why, Jeremiah's going to be real handsome, I thought. I waited a minute, but he said nothing more, and I went back inside to finish the floors.

I had worked my way to the back of the store when I heard the sounds of scuffling, followed by a thud. Then I heard footsteps. Running.

Before I reached the front door, I knew what I'd find. It was Jeremiah, against the wall, thrown there. He groaned and pulled his knees up to his chest.

"Mr. Davis," I called. "Come help me with Jeremiah!" Then kneeling by his side, I asked, "Who was it? Who did this?" But he was in too much pain to answer.

Charlie Davis, his white apron bloody from his butchering, came running from the meat market next door, and together we pulled Jeremiah to a sitting position. "Boy, now let this be a lesson to you. You've got to leave that Wilkins girl alone!" he said, breathing heavily.

Ashen-faced, Jeremiah carefully pulled himself to his feet. "Mr. Davis, I ain't done more than *see* Jean Wilkins since school let out," he said.

"That's what I mean," Mr. Davis said sternly. "You've got to stop seeing her. Now, you know those Wilkinses."

"When I walk by the Wilkinses' house, I see her, but I don't *look* at her," Jeremiah said.

"Well, you're gonna have to walk another way. Miss Lucy, now, he's just gonna have to do that," Charlie Davis said, dusting off his knees, his hands. He stood a minute, looking up and down the now-deserted street. Then he shrugged his shoulders, a shrug that said clearly he had done all he could and went back inside his meat market.

"Come on inside," I said to Jeremiah. "Sit here. In Mama's chair. I'll get you a drink of water."

I brought him a drink and bathed his face with a wet rag.

"Who was it?" I asked again.

"Her brother. And two more. I seen them around."

Sitting in Mama's chair, his clothes rumpled, Jeremiah looked . . . discarded.

"Oh, Jeremiah, what are we going to do?" I said.

"Only thing I know. Next time I be ready."

"What about Queenie? Are you going to tell her about this?"

"Can you keep a secret, Miss Lucy?" he asked.

I thought he meant a secret from his mother about the attack, but he pulled up his pants leg and there, tied to his leg, was a knife, a deer-skinning knife.

"Well, you're going to have to tell Mr. Arnold about that knife," I said.

All afternoon just two customers came in the store. Late in the evening Charlie Davis stuck his head back inside the door. "You all right, Lucinda?" he asked, and when I nodded, he hastily retreated.

Neither one of us wanted to leave the store that day. Jeremiah sat quietly in Mama's chair (I think he dozed off after a while), and I leafed through some fall catalogues, now and then even seeing the illustrations before me.

When the telephone rang, my throat tightened at the thought that it might be Katie. I asked Jeremiah to answer it.

"Yes'um," he said. "Yes'um, I'll tell her." Turning away from the telephone, he said, "Your mama say to come home. They here, and Miss Katie, she done run down to your other sister's and Mrs. Richards say she need you."

"All right, Jeremiah. Come on," I said, but we had not walked a block when I saw Josh's Maxwell turn the corner. "Here's Josh to pick us up," I said. "Now, you watch what you say to him. Mr. Arnold's got a temper, and I don't want him to lose it on account of Munger Wilkins. But you show him that knife, you hear?"

The minute Josh saw us, although there was not a scratch on Jeremiah, he knew. "What's happened?" he said. "Lucy, something's the matter."

"Jeremiah got in a scuffle."

"Why, Jeremiah, that's not like you," Josh said.

When we reached our house, Josh said, "Lucy, I'll stop by later on this evening. Right now I'm going to take Jeremiah home." And as he opened the automobile door and took my hand, he said, "Lucy, Katie's baby girl looks just like you."

Going up the porch steps, I saw the baby in the garden. She was chasing something. A butterfly? And I turned back down the steps. Rounding the corner of the house, I saw that Aunt Catherine, her hands on her hips, stood there smiling, watching the baby.

"Lucy, your mama's in a state," she said when she saw me. "If you'll watch Annabel a minute, I'll run help her."

"What's Mama in a state about?"

"Bob didn't come with Katie. And Katie hasn't said a word about why. Carrie thinks they may have separated."

Sighing, Aunt Catherine went into the house. Bob's not coming, *not coming,* I said to myself to make it real. I felt dismay. Relief. Then I thought, Katie's not been here one hour and already she's got everybody upset.

But here was Annabel running toward me, calling

"Mama, Mama," and not until she had her arms tightly around my knees did she look up. Then she did not release her hold, but "Mama?" she said doubtfully.

"Annabel, your mama will be home in a minute. I'm your Aunt Lucy," I told her, loosening her arms so that I could kneel beside her.

"I know!" she exclaimed. "I know who you are!" And she patted my shoulder, small, comforting pats.

"Let's go swing on the porch," I said, taking her little fat hand in mine. "It's cooler there."

When we reached the swing, I started to help her up, but she said, "No, me do it," climbing up all by herself. Then she turned herself around, sat down, smoothed her dress over her lap and calmly folded her hands.

"Swing," she commanded.

I pushed the swing into motion. Now I could look at her. She had Katie's silvery hair and her pointed chin, but her clear blue eyes were Bob's. She wasn't Bob's child, but somehow she had his eyes. But Josh is right, I thought. Even with Katie's hair and Bob's eyes, she does look a lot like me.

Smiling at me, she quickly stood up and, for balance, put her arms around my neck. I wondered if all babies smelled like Aunt Catherine's herb garden after a warm spring rain.

Down the street, Lillian's door opened and first Lillian, then Katie, came out on the porch. Slowly they walked toward the house, their heads close together, with Edmund following behind but hurrying to take Lillian's arm each time she stepped off a curb or came to a place in the sidewalk pushed up by tree roots.

Walking next to Lillian, Katie looked taller and more slender than I remembered.

I took Annabel's hand in mine. "Here comes your mama," I said.

"Ouch!" Annabel said.

"I'm sorry, Annabel," I told her. "I didn't know I was squeezing."

But Katie, in her easy, careless manner, saying, "Hello, Lucy," leaning forward to kiss me, made those first few minutes easier than I had thought they could be. "Oh, I'm so glad to be home. I couldn't wait for you all to see Annabel. Lucy, Mother Sully says she looks just like you."

"Girls! Edmund, can you get these girls to the supper table? My, my!" Mama said, looking anxiously from my face to Katie's. Then, "My, my," she said again. "Look here at grandmother's angel. You're going to sit by me, Annabel. Right here in the chair your mama used to sit in."

Halfway through supper, Lillian asked, "Why didn't Bob come?"

"Oh, Lucy knows how Mother Sully is, don't you, Lucy? She says they need Bob on the Henrietta ranch and then she says she needs him at the house, and with all that needing, I said 'Bob, I'm going to see my family. If I wait for you, I might never get home.' So here I am."

Mama, clearly relieved, nodded happily. "Let's get away from the table. Let Queenie do up these dishes."

In the parlor, Lillian and Mama told Katie all the news.

"Does Old Man Tyler still scare the children?" Katie asked.

"Yes," I said, thinking I was glad Bob hadn't come with Katie. It was easier.

"And what about Leslie? People in West Texas just can't believe we have our own hermit right here in Bonham."

"Well, we do, and he is the sweetest thing. He got some

more patents. How many did the paper say he has now?"
Aunt Catherine asked.

"Over fifteen, wasn't it, Lillian?" Mama said.

"At least fifteen," Lillian said. "And Jacqueline's still
walking all over the county. But her poor mother. She
can hardly get around."

"So nothing's changed," Katie said.

"Oh, some things have," I said, and told her about Josh
shooting the bottles in the Wilkinses' bottle tree.

Keeping her voice down so Queenie wouldn't hear,
Mama told Katie all about Queenie and Jeremiah and
about Brother Simns's call.

"Mama's right," Katie said when she finished. "The
Richardses had better just stay out of Queenie's business."

But Lillian and Katie had more to talk about than Leslie's patents or Queenie's trouble.

"Lillian, you poor thing," Katie said. "Your feet are so
swollen. My doctor says strong black coffee is the best
thing in the world for that."

And while Edmund read the paper and Annabel fell
asleep in my lap, they talked the rest of the evening
about swelling and nausea and getting their shapes
back.

"I'll take Annabel up and put her to bed," I said, looking at Lillian, at Mama, at the lamp behind them, looking anywhere but at Katie. Somehow, I could not look at
Katie.

When I put Annabel in bed, she stirred and opened her
eyes. "Sing," she said softly.

And I did. " 'Oh, don't you remember a long time ago,
two poor little babies whose names I don't know,' " I
sang, knowing it was the song Mama had sung to Katie,
to all of us when we were babies.

I was almost asleep that night when I heard a light

knock on my door and Katie's whisper. "Lucy, it's me. Can I come in?"

"It's too late," I whispered back.

"Lucy, please. I have to talk to you."

In a minute, she'd wake up the household. I went to the door, opened it a crack. "Come in," I said, turning around and getting back into bed.

She closed the door softly, came over and stood by my bed. "Lucy, I couldn't help it!" she gasped. Then she was crying, pinched whimpering sounds that made her seem far away.

"Come on," I said grimly, getting out of bed. "You'll have Mama in here in a minute."

Tiptoeing downstairs and out to the porch, we eased into the porch swing.

Katie bent over, picked up the hem of her gown, and wiped her tears away. "Lucy, I had to marry," she said, between short little gasps. "Oh, you don't know what's it's like. Getting fatter every day, and *nobody* knowing and doing everything you ever heard of—jumping off tables and bathing in scalding hot water, and knowing all the time how ashamed everybody will be."

I didn't answer. But in a minute she was calmer, the small gasps becoming an occasional sniffle.

"But Bob and I, we were promised," I said, wiping away the tears that now had begun to run down *my* cheeks.

Katie started to cry again, deep wrenching sobs. "I'm so sorry, Lucy."

Curled up sideways in the swing, her face buried in the crook of her arm, her voice was muffled so I had to strain to hear. "One of the worst parts of it is that Bob's sorry too," she said, sighing a long, shuddering sigh.

"I don't want an apology from Bob," I said.

"I mean he's sorry he married me. The way he looks at

me sometimes, his eyes hard as marbles, I know he's mad it's me and not you there with him. And his mother, she even said it. Mrs. Sully said, 'You're not one thing like your sister.' "

Well.

Here was something else. I remembered the times Mrs. Sully had looked at me like she had just bitten into a peach and found a worm. I could see it all—Bob's blue eyes like stones, and his mother sitting there in a silence as cold as a Sunday stove, both of them looking at Katie.

Crumpled up in the swing, Katie looked small. Defenseless.

"I am glad we've got Annabel," I offered.

Katie smiled. We sat together in the swing. It was the quietest night. I started to say, "It's all right," but I wasn't sure it was. Then I said, "Let's try . . ." and I stopped, wondering what we could try.

Katie sat up. "From now on, I'm going to be such a good sister. Lucy, you won't know me, I'll be so good."

The hardness that had been there, around my heart, whenever I thought about Katie or Bob—I don't know, but I think it began to melt away that very minute. I felt better all over.

I leaned over and gave Katie a quick little hug. "I'll always know you," I said, "no matter how good you are. And you'll always be my sister."

Not until I had gone back to bed that night did I realize that Josh had not come by after all.

Early the next morning he came. His left eye was almost swollen shut, and he had a cut on his lip.

"Good morning, ladies," he said.

"Josh, what happened?" Katie asked.

"You should have seen the other fellow," he said,

laughing, but not answering, either, and I knew it had something to do with the Wilkinses and Jeremiah.

As Josh and I sat in the swing that night, I said, "Josh, tell me what happened. Did you get into a fight with Munger Wilkins? I can't believe you'd lower yourself to fight with him."

Josh threw back his head and laughed. "Lucy, I went down there to talk to Munger. I don't care a thing in the world about fighting, but sometimes with a fool like Munger that's all that's left. I could stand there or hit him. So I hit him."

Josh looked so pleased about the whole thing that I just said "Good night, Josh," and went to bed.

During the next few days (can anybody pinpoint the moment or the incident that brings it on?), I grew more and more restless, so restless I didn't know what to do. For one thing, Katie, trying to be the best sister in the world, *took over.* The hardware store. Lillian. The house. It wasn't that *she* did anything, but she told everybody else what to do.

That first Monday morning, looking in the mirror, she put her hair up on top, then, frowning, she pulled it to one side. Pursing her lips to bring out her cheekbones (she has always thought she had nice cheekbones), she said, "Mama, you need some help at the store, someone to open up early every single morning and to close every day at six o'clock. It's too much for you and Lucy."

"I've been thinking along those lines," Mama said. And she hired the Walkers' nephew.

Katie was especially strict with Lillian. "You're not getting enough exercise," she told her. "My doctor told me a long walk every day and a few household chores were the best things in the world for a lady expecting."

"Well, I'm not about to go out in public now," Lillian said. "Not like this!"

"Lillian's right, Katie," Mama said. "She's too far along."

"She can walk after dark, Mama. Be cooler then, anyway."

I'll be glad when Katie leaves, I thought, trying to decide whether it was being a good sister or having her own bank account that made her so bossy.

But Annabel! That was different! She filled up the house with her sweetness, drawing us all to her like a magnet. Early in the morning, she might be found anywhere. Sometimes she'd slip into my bed. "Aunt Lucy, read," she'd say. Or before the neighbors were up, she'd coax me, still in my gown, out into the garden. We'd look for little tomato worms and rolly bugs, and we'd find a bee in a hollyhock blossom and fold over the bloom, imprisoning it for a minute before releasing it to buzz angrily away.

One night Lillian and I helped her catch lightning bugs (Lillian lumbering about the garden with a butterfly net, and Edmund and Mama calling, "Lillian, be careful!" and "Lillian, darling!"), and Josh put them in a small jar with a string around it. "Now you've got your very own lantern," he told her.

Annabel adored Lillian, and soon she was as protective of her as Edmund. When she saw her coming, she'd run to meet her and, holding her hand, she would solemnly lead her up the steps and ease her into the swing. Then she'd pat her knee and push the swing, so gently that it was impossible to tell if it moved.

The end of the week, Katie got a letter from Bob. "He won't be coming for us until the end of September," Katie said. "But that's better. It will be a little cooler for traveling. And I'll be here to see about Lillian's baby."

Katie had begun to go about again, seeing friends, going to the theater. Shopping. With her *very own check-*

ing account, a husband, and a baby, it's no wonder everybody listens to her, I thought.

Still, everything was better. Easier between us. And Mama's business was good, and Lillian felt well. Aunt Catherine was like her old self.

"Miss Catherine, you are so much improved," Dr. Grey told her. "I can hardly believe it. The summer's helped you. And the rest and good food."

"And Annabel, Dr. Grey. She's just a little sunbeam," Aunt Catherine said.

"The tuberculosis is in remission. You may never have any more trouble, but I'd still take every precaution around the baby."

With Aunt Catherine well again and the business good and Annabel cheering us up, it seemed to me that I should have been happy. But as I watched Edmund doting on Lillian and Katie managing the household and Mama cheerful and Aunt Catherine well again, with each day that passed I grew more and more restless.

19

IT WAS THIS vague sense of unrest that caused me to sleep so lightly that Saturday night, so lightly that I heard, or thought I heard, someone opening the kitchen door, the squeak of a floor board, the scraping of a chair being pulled away from the table. Thinking it was Aunt Catherine and that she might need me, I slipped on my wrapper and went quietly down the stairs, staying close to the wall so the stairs wouldn't squeak.

Outside, a pale moon cast a faint light through the kitchen windows. "Aunt Catherine," I whispered into the darkness.

"It Queenie, Miss Lucy."

Too sleepy for surprise, I turned on the light. "Queenie, what are you doing here in the dark?"

"Jeremiah, he ain't come home. Not all night."

My heart sank. What we'd all been saying had come true. Something bad had happened to Jeremiah. And Queenie knew it. Sitting at the kitchen table, she looked worn out. Shrunken. It was as if all her bones had collapsed inward, her rib cage and the bones in her shoulders and her back. Looking at me, she put her hands over her mouth as if to prevent a final collapse.

The kitchen, with its cold stove and without the usual smells of coffee perking and bread in the oven—it, too, had taken on an air of disaster. I went to the stove, lit the fire, put on a pot of coffee.

Queenie shifted in her chair. "I told Uncle Jerry," she said. "He gone to tell Mr. Arnold."

Conscious of Aunt Catherine, asleep just off the kitchen, we spoke in whispers.

"We'll find him, Queenie. I know we'll find him."

I handed her a cup of coffee and poured one for myself. Then I drew my chair up to the table and sat down across from Queenie, and in the silence we waited.

It was a good hour before Josh came back. "Queenie, I went over to the Wilkinses'. Woke them up. And I asked every one of them, from Munger on down, about Jeremiah. Munger and his boys kicked the floor, looked down, said they didn't know a thing about it. But there were two others there, cousins visiting from Georgia, and some of them, maybe all of them, know something about Jeremiah. They're mighty nervous about something. Munger was shaking so badly he had to set his coffee down to keep from spilling it."

I handed Josh a cup of coffee. He sat down at the table, drank a little of it, and then, abruptly, put the cup on the table and stood up.

"It's after seven," he said. "I'm going over to the sheriff's house. I'll talk to him. If he'd bring the whole bunch in, we might find out something."

As soon as Josh left, I got up from the table. "I'm going to fix us all some breakfast," I told Queenie. "Now, you just sit still."

"I got to do something," she said, "If I don't I'll go crazy."

While I set the table and fried bacon, she stirred up a pan of biscuits and got the eggs out, ready to scramble.

As first Aunt Catherine and then Mama came to breakfast, I told them about Jeremiah. Mama's first impulse was one of generosity. She hugged Queenie and said she was sorry, but when Josh returned, telling us the sheriff had said he had to have something more than suspicion to go on before bringing the Wilkinses in for

questioning, a frown appeared on her forehead and I
knew she wished we had stayed out of Queenie's problems.

"Queenie, we'll find your boy," Josh promised. "Sheriff
Hayes agreed that with the violence against Jeremiah
and the fire at Queenie's, we should organize a search
party. So let's get to work on that. Mrs. Richards, you ask
your preacher to announce it at church," he said, and
sticking his head out the back door, "Uncle Jerry, you go
on down to Pig Branch and tell the folks down there that
we're going to meet on the courthouse lawn right after
dinner, no later than one o'clock."

I called up Dr. Grey, who said he'd come if he could,
and I called Edmund. I knew he'd help. When I asked
Mr. Rather, there was a long silence before he said he'd
be there, but Mr. Mosley spoke up right away. "That's
terrible. I'll sure help," he said. Then I called Mr. Green
at the hotel, and he said he'd come. Mr. Davis said, "Lucinda, after what happened outside your mama's store
the other day, I knew this was bound to come," but he
said he'd be there.

Knowing Mr. O'Dwyer, the owner of the mill, was
civic-minded, Aunt Catherine marched right to the telephone and called him up. Mr. O'Dwyer said he'd drive
out to South Bonham and round up some of his mill
hands to join the search. Mama even called up Brother
Simns, thinking he'd announce it to *his* congregation.
He said he'd heard it and that he was sorry. "It's too bad,
but I've warned about going against the Bible," he
added. He started to say more, but Mama hung up before
he could.

A little before one Josh started out the door. "I'm coming with you," I said.

"Lucy, you can't go with me. A search party is no place
for a woman."

"I'm coming as far as the square," I said. "If you won't take me, I'll walk."

"Get in the car," he said.

I was surprised at how many people were there when we arrived. There were a good many coloreds, and Mr. Rather and Mr. Davis were there. And sitting at the foot of the monument to the Confederate soldier was Maggie's father. I hadn't thought to call him. Jake William was there, and some other mill hands I didn't know. And Bill Porterfield came driving up.

"Maggie said not to come home until Jeremiah's found," he grinned. "She said if I find him she'd give me three kisses!"

Now, isn't that just like Maggie, I thought. Making everything personal. Watching the crowd grow, I was so glad there were this many. "I didn't think there would be this many people," I said.

"Well, we're bound to find him. I just hope he's alive when we do," Josh said.

The words hurt my heart. I had never thought Jeremiah might not be alive when we found him.

Sheriff Hayes came over to Josh's car. He put his foot on the running board and tipped his hat back.

"Mr. Arnold, I've divided this bunch into four different search parties, giving each one the area they're best acquainted with. Now, that will put the coloreds around Pig Branch and the mill hands in South Bonham. I've asked those with motorcars to drive around the fairgrounds and those on horses to ride through the river bottoms. The Reverend Cook and you and I can take the woods behind Old Man Tyler's and Munger Wilkins's places and, well, speak of the devil! Here comes Tyler now."

I was surprised to see him out from under his car. Walking as if his feet were bound, he snatched his hat off his head when he saw us. "Is it a nigger or a white boy missing?" he asked. "Well, it don't matter. I come to help." His hat, quivering in his trembling hands, gave him an aspect of feeble eagerness despite his rheumy eyes.

Sheriff Hayes walked over to stand at the base of the Confederate soldier and began to speak.

"Now, this is a good town, with good folks in the town," he said. "And we don't want no harm to come to nobody, no matter what color they are or"—glancing at Josh who moved as if to interrupt—"what folks *say* their color is. We are all law abiding. So let's get on with it and find that boy that most of us *think*"—and he paused and looked at Josh—"is white."

But by five o'clock that afternoon, most of the searchers, disheartened by the heat and by the mosquitoes along the riverbank and creekbeds, had given up and gone home. Only a few searched until dark.

The next morning the men, by now only about a dozen in number, went out again. About two in the afternoon, Mr. Davis stopped by the store and said what everybody was thinking. "No use in wearing everybody out. The boy's dead. Might as well wait until a hunter comes upon the body, or a fisherman snags it."

But Josh meant to keep on looking. "Queenie, I'm going to find your boy," he said. Then he looked at me. "At least I'm going to look until I leave Bonham. I'm not giving up on anything until then."

That was the closest Josh came to mentioning his proposal again.

Late Tuesday afternoon Josh, who had just returned from another long day of searching, and I were in the garden with Annabel. By the time the sun set, Jeremiah would have been gone three full days and nights, and I hated for the day to end. I had just about given up, but

Queenie hadn't. Playing with Annabel, I saw her stand for a minute at the window in the kitchen. A little later, she appeared at the living room window, then the dining room window. Josh had seen her too.

"It's hope that keeps her going," he said.

"Mama told her to stay home and rest. But she said if she didn't do something, she'd go crazy," I said.

Just then I saw Annabel squat down behind a rose bush. I rushed over to her. "Not here, Annabel," I said, thinking she needed to go to the privy.

"A dirl," she whispered. "See dat dirl!"

I looked where she pointed. A ruffled umbrella swaying down the walk, and underneath it, Jacqueline Balfour. Dressed in pale chiffon, as for a tea, she wandered down the sidewalk toward us. From this distance the lines on her face were invisible; she looked young. I sat back on my knees, wondering where on earth she was going on a day still so hot, even with the sun low in the sky.

Surprisingly, when she reached our front sidewalk she turned in and walked up to our front door. She tapped so softly with the door knocker that the door would have gone unanswered had I not seen her there on the porch.

"That lady's come to see us," I told Annabel, taking her hand.

Josh and Annabel and I walked up the porch steps behind Jacqueline.

"Good afternoon, Miss Balfour," I said.

"Hello, Lucinda."

I introduced her to Josh, and she extended her hand. To Annabel she said, "Hello, little girl." Then, taking a tattered handkerchief from her purse, she dabbed at the beads of perspiration on her upper lip.

"Well. Let's go right in. It's cooler inside the house than out today," I said.

"Is this a convenient time for company?" she asked softly.

"Why, yes," I said. "Now, come in and sit down. I'll run fix us all a glass of iced tea."

I hurried to the kitchen, Annabel trotting along behind.

"Queenie," I said, "it's Miss Jacqueline Balfour, come to see us. Can you believe it?"

But not even a visit from Jacqueline could shake Queenie from her air of lassitude and melancholy. Nevertheless, she helped me chip the ice, cut a lemon, get out a tray.

Returning to the silent parlor, it struck me that for once Josh Arnold was at a loss for words. So I said, "Miss Balfour, everybody's gone but Annabel and Josh and me. You know, Annabel is Katie's little girl."

Jacqueline smiled at Annabel, a nebulous, uncertain smile. Up close the wrinkles on her face shot up into her eyebrows, out from her eyes and the corners of her mouth.

"These are mighty good cookies," she said, not noticing that she hadn't yet tasted one.

Casting around for something to say, I asked, "How's your mama, Miss Balfour?"

She took a cookie from the tray. "Oh, Mama's fine," she said. "Every Sunday, I take her for an automobile ride in the country."

This was news to me. I hadn't known they had a motorcar.

She took a bite from the cookie and *replaced it on the tray*. Carefully repositioning her napkin under her glass, she sipped her tea.

"That's very nice," I said. "Did you go riding this past Sunday?"

"Oh. Yes," she said vaguely.

Jacqueline has a lyrical voice, one that sounds as if at any minute she might break into song, so that speaking she seems always to be on the verge of singing. After a pause, during which she held her glass of tea up to the light, examining it closely, she said, "We drove out on the Honey Grove road. When we got way out in the country, I stopped the car."

Annabel, warming to Jacqueline, moved closer to her, and put *her* half-eaten cookie back on the tray. Naturally, I couldn't correct her, but I picked up the conversation.

"It is pretty out there, even this time of year," I said, thinking she had stopped so she and her mother could admire the view.

As if she hadn't heard, Jacqueline continued. "And when I stopped the car, I said, 'Mama, get out!' Mama didn't want to get out, but I said, 'Now, Mama, you get out!'" Although Jacqueline spoke more emphatically, now there was a note of bewilderment in her voice. "So Mama got out!" Now Jacqueline leaned forward and patted Annabel's head. Looking at Josh, at me, at Annabel, her tilted head, her slight movements made me think of a little sparrow. "Then I said, 'Run, Mama!' but Mama didn't want to run. So I said, 'Mama, now you run!' So Mama started running and I tried to run over her. She'd run this way," said Jacqueline, leaning delicately to the left, "and I'd go that way, but then she'd run that way," now leaning to the right, "and I'd turn that way. I tried and tried, but I couldn't run over her," she said sadly. "So we came home."

I closed my eyes and opened them. Jacqueline was still there. I cleared my throat. Josh shifted in his chair. Nobody said a word. Hardly breathing, Josh and I sat, fascinated by the horror of her tale and the gentleness with which it was told. Then Annabel, completely won over (I can only suppose), by the lilting sweetness of her voice, was leaning on her knee, patting it. Both reached for another cookie. Annabel took one. Jacqueline's hand hovered over the plate, her index finger moving this way and that. She chose one and sat up straight in her chair. "I know where that young man is," she said, "the one you all been looking for."

"Oh, Jacqueline, do you?" I asked, jumping up to tell Queenie.

"Wait a minute, Lucy," Josh said, "Don't say anything to Queenie yet."

He's right, I thought. Jacqueline probably hasn't the faintest idea where Jeremiah is.

"Miss Balfour, would you show us where Jeremiah is?" he asked gently.

"Why, yes," she said.

While Jacqueline and Josh made their way out of the house and down the sidewalk, I ran to ask Queenie to mind Annabel. "Watch Annabel for a little while," I told her. "Josh and I are going to drive Miss Balfour home."

But when Josh and I started toward the car, Jacqueline said, "Oh, we'll have to walk. I don't think we *could* drive there."

So we walked, the three of us. On that hot day without any real hope at all we walked. We walked past blocks of houses and then past the Big Pasture. When we turned off onto a dirt road, little more than a trail, right after we passed the Wilkinses' place, I thought, Maybe Jacqueline does know something about Jeremiah. We walked along the trail until it intersected an unused logging road, and we walked all the way down the logging road. At its end, the land fell away into a dry creek bed. There, halfway hidden under a pile of brush, we found Jeremiah, bound and gagged. He was unconscious, but he was alive.

Leaving Josh to tend Jeremiah, I ran to Dr. Grey's house. Thank goodness, he was there! Dr. Grey brought his car, and together he and Josh carried Jeremiah to where we had left it, at the end of the logging trail. We took him straight to the colored hospital, and Dr. Grey sent for Mrs. Camp to come from the white hospital and help. "We gonna have to have a nurse out here with him or else move him into our hospital," he grumbled.

When Mrs. Camp came out, he told her, "Lying out there in the heat three days, it's a wonder the boy's still alive. We got to get some water in him."

Josh and I watched from the door as Mrs. Camp bathed Jeremiah's arms and legs, and Dr. Grey held a wet rag to his lips, now and then squeezing a few drops of water into his mouth. After a few minutes Dr. Grey said, "Good. He can swallow. Lucy, you go and call Queenie. Tell her we found Jeremiah and that he's going to be all right."

The colored hospital didn't have a telephone, so I went into our hospital to call. I asked Miss Opal to ring number twelve. "Hurry, Miss Opal," I said. "This is very important!"

When I told Queenie, she said, "Praise God! Praise God! He answered my prayers!"

"Josh is coming to get you," I said. "He's in Dr. Grey's car. He'll be there by the time—"

Queenie had already hung up, but Miss Opal, still on the line, said, "I'm real glad you found him, Lucinda." By then, turning away from the telephone, I was crying so, I could no longer speak.

A few minutes later Queenie came in. Rubbing Jeremiah's forehead, whispering, "Thank you, God, thank you," holding a piece of ice to his lips, she never took her eyes from his face. Once I saw Jeremiah's eyes flicker open for a second. And soon after, Dr. Grey said, "Queenie, I'm going to keep him here a day or two, but as young as he is and with you here to nurse him, he'll recover. He'll be just fine."

After Dr. Grey left, Josh and I tiptoed out of the room. It was not until we reached the front steps of the hospital that I suddenly remembered Jacqueline. We looked everywhere for her, but Jacqueline had gone, leaving her ruffled parasol behind.

It was three days before I saw her walk past our house again. I grabbed her parasol, hurried out of the house, and ran to catch up with her. I handed the parasol to her and walked along by her side.

"Jacqueline, how did you know where Jeremiah was? Did you see someone drag him into the woods? Or take him down into the creekbed?"

Jacqueline looked up at the parasol, tightening her grip on its handle. She stopped walking and looked into my face. "Bound things cry," she whispered. And that is all she would say. Somehow I knew that no other answer would be forthcoming, and at the corner of the next block I left her to continue her solitary journey.

Later that night, Josh and I sat in the swing. It was still hot, but the heat was not so oppressive. "Jacqueline's mother never wanted her to marry," I said. "Every time she got a beau, her mother took to her bed, and Jacqueline had to nurse her."

Chuckling, Josh put his arm around my shoulder and pulled me close. "That's enough to make a girl want to run over her mother. It's good she doesn't have a motorcar," he said.

The next morning I woke up thinking of Jacqueline. And there was a little note of panic in my awakening. I wondered what Jacqueline thought this morning, how she felt. It seemed to me that the path she had chosen was lonely.

When Jeremiah came home from the hospital he told us what had happened. He said four or five men had jumped him as he walked home from our house after dark that night. They tied his hands behind his back and blindfolded him. Then they made him walk, blindfolded and stumbling, down to the creekbed, where they wrapped a rope around him and tied him up so tightly that he couldn't move, could hardly breathe. The whole time only one of them, talking very slowly, said a word. "Not me, I ain't in it for no murder," he had said. Jeremiah had not recognized the voice.

That same day the sheriff went over to the Wilkinses' and found the two cousins gone. Munger denied the whole thing. I could imagine him spitting tobacco and hitching up his overall strap and shaking his head. The sheriff said there was nothing he could do without more evidence.

That week Josh had long visits with Jeremiah and Queenie. I'd see him talking to one or the other of them, sometimes both of them, in the garden, the backyard, in the kitchen.

I knew he was worried about what might happen to them when he left. "It's a strange thing," he said one evening, "but the closer the war comes to our shores, the more suspicion and hate we have right here in Bonham."

"What does the war have to do with Jeremiah?" Mama asked.

"I'm not sure," Josh said. "But when people are afraid, their thinking gets crossed. And fear gives people like Brother Simns an excuse for preaching fear and destruction. Whatever the reason is, I don't think Jeremiah can stay here. I honestly fear for his life."

One afternoon, late, Josh joined me in the swing. "We've got it worked out," he said, smoothing my hair from my face. "Jeremiah's coming to Sweet Shrub for a few months. I can find him a place to live, and until he finds a job, Queenie has a little burial money he can use for room and board. He'll be coming to my school, and I can keep an eye on him."

"A colored boy in your school?"

"We're pretty sure he's white," Josh said, "and what difference does it make?"

I'd have to think about that. I wasn't sure what Josh had meant when he said it.

"Jeremiah said he never intends to be white."

"He's going to try," Josh said. "And Queenie wants that for him. She promised Jeremiah she'd be visiting him before Christmas."

Somehow Josh made it all—a place for Jeremiah to live, a job, his mother visiting—seem possible.

I thought about what the days ahead would be like when Josh left. Mama and Aunt Catherine and my sisters. Katie with a bank account, a husband, and a baby. Lillian with a husband, and soon, a baby. I didn't think Edmund would ever agree to a bank account.

Josh took my face in his hands and kissed me, a long, leisurely kiss that made me want to go on kissing him forever. All at once I felt the way I had as a child when, standing on a high bank by the river, I'd grab a rope and swing way out over the water. Breathless, I'd close my eyes just before I let go of the rope.

I took a deep breath and closed my eyes. "I'll marry you, Josh."

The words were out. I had left the bank. I was swinging out, way out over the water.

Josh turned to me, pulled me to him, and kissed me again. His eyes changed color. They were greener, larger than I had known them. Closing my eyes, kissing Josh, I let go of the rope.

20

MY MOTHER'S HOUSE was full of plans. They spilled out of George's room, where Miss Brim sewed my trousseau. Patterns and pins and scissors, and the Singer sewing machine brought up. Soft cottons, and yards of blue velvet. Silks and pretty buttons and ribbons. And slips and step-ins and dresses to be mended. All filled the room, spilled out in a frenzy of preparation. The *whirr* of the machine, from early in the morning until late at night, soon became so familiar, we no longer heard it.

Fitting a rose-colored wool dress on me, her mouth full of pins, Miss Brim said, "Lucinda Richards, two weeks is just not enough time to get ready for a wedding. Your Mama's right. If you'd put this off until Christmas, we could have everything real nice."

But how to explain to Mama, to Miss Brim, to *anybody* that I had already let go of the rope.

Aunt Catherine's room was filled with plans: the flowers, the food, the guests to be invited. By the middle of August, not many flowers would still be in bloom, but "August is the best month for zinnias," Aunt Catherine said, "and Mrs. Walker has those climbing roses that bloom late, and the Weatherbees have a whole fence row of crepe myrtle." Queenie would prepare most of the food, but Aunt Catherine planned to make the six-layer jam cake herself. That left the invitations. We were only inviting relatives and close friends. But as Aunt Catherine wrote invitations those first two days, and a few more the next day, and some more after that, we gave up the idea of a small wedding.

My almost empty hope chest worried Mama. "Lucy, you can't set up housekeeping with two quilts and a pair of pillowcases," she said, and she set herself the task of filling it up. First she called up Lillian. "Now, you can certainly give your sister one of your egg poachers. Nobody needs two," she told her.

Lillian outdid herself. That very day she brought down a tea strainer and a tea kettle, six glasses she had got with Lipton's coupons, and the egg poacher. After I went down to the hardware store and picked out a skillet, a saucepan, and a set of blue and white everyday dishes, Mama began to feel better about the wedding.

The plans spilled over into Maggie's house, where I went every day to talk about the wedding. Since Lillian was in no shape for a wedding, Maggie would be my only attendant. "Me?" Maggie said. "Me, and not Katie?"

"One day Katie and I will be close again," I said, "closer than ever. But now I'm just not ready to have Katie in my wedding. Annabel's going to throw rose petals, and Katie's pleased about that."

"Lucy, that will hurt your sister's feelings," Mama said when I told her I'd asked Maggie.

"Carrie Belle, it's Lucy's wedding," Aunt Catherine told her, and Mama said no more about it.

Maggie was already writing up the wedding for the *Bonham Daily Favorite,* describing the flowers, my wedding dress, my first-day dress, my second-day dress. She said she was glad George and Inez were coming because then she'd have out-of-town guests to write about, but I knew she couldn't wait to see George again.

Josh had decided not to tell his family about the wedding until after we were married. "Mama's not been well. She couldn't travel to Texas even if she knew about the wedding," he said. "It'll be easier for her if I don't tell her until afterward."

Well! That was enough to set Mama off, worrying about Siamese twins. Since the summer when the circus had come to town with Siamese twins in their sideshow (Katie had seen them with her own eyes), Siamese twins had been one of Mama's concerns.

"Lucy, you don't suppose . . . you don't suppose that there's anything like that in Josh's family! Something like that *would* keep a family from coming to a wedding, now, wouldn't it?"

"Mama!" I said laughing. "I promise you there are no Siamese twins in Josh's family." But her mind wasn't easy until she asked Josh about it. I have never seen him so astonished, but then he broke into a gale of laughter. "Just like Mr. Walker," Mama said, but she was convinced by his merriment.

A few days after we told my family we'd be getting married, Josh, bemused by the furious whirlwind of preparation that swept through the house, watched quietly. For a while he sat at the kitchen table, but Mama needed that space for dishes and pots and pans and cup towels, all the things she was gathering for my hope chest. Then he moved to the parlor and watched from there, until Miss Brim brought down some dresses that had to be fitted.

"Stand up here on this stool," she said to me, and nodding toward Josh, "you'll have to excuse us, Mr. Arnold. I have to take the hems on these dresses, and I can't do it upstairs without breaking my back."

That night Josh told me he had decided to go to Sweet Shrub. "Lucy, this next week there's not one thing around here I can do. I'm going to Arkansas to find a house for us to live in and a room for Jeremiah, maybe even a job. I can do that and be back the day before the wedding at the latest."

"Josh, please find us a pretty house. I'd like one with a porch and a garden, and with enough room, besides, for a croquet court," I said, enjoying the thought of my very own home. Then I remembered. "But what about Jeremiah?" I asked. "Queenie's terrified that something else is going to happen to him. And he's still got that knife. He could hurt somebody with it."

Jeremiah had told Josh about the knife, but Josh had let him keep it. "It's his knife," Josh had said. "And if somebody jumps on him again, he'll need more than a knife."

"Josh, you've got to take him with you when you leave," I said now.

Josh thought it was a good idea, but Jeremiah wasn't sure he wanted to go to Arkansas.

"You got to do it, son. You got to go," Queenie told him. "When you safe in Arkansas, your mama can rest easy at night."

So it was settled. Jeremiah would go with Josh.

Josh warned us not to tell anybody where Jeremiah was going. "It's nobody's business," he said. "We'll just drive out of here before daylight, and it will be a while before the Wilkinses, or anybody else, even know he's gone."

Mama agreed it was best, but "Trouble follows trouble," she warned.

To get Jeremiah ready in one day's time, my wedding plans came to a halt. Katie bought him a new suit, and Mama got him a shirt and tie to go with it. Lillian brought up a pair of Edmund's shoes that had always pinched his feet. When Jeremiah put them on with two pairs of thick socks, they fit just fine. In no time Queenie, even ironing his socks and underwear, had his clothes all ready.

The next morning we stood on the porch to see them off, all but Queenie. "Now, Jeremiah, you go along," she said, bustling around in the kitchen. "You go on up to Arkansas. And you work hard and you tell the truth and you learn. And remember, white or colored, you always my son."

As we stood on the porch, before good daylight, to wave good-bye, the whole town was quiet, except for the insistent cooing of a mourning dove. Then, catching the fragrance of Josh's tobacco smoke, all at once I hated to see him leave. And as Josh hugged Mama and Aunt Catherine, and gave me a quick kiss, I felt an uneasiness verging on dread.

"Let's go, Jeremiah," Josh said. Whistling, he walked to the car, opened the door, and stood there for a long minute, looking back at me. He must have sensed how I was feeling, for with a few long strides he was back on the porch, had swept me up into his arms and carried me out to the car. There he put me down and kissed me. A long, hard kiss.

"Goodness!" Mama said from the porch.

Josh laughed. "That's what this girl is to me, Mrs. Richards. She's goodness itself."

Then he was in the car, and turning the corner, he disappeared from view.

I went back into the kitchen and found Queenie wiping her eyes, putting her handkerchief into her apron pocket. "I do know it the best thing, Miss Lucy. It the only way for Jeremiah to be what he *can* be. And I be up there to see him right soon." She took out her handkerchief again, wiped her eyes, blew her nose. "Now we got to get busy. We got us a wedding to get ready for."

But the next few days, with Josh out of the house and

Miss Brim sewing and with all the cleaning and baking, it began to seem like we were only getting ready for a party. Or Christmas. No more than that. I had to remind myself that it was my wedding that was just around the corner; tell myself there was no turning back now.

Inez wired that she and George would arrive the day before the wedding, "and we have a wonderful surprise for you."

Maggie said that Inez must be expecting. "What else could it be?" she asked sadly. When I told Mama and Aunt Catherine, they agreed with Maggie. But I thought the surprise was a present for me.

With each passing day, I felt more loved. Mrs. Walker gave me her mother's china, every piece hand painted. "Lucy, living down the street from you, watching you grow up, well, you've been almost like a daughter to Harry and me," she said.

I knew the Walkers liked me, but I hadn't known they liked me *that* much.

That same day Aunt Catherine asked me to come into her room. "Honey, I'm glad you're going to marry Josh. He's a man you can count on. Now, I've been saving this for you," she said, opening her cedar chest, unwrapping layer after layer of newspaper from around a package. "It's sterling and it's never been used. There!"

It was a coffeepot, luminous and graceful, so beautiful it was the only thing you saw in Aunt Catherine's room, the only thing to see in any room. Looking at it, I thought of the first time I had seen a morning-glory. And a West Texas sunset.

I picked it up, held its silvery grace in my hands. "Aunt Catherine, it's a thing to live up to."

"It is pretty, isn't it? One time, oh, a long time ago, a man I loved gave this to me. That was when I thought I'd have a home of my own," she said.

"What happened?" I asked, wondering if someone had eloped with *her* true love.

"I'm not sure," she said. "Looking back, I think that maybe we just waited too long."

I knew, then, what had happened. She had never swung out over the water, had never let go of the rope.

And all at once a wave of happiness, so unexpected that I had to catch my breath, swept over me. I was glad to be marrying Josh, happy to be going off to a house of my own. Giving Aunt Catherine a hug, I ran all the way down to Maggie's. I couldn't wait to tell her about the house I would have in Sweet Shrub, a house with a front porch and a garden and, maybe, a croquet court. And on the dining room table a silver coffeepot.

The last few days before my wedding, nothing, not Lillian's backache or Katie's pleas to go with her to the theater, could persuade Mama to leave me. She alternated between sighing deeply and chattering away.

"Lucy, when you and Josh first told me, I was a little sad. I admit it. But I knew the first time Josh ever stepped inside this house, he would be the one to take you away. I just knew it. And I do like Josh. I just wish he had been a Bonham boy."

I laughed, imagining Josh's reaction to being called a boy.

Even Lillian hated for me to leave. "You won't be here to see the baby," she said.

"Oh, Lillian, you know we'll come see the baby. It's not that far from Arkansas. I can come home anytime on the train."

With each passing day, my family and my friends, the magnolia tree in the front yard, the houses in the neighborhood, the monument to the Confederate soldier—all took on an air of sweet significance. I wanted to gather them up, take them all with me.

Thursday, George and Inez arrived for the wedding.

"Look! Look at your surprise, Lucy!"

His eyes dancing, George held a large cage high in the air. In the cage sat a bright blue bird with a great yellow beak.

"A parrot!" I cried. "It is a parrot, isn't it?"

George, smiling with pleasure over his gift for me, said, "It's a blue hyacinth macaw. We bought it in New Orleans. Inez picked it out."

"And the best thing about this present is you'll have it forever. They can live to be seventy-five years old," Inez said proudly. "I told George maybe we should get one for Lillian too."

Mama and Aunt Catherine raised their eyebrows, looked at each other. After George and Inez left to get settled at the Alexander, Mama said, "Inez hasn't any sense at all, giving Lucy a thing like that! Why, that thing's liable to outlive us all. Imagine giving somebody a present they'll have to take care of for seventy-five years!"

But I liked the present. I stood by his cage and watched him. He was beautiful, his color such a bright blue, his beak so yellow. I liked him as much as the coffeepot. Oh, what a house Josh and I were going to have, one like no other, in Sweet Shrub. I couldn't wait for Josh to get home so I could show him the presents.

On Friday night, a handful of pebbles thrown against my window woke me up. It was Josh.

"Lucy, come down here and let me put my arms around you," he whispered up to my window. Before I could answer I heard Mama call, "Who's that? Oh, is that you, Josh? Why, it's almost midnight."

"Mama, I'm going to show Josh our present from George and Inez," I told her, throwing a shawl around my shoulders, running down the stairs before she had a chance to answer.

Josh threw back his head and laughed when I told him what Mama had said about the macaw. "Now tell me about our house," I said, after he had hugged and kissed me.

"I'll tell you all that on the way to Sweet Shrub," he said, taking out his watch and looking at it. He kissed me again. Then he said quietly, "Lucy, it's our wedding day."

It was. Suddenly (where had the days gone?) it was our wedding day. Standing before the fireplace garlanded with roses, Josh and I exchanged vows. Professor Bucinni stood up for Josh, and Maggie, sobbing all the way through the ceremony, stood up for me. Afterward, Mama moved briskly (the way she always moves when she thinks we're in the middle of a crisis), through the parlor and the dining room, greeting our guests and thanking them for coming. I glimpsed Lillian, so far along that I had had to persuade her to come, half hidden by the dining room door, shyly throwing me a kiss. And Katie. When the wedding had begun, Annabel had come in with her basket of rose petals, but seeing all the strangers, so many of them, she stood a minute, frozen. And then she began to cry, so Katie had picked her up and taken her out. So Katie missed my wedding . . . as I had missed hers.

Inez, in a yellow dress with a white organdy collar, wearing yellow shoes to match, looked every bit as exotic as the macaw. She hugged me. "Lucy, you're the prettiest bride I ever saw," she said seriously.

During the party, Inez, teasing George, laughing, talking to all our guests, and drinking her little glasses of sherry (I was sure of it, although it was grape punch we served), had more fun than anybody. She was soon out in the garden, taking the macaw (and most of the wedding guests) with her. Hanging the cage from the magnolia tree, she tilted her head to one side. "Lucy, you've got to give him a name," she said.

He was so beautiful, hanging there against the blue of the sky and the deep green of the magnolia leaves, his color in perfect accord with Inez's dress, that I wanted to call him Inez, but then Josh was there, too, with his arm around me, saying seriously, "Why, his name is Keats," he said. "What else could it be?"

And gathered there, under all this beauty, we laughed and clapped our hands with the joy of it, and I knew it was a moment I'd never forget.

Then we were in the car, waving good-bye. Aunt Catherine and Mama were waving, too, their white handkerchiefs little flags of love and sorrow, and Annabel was crying and running after the automobile. And then I was crying too.

But after we had left Bonham behind, I dried my eyes and thought about how much I had enjoyed the day. "Weddings are fun," I said to Josh, leaning over the backseat to be sure Keats was settled. Josh's look told me he didn't think so, but I had loved it.

I had loved dressing that morning, knowing that every single thing I put on was new, except for something borrowed and the penny in my shoe. And I had loved seeing all my family together, and the house prettier than it had ever been. And the solemn words from the Bible, words that marched along so majestically, I had loved hearing them said.

When we were well on the way to Paris (and on our wedding day the small East Texas town sounded exotic, mysterious), Josh took off his coat and loosened his tie.

"Josh, you look like you're going on a picnic," I said.

He threw back his head and laughed. "That's exactly where we are going. If I have anything at all to say about it, our life together is going to be just like a picnic."

It sounded nice. I leaned over, unbuttoned my shoes, kicked them off. Then the thought struck me: tonight I'd be getting into bed with Josh! Quietly, unobtrusively, I put my shoes back on.

21

THAT AFTERNOON WE drove all the way to Paris, just sailed along at twenty miles an hour. Every now and then we'd meet another automobile, and Josh knew them all. "A Ford." "A Pierce-Arrow." Or, once, enthusiastically, "That's a Cadillac and it's cranked, lighted, and ignited from its own electric plant."

The long, black car passed us so fast I saw only that it was driven by a man, traveling alone.

"Why, he's got to be making at least thirty-five miles an hour," Josh said. "But the fact that he's going downhill accounts for some of that."

I wondered about the man driving such a car. Was his haste in response to some urgent message? He could be hurrying to the bedside of his sweetheart, who even now might be breathing her last breath. I hoped he would arrive in time.

We reached our hotel just before sunset, and a short man and his even shorter wife, expressing their amazed delight over Keats, welcomed us and showed us to our room. The room was light and airy. Its dainty, rose-sprigged wallpaper and the even daintier white lace curtains on the windows, which overlooked the front porch, contrasted sharply with the high, carved headboard of the mahogany bed. In the corner was a tin lavatory with white enameled faucets, and on the floor beside it, a small round tub.

"We've let you folks have the best room," the man said. "It being your honeymoon and all."

"It's just lovely," I said, wondering how he had known, feeling unable to look anywhere but at the massive bed.

"If you need them, there are towels here," his wife said.

Tearing my eyes away from the bed, I saw the dresser drawer she was opening. "You want a bath, two or three pitcherfuls will give you plenty of water and"—bending toward me, lowering her voice—"the privy's out back." She turned and looked at Josh. "If you want a bath, we got another tub the end of the hall," she said sternly.

"I wrote that I wanted a room to remember," Josh said when they had left the room, "but I think it's the innkeepers we'll remember."

Standing there, smiling down at me, he looked sure, *knowing*. But shouldn't he? I told myself in answer to the twinge of resentment I felt. Isn't that the way of the world?

"Let's have an early supper and take a stroll around the town," Josh said.

I splashed some water on my face, brushed my hair, and put it up again. "Let's take Keats down with us," I said. "The other guests will enjoy seeing a blue hyacinth macaw."

And I was right. "The folks here in Paris, they're gonna look twice at this," Mr. Garvy, for that was his name, said, taking us to a table by the window.

The potato soup was cold! And the green tops of spring onions were sprinkled on top. And Mrs. Garvy served thick slices of homemade bread with it, and, for dessert, she gave us stewed peaches with thick cream. I decided I'd write Inez about the food.

The other diners, a man who was traveling alone, and an older man and his wife, smiled and nodded at us all through the meal. I felt sure they knew I was a bride. And outside, a small crowd gathered to peer through the windows at Keats. After supper, Mr. Garvy asked if we'd leave Keats in the dining room as long as we stayed in Paris. "Give more folks the chance to see him," he said.

We were glad to do that. "Throw a towel over his cage at bedtime, and you won't hear a peep out of him," I said.

Then we took a walk around the square and looked at their Confederate monument. Afterward, walking up the hotel steps, Josh said, "Lucy, I'll sit out here on the porch and have a smoke while you get ready for bed."

In our room, as I unbuttoned my shoes and slipped off my silk stockings, I caught the fragrance of Josh's cigarette smoke coming in through the open window, and my heart beat faster. I got out my new white silk nightgown and my China silk shawl, both embroidered with pale pink rosebuds, and laid them across the bed. Then I filled the tub, recklessly pouring in pitcher after pitcher of water. Hurrying just a little, I bathed, and then, stepping out of the tub, I saw my bare reflection in the dresser mirror, a reflection darkened by the shadows that were already beginning to fill the room, and I stood there gazing at it. Had it been the light of day or even if the room had been lit by electricity, I would not have looked so shamelessly at my rounded shoulders, not yet dry from the bath; my high, round breasts tipped by light-brown nipples; the dark button of my navel and, below, the black brush of hair between my legs, startlingly black in contrast to the whiteness of my skin.

Hearing Josh's footsteps on the stairs, I quickly put on my gown, slipped into bed and pulled up the covers.

Josh came and sat on the edge of the bed. He gathered me in his arms and kissed my lips, my eyes, the hollow of my neck.

"Lucy, you're a beautiful woman," he said, tracing my lips with his finger. "Did you know that?"

Feeling the warmth of his breath, I opened my eyes and looked into his, now a liquid black. He kissed me again, and then, getting up from the bed, he said hoarsely, "Just a minute." Hearing the light, muffled sounds of his clothes falling to the floor, I opened my eyes and saw Josh, saw him coming toward me. Goodness! I thought, closing my eyes, I had never imagined there would be so much . . . *maleness* there.

Josh sat on the bed, held me in his arms, kissed me. Then he was kissing me where I had never been kissed before, his gentle urgency sweeping away all my uncertainties, my shyness, until I, feeling the hunger of his kisses, opened my mouth to his and drew him down beside me, answering his sweet urgency with my own. Then he pulled away the sheet that lay between us and I slipped my gown up over my hips and there was nothing between us and then—and oh, the sweetness of it!—my body of its own accord arched to his, and the small pain was nothing, and afterward, lying splendidly at ease in Josh's arms, I knew that what had happened between us was a wondrous thing.

I woke the next morning happy. Elated. Now I was married, and dressing for breakfast (Josh had already gone downstairs) I thought about the night before. Putting the combs in my hair, feeling wise and sure, I smiled at my reflection in the mirror. I wondered how it would be tonight. I thought that when we reached Texarkana, we might have an earlier dinner, a briefer walk.

Going down the steps, I remembered Josh as he had walked toward me in the darkening room, and I saw again what I had seen in one quick glimpse. How is it that men manage to walk and run so easily? And even dance! I wondered. And entering the hotel dining room, I thought how very glad I was to be a woman.

* * *

The one night we had planned to spend in Texarkana stretched into three. The town was beautiful, more beautiful even than Bonham, with the branches of sycamore and oak trees meeting so that they formed tunnels of shade over the red-brick streets along which we walked. On two afternoons big clouds swept over the town (Josh said they were from the Gulf), bringing fresh, cool showers, and then, even though it was not yet fall, the *promise* of spring was all about us in the rich earth smells as every leaf, every flower, every blade of grass was sharpened, made cleaner and brighter by the rain.

And each evening we went to bed a little earlier and each morning we slept a little later. One time we woke together in the night (I don't know what time it was), and we lay close in bed and Josh named all the cities we would someday visit and the oceans we would cross and the languages we would hear. And another time, in the midst of our love-making, it began to rain and I thought, well, *this* is what it's all about! This is what we're here for, all of us; this is what we were created for. To love and be loved.

That next morning, I opened my eyes and saw that Josh, propped up on his elbow, watched me while I slept. He kissed me and said, "Stay there." Dressing, he left the room and was soon back with a breakfast tray of hot biscuits and ham and strong black coffee.

"Josh, in my whole life, I've never had breakfast in bed unless I was sick," I told him.

After breakfast we loved each other and slept again and got up in time for an afternoon walk and an early supper of scrambled eggs and biscuits and strawberry preserves.

Our last morning in Texarkana, I woke up before Josh.

Throwing my shawl around my shoulders, I walked to the window. A milk wagon rumbled slowly down the street and from far away came the whistle of a train. I turned back to the bed and saw that Josh was awake and smiling. His eyes had never looked greener. He stretched his hand out to me. "What is it, sweetheart?"

"Josh, I want to go home," I said.

The look of surprise, of alarm, that swept over his face made me laugh out loud. "Not Bonham," I said. "I want to go to Sweet Shrub. I want to see what it's like. I want to get things ready for a spring garden and meet our neighbors and make curtains for the windows. I want to clean house and have company over for dinner. I want to go home."

That afternoon we left Texarkana, and as we drove into Arkansas, Josh told me about Sweet Shrub and the house he had found for us and what he thought our life would be like there.

And we knew that our life there would be bliss. After all, how could it be otherwise in a town with a name like Sweet Shrub?

PART TWO

JEREMIAH

22

JOSH HAD THOUGHT the trip from Texarkana to Sweet Shrub would take three days. It took seven. As we drove farther and farther into eastern Arkansas, the countryside took on an aspect of strange, lush beauty. For one thing, the land was more sparsely settled than in East Texas, and the roads were not as well traveled. Except for the cotton plantations that sometimes bordered the roads, the land was more heavily forested than any I had seen. And there were more rivers, so many I lost count. And the deer! Several times we saw them, sometimes two or three at once. Watching them bound effortlessly across the road to sail over underbrush or across a ditch, I thought they were the most graceful creatures in the world. And driving into a land that became stranger with each day's passing, I sometimes felt that the man I had married was as exciting and as full of surprises as the land through which we drove.

That first day, as we left Texarkana, Josh told me about our house. "For now we'll be rooming with a lady named Mrs. Elam. Mildred Elam."

"Rooming? Josh, I thought we were going to have a house of our own, with a front porch and a garden," I said, dismayed at the thought of living in a house with strangers. And I thought that he should have told me sooner.

"Lucy, in Sweet Shrub there are not many empty houses. I looked at three, and none were places I'd want you to live in," he said. Seeing the expression on my face, he pulled over to the side of the road and stopped the car. "Honey, this is a place to live for a few weeks. Together, you and I will find a house. Why, that's the first thing on my list," he said.

"I wish you had told me this earlier."

"It didn't seem that important. There was so much else to talk about," he said earnestly. Frowning a little, he sat still a minute, and when I said nothing more, he started the car again.

I thought about it. Josh was right. Living in a house with other people for a few days or even weeks might be nice, a way to make friends.

"It'll be fun to find a house together," I said, after a minute. "I'm glad you waited."

At this he smiled at me, pushed his hat back on his head, and began to whistle. "You made me love you," he whistled, looking happy, self-satisfied.

Leaning over to kiss him, I blocked his view for a minute so that we almost went off the road. He stopped the car again and kissed me, a nice long kiss.

"Tell me about Mrs. Elam," I said, when we were again on our way. "Is she anything like Mrs. Lace?" I asked, wondering if ladies who run boarding houses might not, in some way, be similar.

"No. Mildred Elam seems too sad to be anything like Mrs. Lace. But she's interesting. Her grandfather was a general in the Civil War, and before the war her family owned a great river plantation just outside Memphis. But I believe the main reason for her melancholy is that she's recently widowed. And she's been forced to take in paying guests."

I disliked the idea of anyone's being forced to have me as a paying guest, but then I said to myself, *Lucy, for goodness sakes! Stop thinking about yourself. Think about that poor woman and how she must feel. Losing a husband and being forced to take in strangers.*

"It's a large downstairs room," Josh was saying, and I realized he was describing the room where we would live. "It was once the library, and so it has plenty of shelves for books. And with windows off the porch and on the side, it's the coolest room in the house. Good cross ventilation. Lucy, finding the room was a stroke of luck. You and Mildred Elam will enjoy each other."

Josh was right. Maybe she'd be my best chum in Sweet Shrub. "And Jeremiah? What about him?"

"Mrs. Elam was kind enough to call the owner of the hotel, a Mr. Wickham, and he said that Jeremiah could have room and board in return for some heavy cleaning and gardening. Jeremiah looked mighty lonesome when I left. He'll be glad to see us."

How kind she must be, I thought. Thanks to her, Jeremiah had a place to live, and we had a temporary home. Josh had not told me what she looked like. And I wondered how old she was.

The countryside through which we were driving was filled with soft, low hills, the trees on either side of the road tall and straight, the underbrush thick and green. It was somewhat like Bonham, but there was not as much cleared land and everything was greener.

By the time we drove into Little Rock it was dusk, and after a late supper, I left Josh to smoke a cigar on the front porch of the hotel and went upstairs. I bathed, went to bed, and slept soundly all night, not even stirring when Josh came to bed.

The next morning, eager to reach Sweet Shrub, we were up before dawn. The kitchen was not yet open when we came down, but the cook scrounged up ham and cold biscuits for us and made a fresh pot of good strong coffee. Josh asked him to fix a hamper of food for the trip.

"For a picnic?" I asked, pleased with the idea.

"This part of the country's so pleasant that I thought we'd camp out. Besides, between here and Helena, there are not many towns large enough to have hotels."

I had never in my whole life camped out. I liked the idea of it. Sleeping under the stars with Josh, listening to the night sounds. But I was glad Mama didn't know about it. She'd have been worried to death.

As we drove farther into Arkansas that day, we came to more and more rivers, and crossing them, unless there was a bridge, almost always involved a considerable amount of time. We often had to wait for the ferry, and when it came, it seemed to me that we crossed strictly at the ferryman's whim. Mostly these were silent men who would nod, step off the ferry onto the riverbank, secure the ferry, and then stand, gazing quietly at the river as if they had not seen it before. Then (and I could only suppose some inner signal told them when it was time to begin another crossing), they'd swing on board, nod to Josh to drive the car onto the ferry, and take us across.

Josh would get out of the car and stride back and forth across the deck, looking at the water, the sky, the riverbanks. Talking enthusiastically to the boatman and to me, not noticing (or caring) that the boatman did not often respond, he would tell us about the great rivers of the world and the great civilizations that had begun on these rivers. With the wind blowing his black hair and the water swirling around him, Josh seemed a part of the river itself. There was an undefined wildness about him. He had never seemed so attractive, so mysterious to me. I'd sit quietly, watching him, and, more than once, had it not been for the ferryman, I would have thrown my arms around his neck and silenced him with a kiss.

"Lucy, wait until you see the Mississippi," he said, just after we had crossed the White River. "Wait until we cross it! It's one of the world's finest rivers, and Mark Twain himself said that Helena is the most beautiful spot on the river. We'll see both of them day after tomorrow."

"What about Sweet Shrub?"

"Sweet Shrub's not on the Mississippi. It's on a cypress lake, a lake that in its own quiet way is very beautiful. In fact, I'd like to build a house for you right on the lake."

I was imagining a house on a calm, blue lake, when the automobile's steering wheel came off in Josh's hands! Holding it up in disbelief, he continued turning the wheel, although it was no longer attached to the car, while he applied the brakes. But before he could stop, we were off the road and in a ditch, the car caught gently by the underbrush that grew there.

"Lucy, are you all right?" he said, climbing hastily out. "Goldurn it! Next time we'll take the train!"

"Josh, if you could have seen your . . ." and I could say no more. The thought of Josh, wide-eyed with astonishment, vigorously turning a steering wheel no longer attached to the car, was too much. Clutching my sides, bent over with laughter, I climbed out of the car and up to the road. "Josh, that was the funniest sight I've ever . . ." I began, but a look at Josh's face told me he saw nothing funny about it. Biting my lip to stop laughing, turning my back, I heard a thump behind me.

"Here. You can sit on this," Josh said, and I saw he had brought up a suitcase for me.

Just then we heard the *squawk, squawk* of Keats and, at first startled, then laughing again, I found him just behind the car. Still in his cage (although it was upside down), he looked fiercely around.

I righted the cage and put it on the ground beside the suitcase. Then I found a dried apple in our food hamper and gave it to Keats to calm him.

"Keats, it's all right," I said, talking to Josh as much as to Keats. "Nobody's hurt."

Josh, grimly examining the car, ignored me.

"Is the car all right?"

"I don't know," he said shortly.

Silently, I watched Josh take his tool box and a tow rope from the car. I stood up and looked around. The road that stretched in front of us was as flat as any in West Texas. Except for a small clearing on the right, the trees and the undergrowth grew right up to the road's edge. In the clearing the skins of small animals (rabbits, squirrels, possums?) hung from a line stretched between two trees.

"Josh, look," I said.

"Belongs to a trapper. I'm going over there to see if I can find some help. But if someone comes along, flag him down."

His voice was impatient. He did not look at me as he spoke.

Well!

I had not come all the way to Arkansas with Josh Arnold, a man I had nearly refused to marry, to be treated in such a fashion. I did not reply. Instead, I sat down again and watched him walk to the trapper's line and, in a few more steps, disappear into the underbrush. For a minute or two I could hear him making his way through the thicket, but that sound soon disappeared as well.

Looking around, I thought it was not an unpleasant place to wait. On my left I could see a lake through the trees. Through the branches of a pine tree nearby, I saw an owl perched on a topmost branch. Bigger than Keats, the owl sat perfectly still, waiting, I suppose, for nightfall so it could begin its nocturnal search for food.

I heard someone coming through the underbrush. Josh, I thought. But it was a dog, a big black dog that trotted from the forest on my left. I sat still, hoping the dog would not see me. Then a man came out of the woods and, even at this distance, I could tell that he was big. Relieved that the dog's master was in sight, I patted Keats's cage. "It's all right, Keats," I told him.

Both saw me at the same time, for both stopped, the dog leaning into the wind, sniffing, his hackles up. And the man! He, too, leaned forward, not moving, and stared at me. At that moment Keats, braver than I, emitted a series of ferocious squawks, and this infuriated the dog. Although he still did not bark (and his not barking made him appear even more vicious), he bounded forward, his teeth bared.

"Blackie! Down!" the man shouted. At his command, Blackie crouched to the ground, but still he crawled toward us, and now I could hear the growls that came from deep in his throat.

I jumped to my feet, grabbed the cage, and held it high in the air. "Squawk! Squawk!" said Keats, daring Blackie. A part of me felt the humor of it, but I was too frightened to laugh. Now the man took three quick strides forward and kicked the dog with such violence that he slid off the road into the ditch.

"Our steering wheel came off," I said, "and I don't think you should have kicked your dog."

The man looked at the steering wheel and then extended his hands and looked at them as carefully as he had looked, a second earlier, at the steering wheel. He had the whitest hands I had ever seen, but then I knew they only seemed so white because of the long black hairs that grew on the back of his hands. Apparently what he saw in his hands satisfied the man for, moving quickly, he picked up the tow rope Josh had found, attached it to the car, and held the end of the rope out to me.

"Thank you," I said, unsure of what he planned to do.

I put Keats down on top of the suitcase and took the rope from his hand. Neither of us said a word while he searched for and found a rock of the size and shape that suited him. Holding the rock in one hand, he scrambled down the bank and put his shoulder to the back of the car.

"Now!" he growled.

With all my strength I pulled on the rope and the car moved forward, slanting up the incline, maybe as much as five or six inches, before he jammed the rock under the rear wheel. He straightened, took a deep breath, and put his shoulder to the car again.

"Pull!" he said again, sounding a lot like his dog.

The car moved at least a foot. Now I caught the rhythm of the task and no longer waited for the trapper's command. When he put his shoulder to the wheel, dug his foot in, I was ready. And we soon had the car back up on the road.

"Oh, thank you," I said, but he was already moving away, taking the exact path Josh had taken earlier, and then he, too, disappeared. I wondered about his dog, wondered whether it was alive or dead, but when I looked at the place where the dog had lain, whimpering, it was empty.

In a little while, I again heard someone making his way through the underbrush. It was Josh. He was about twenty feet away when he noticed the car was out of the ditch.

"Lucy! Sweetheart," he called, as if he had never in his life been cross, "how did you get the car back on the road?"

"The trapper did it. Didn't you see him?"

"I didn't see a soul."

Then I told Josh how we had managed, the trapper and I, to get the car out of the ditch, but I did not tell him about the fight between Keats and the dog. Sadly I watched Josh examine the car, thinking how much fun it would have been to tell him about the fight. Just this time yesterday, how he would have laughed. But now, since he had lost his sense of humor, what was the point?

Josh walked around the car again, kicked the tires, looked at the car and at the place where the trapper had disappeared. Then he smiled at me, and holding out his arms, he said, "Come here."

I stayed where I was.

"Lucy, I'm a damn fool," he said. "I've got this god-awful temper when I'm scared. And just now, I was afraid you might be hurt. But you were right to laugh. It was funny. Damn funny."

Chuckling, Josh held out his arms again, and I walked close and felt the goodness of his arms around me. He pulled me closer, pulled me close between his legs, tightened his arms and kissed me.

And then I could tell him about Keats and the dog and about how brave Keats had been even as the dog ran toward him.

He threw back his head and laughed. I do love to hear Josh laugh. "I wish I could have seen it," he said. "Keats, next time you'd better pick on something your own size," he said, between his kisses.

After a while he turned to get our other suitcases from

the car. "In the morning I'll see about the steering wheel," he said. "I think it can be bolted back into place again. But right now we need to find a good campsite and get settled before dark."

"What about that man?"

"What man? Oh, the trapper. Why? Are you worried about him? Honey, that man's not going to bother us. He's probably running his traps right now, wondering where you found a bird like Keats and how I ever found a woman like you."

Silly, I thought. Josh is right. Taking Keats in one hand and the food hamper in the other, I followed him through the trees and along the lake's edge. Now the lakeshore curved sharply around to the left and, following this curve, we found that the water we had seen from the road was only a finger of the lake, for now the lake opened out, and we saw that it was as wide as the White River we had crossed earlier. And as we could not see either end of the lake, only the stillness of the water told us it was a lake rather than a river.

We walked under tall loblolly pines along the lakeshore to the crest of a small knoll that was at the widest part of the lake. "Here. This is perfect," I said, setting the cage and the food hamper down on a cushion of pine needles. Josh put down the suitcases and spread a blanket close against the trunk of a pine tree. Then he left to finish unloading the car. I gathered sticks and pine cones for a fire and, for our supper, found a can of beans and cut two thick slices of ham from the generous portion the hotel had provided.

When Josh returned, "Lucy, I'll make a pan of cold-water cornbread," he said and, seeing the expression on my face, assured, "No, it's good, hot bread. You'll like it. It's Tennessee bread."

While Josh stirred up the bread and poured it into a

hot skillet he had set on the fire, I picked a few wood violets and some wild grape leaves and put them in the middle of the blanket.

After supper (and the best part of the meal was the hot cornbread), we sat and watched the night come on, watched the sillouettes of the lake grasses, the trees, the shoreline—against a pale gold sky that faded into bright oranges and pinks that became pale shades of violet. I had to close my eyes from time to time so that my mind could grow accustomed to a sight so beautiful. Then the white faded from Josh's shirt and from his face, and the lake and the shore became more and more dense until it was completely dark. And in the darkness I could smell the lake more strongly, and the night sounds—the *slap* of a fish as it leapt, the *plop* of a frog jumping into the water—became louder.

When it was dark, so dark that the stars in the sky seemed small and far away, I heard the birds. At first, the sound they made was a hum like a running stream. Then the darkness became darker still, and I heard the flappings of their wings and, although I could not see them, I heard them splashing lightly onto the lake's surface and rustling into the grasses on the lake's shore and into the tops of trees around the lake.

The next morning, Josh said, "Lucy, wake up!" and I opened my eyes to see that the lake was covered with ducks and geese and other water birds I did not recognize. As I watched, the birds in the center of the lake, the very center, some twenty or thirty of them, swirled up and up into a small whirlwind of birds that whirled still, and, whirling, caught up other birds in the circular movement and still others and more still until the swirling mass of birds reached the lake's edge, and there still more birds were caught up in the ever-widening sphere of birds. Now the lake was filled with the dense cloud of swirling birds, so dense that it seemed as if they had been stirred by some great tidal wind. And Keats, excited by the noise of the beating wings and the birds' callings, frantically beat his own wings against his cage, and my heart stirred to think that he could join the flight, find some place in it. But as I moved to open his cage, Josh's "No, Lucy," stopped me and I knew he was right. Keats's best chance was with us.

Then the birds were gone and I do not know why, perhaps there were no words for it, but neither of us spoke of it again.

Josh made a fire and we boiled coffee over it and reheated the leftover bread. After breakfast we repacked our things and made our way back to the car.

Almost immediately, Josh found the bolt from the steering wheel on the floorboard of the car, and in his toolbox he found a nut that fit well enough. We drove to the next town and there the Maxwell was made roadworthy again.

Oh, I was glad to reach Helena that night. Even before Josh had brought up our suitcases, I had filled the tub. I washed my hair and sat a long time in the water, soaking. Then, standing before the mirror, I dried my hair with a towel, pleased with the reflection I saw there. I dressed slowly, wondering if Josh might not return from bathing and dressing down the hall before I finished.

We had a light supper at Habib's, the finest restaurant in Helena. It was an elegant evening, the food and the service as fine as any in Dallas; and the restaurant itself, with its resplendent staircase, its painted, hand-pressed metal walls, its brass chandeliers, was the most beautiful I had ever seen.

After dinner we walked over to the Mississippi River,

and it was, just as Josh had said, magnificent, but when I went to bed that night, it was the lake and the sunset and the great swirl of birds that I saw again and again in my mind.

23

ABOUT NOON THE next day, just as a Memphis–Helena–Louisiana train slowly overtook us, we had our first glimpse of Cypress Lake. After the train passed we had a clear view of the lake, for the land all the way across the railroad tracks and right down to the edge of the lake had been cleared. But on the far eastern side, the forest came almost to the lake shore, and the huge cypress trees growing up out of the still, silvery water gave the impression that the forest itself was stepping out across the lake.

After a mile or so we saw fifteen or twenty cabins scattered about in a more or less circular pattern between the railroad tracks and the lake, some within a few feet of the lake itself. Colored town. All were identical two-roomed cabins, each with a brick chimney, each with its own garden. Most of the gardens were behind the cabins, but a few were alongside and one or two were in front. The cabins were connected by worn paths, which from a distance looked like faded ribbons winding in and out among the cabins and out again toward the town and down toward the lake.

About a hundred yards past the cabins, there was a house—weathered, rambling, a house unlike any I had ever seen. Half of it, the two-storied half, was built on shore, and the other half, a single story, rested on supports out over the lake.

"Why, it's almost the color of the lake," I told Josh.

"It's cypress. That wood weathers to that silvery gray color. It's nice, isn't it?"

I had never seen a house that looked so much like it *should* be there, like it had always been there.

"Think of living in it, of sitting on the porch and watching the sun come up over the lake."

"It looks deserted," Josh said.

Deserted. I knew I'd like to live there. And if it were deserted, we probably could. I decided to look into it immediately.

Now a lumber mill appeared on our right, with big red letters, WICKHAM'S LUMBER CO., on its side, and then, in quick succession, MORRIS'S WATER COMPANY and LAMBERT'S GAS AND ELECTRIC COMPANY came into view and, in a hundred yards or so, Wickham's again, this time WICKHAM'S GIN.

Off to the right I saw a small frame house, and another, and then a cluster of houses. We were in Sweet Shrub.

Turning onto Main Street, we passed a small, two-storied building, a sign in the window saying SHERIFF, and above it, a room with bars on the windows. The jail.

Then we were in the middle of town. "That's where Jeremiah lives," Josh said, pointing to a small hotel, Wickham's *again,* that advertised its eight sleeping rooms and, in smaller, red letters, boasted of a barber's chair and pool table in the living room.

I wondered what Jeremiah was doing that very minute. I'd have to see him tomorrow so that I could write Queenie and tell her he was just fine.

The Trumper Drugstore was across the street from the hotel, and on a sign written across the front glass I saw Sweet Shrub's first sign of culture, LADIES' TEA ROOM, in dancing green letters. All the businesses seemed to be

within this two-block area; here I would shop for everything from groceries to hardware.

Josh's school sat at the end of Main Street. Newly
painted white with bright green trim, its windows sparkling clean, it looked perfect and untouched, like a new
box of crayons. And the playground, with its new merry-
go-round and swings, was immaculate. Seeing the
school like that, waiting and *hopeful,* I experienced a
feeling of regret that, being married, I could not teach
there, or anywhere.

We circled around the school, came to Main Street
again and drove past several blocks of medium-sized
houses. After that, the houses we saw were quite large,
their grounds extensive. Mrs. Elam's house was one of
these. It sat in the middle of several acres, and a
wrought iron fence encircled the entire property.

The tall gates stood open, but even before Josh drove
between them I saw that all along the drive, and on both
sides, the trees had been cut down. The huge stumps and
the few leaves of new growth on the stumps were all
that remained of what had once been a drive of stately
old magnolias. It was shocking! The stumps showed the
axe marks still, and some of the trees, not yet cleared
away, lay where they had fallen, mortally wounded.

"What in the world happened!" Josh said. "It must
have been some terrible disease. I can't imagine any
other reason why a magnificent stand of trees would be
cut. When I was here last week, I thought that this was
one of the most beautiful approaches to a house I had
ever seen."

Reaching the house, we got out of the car and walked
up the steps. On our left was a circular-shaped porch,
covered with a generous roof. Rocking chairs and hanging baskets of ivy and ferns gave it an aspect of shady

welcome. I thought of Aunt Catherine and of how she would have approved its generous size.

Josh's knock was answered by a solemn Negro girl. At first I thought she was no more than twelve or thirteen, but as she stepped aside so we could enter, I saw that it was only the slenderness of her body that made her appear so childlike. Her face, although it was unmarked by wrinkles or blemishes of any kind, held the marks of resignation that I had seen only in the faces of a few very old people. There was no eagerness in it; there was nothing in it, not even the ability to show interest in a creature as beautiful and as exotic as Keats.

"Miss Elam, she resting now. She say she see you at the table tonight."

"And what might your name be?" Josh asked as we stepped inside a spacious entrance hall from which a wide mahogany stairway rose to the second floor.

"I Sudie," she said.

As Sudie opened the door on our left and moved with us into the room, she seemed mildly distracted. She stood at a window and looked out, and then she moved to the west side of the room and another window, and stood gazing outside.

The room was large, so large that the massive bedstead, the dresser, the chiffonier looked almost small. Just inside the front windows there was a small round table with a reading lamp on it. On one side of the table a gentleman's chair was placed, and on the other side, a small rocker.

Suddenly tired, I felt relieved that we had been welcomed only by a quiet maid, however distracted, and a comfortable room. Josh brought in our bags, and I asked Sudie for bath water. Then Josh, saying he'd relax a little while, found a *Liberty* magazine and settled down with it on the porch just outside our windows. While

Sudie filled the wash basin, I unpacked one of my suitcases. The house was wonderfully still. Slipping out of
my clothes, I took a sponge bath, put on my coolest gown
and, almost at once, fell asleep.

"Sweetheart, you were tired." Josh was there, sitting
on the bed beside me. "I'm going to rustle up a cool drink
for us. Lemonade. Iced tea. Which?"

"Anything cold sounds wonderful."

Josh turned on the electric fan as he left the room, and
the breeze it stirred helped me wake up. I splashed water on my face and rose water on the back of my neck
and behind my ears. Then I brushed my hair and put it
up, both for coolness and because I was a married lady
now. I chose a buttercup-yellow dimity dress to wear to
the supper table. The dress was a little wrinkled (Mama
would have insisted I press it), but I knew the wrinkles
would shake out.

Then I sat down in the small rocker and looked around
the room. There was nothing in it that said "Lucy," nothing that would say to anyone, "This is Lucy's house."

Well. I'd fix that!

First, I unpacked my silver coffeepot. There! Sitting on
the table by the reading lamp, it transformed the room,
giving it a quiet elegance. Then I put my silver comb
and brush set on the dressing table and arranged all the
pictures—Mama's, Aunt Catherine's, Lillian's, and after
a minute, Katie's too, on the chiffonier. I put a picture of
George and Inez, looking quite dashing in their Pierce-
Arrow motorcar, and one of Annabel on the reading table with my coffeepot.

This was better. And when my hope chest arrived, I'd
put my China silk shawl on the table and hang my hat
on the wall. Perhaps we could take some of our meals in
here, at our own little table. I'd ask Mrs. Elam about it.

Just as Josh reappeared, a gong sounded.

"A half hour until supper," Josh said, handing me a glass of lemonade, giving me a kiss at the same time, "and you look beautiful."

"Josh, look at the room. Do you like it? Doesn't it seem more like ours?"

Josh grinned. "I like any room you're in," he said. "And the room looks wonderful! Now, would you like to join your husband on the front porch?"

At that moment Josh looked so handsome, I thought that I'd much rather join him in bed. Wondering what he would think if I said such a thing out loud, I held out my hand to him, and together we walked out to the front porch.

Pulling two of the chairs close together we sat down, and a minute later we were joined on the porch by a couple who were about our age. The man's brown hair fell in waves over his forehead. Above the deep cleft in his chin his lips were short and full.

"I'm Timothy Massie and this is my wife," Timothy said, looking pleased with his wife, with finding us on the porch, with the world.

"Call me Lassie!" the woman said, settling into the rocker Timothy placed for her.

"What?"

"Lassie Massie," she giggled. "I almost didn't marry Timothy because of the rhyme. Before that I was Lassie Smith. But I married him in spite of what it did to my name. I'm a singer, *rilly*. If I go back to the stage I'll use my maiden name."

"You won't have to go back," Timothy said proudly. "By this time next year, I can buy you anything you want."

I hated to be nosy, but his comment invited a question. "What do you do?" I asked.

"We've just opened a broom factory right here in Sweet Shrub," Timothy said.

A broom factory. It sounded chancy. I looked at Lassie. Her smile was wide. Her black hair, glowing into russet at the ends, set off her round blue eyes. Her bright blue cotton dress strained across her full breasts. Crossing her legs, she flipped her skirts so that I caught a glimpse of white lace. I glanced at Josh. Apparently, he hadn't noticed; he looked as casual as he had looked a minute earlier.

Lassie put her hand on her hip, leaned forward. "What did you give up?" she said. "To marry, I mean. I gave up the stage."

I thought for a minute. I had left my family and the town I loved. If I had stayed . . .

"I suppose . . . a different life," I said carefully. "Teaching. I did that one year, and I liked it."

"I know just what you mean," Lassie said. And then, jumping up out of her chair, "No, Tim, darling. Don't get another chair. I'll sit in your lap."

Even before that, I had known Lassie was a little fast. But I liked her. She made me feel . . . different. Older and younger at the same time.

Josh looked at me and winked. Leaning back in the rocking chair, I thought of crossing my legs and immediately heard Mama's "Lucy, ladies do not cross their limbs in public."

"Hush!" I told her silently, and flipping my skirt up out of the way, I crossed my legs.

When the supper gong sounded, we went inside just as the most beautiful woman I had ever seen came down the stairs. Tall, slender, she came gracefully, lightly, her soft gray dress brushing each step as she came. And a surprising thing: When she reached the bottom of the stairs, I saw that she must be forty. At least!

I looked at Josh, who was smiling, a little foolishly I thought, at Mrs. Elam as she held out her hand to me.

"You're our bride. And you're lovely," she said. Her voice was liquid. Warm. "I'm so pleased to have you and your husband as our guests. You've met the Massies and here's our other guest, Louis Sullivan. Louis is my cousin, just down from Memphis. Come to help me with my affairs."

Mr. Sullivan was a bear of a man, with unruly hair and a coat that was hardly big enough and pants a little rumpled.

"As a widow, I've had to rely on kin a good bit lately," Mrs. Elam continued.

I wondered when Mrs. Elam's husband had died, how long she had been a widow.

Just as we had taken our places at the table, Mrs. Elam and her cousin at either end, and Josh and I across from the Massies, we heard heavy footsteps on the front porch, followed by a faint, almost apologetic knock on the door.

A smile crossed Mrs. Elam's face. "That will be Mr. Wickham," she said gently. "Louis, if you'll show him in, I'll just tell Sudie to set another place."

Mr. Wickham, his head carried slightly forward, came into the room. Remembering all the Wickham signs I had seen in town, I thought: So here is the man who owns half of Sweet Shrub; and he walked like it, his feet coming down squarely on the floor with each step he took. But then he smiled, and perhaps it was his stained teeth that made it so, but his smile was cautious; in it there was none of the power that I had seen when he first entered the room. In fact, his sphere-shaped body, the tense cords in his thick neck, and his broad, rather short arms and legs caused me to think fleetingly of a turtle, and when I looked again at his face, at his slightly hooded eyes, the curious creature came to mind again.

Now Mrs. Elam was back in the room, gesturing to the men to remain seated, and Sudie, still with her distracted air, was bringing another place setting to the table.

"Mrs. Elam, am I too late to join you? Unexpected business requires my presence in Sweet Shrub tonight."

"Certainly not, Mr. Wickham. We're delighted. Sudie, Mr. Wickham will sit here, at my right."

After chairs were shifted to make room for Mr. Wickham, Mrs. Elam introduced Josh and me.

Mr. Wickham looked at Josh. "Mr. Arnold, aren't you our new principal?"

"Yes, I am. Are you connected with the high school, Mr. Wickham?"

"Only indirectly. My wife and I have not been blessed with children."

"You have fine teachers here, a good building. And the beginnings of a library," Josh said. "You have a school to be proud of. And I think it can be even better."

"Well, improvement of any kind takes years," Mr. Wickham said.

"Mr. Wickham, we don't have years. These boys and girls need the best education we can give them now, and we plan to begin this fall. We're going to add Latin and Greek to the high school program, and art and music to the elementary grades. In fact, we'll be needing two more teachers right away."

"Sounds like these improvements you're talking about might get right expensive. Now, the people in Sweet Shrub won't go along with that."

Josh smiled courteously. "I'm sure that the people here in Sweet Shrub know the value of a good education.

They'll give up a lot for their children. And businesses like yours can help."

I knew that behind Josh's smile, he was already planning how to win Sweet Shrub's support for better schools, and I knew how persuasive Josh could be. I smiled at Mr. Wickham. He had no idea about the changes that would be coming with Josh in town.

The talk at supper soon turned to cotton. Mr. Wickham was convinced that the long staple cotton he planned to grow after the timber was cleared from his land would be the finest in the nation. But then we spoke of the war and of the Allies' mounting losses in the trenches. Josh said he was much disheartened by the failure of a second landing at Gallipoli because for a time the Allies had held six positions. Mr. Wickham said wars were not good for commerce and the sooner the war was over, the sooner trade between the United States and Europe would flourish.

Then Josh said, "But the real tragedy of the war is the loss of life. In a single day this past month nearly a thousand men died in France."

"Oh, Mr. Arnold, you speak for us all, in saying that," Mr. Wickham said. And his eyelids partially closed over his eyes and his head sunk a little into his neck.

Sudie was just bringing in our dessert when we heard a knock, this time a rather bold knock, at the back door.

In a minute Sudie was back, and standing by Mrs. Elam's chair, almost in a whisper, she said, "He here, asking about Mary again."

"Sudie, did he say 'Mary'?"

"No'm. He say 'Mrs. Johnson' when he ask."

Mrs. Elam looked at her cousin. "Louis, this kind of thing. This is what frightens me so."

A glance at Josh told me he was as puzzled as I.

"Sudie, just tell him again that there is no Mrs. Johnson here." Mrs. Elam's voice was tremulous.

Mr. Wickham jumped from his chair. "I'll take care of it, Sudie." Then, as if remembering his manners, he said, "Mildred, let me see about this for you."

And now Mr. Sullivan was on his feet, saying briskly, "Russ, I'll go," but Mr. Wickham was already at the kitchen door.

Even through the closed door we could hear Mr. Wickham saying, "There is no Mrs. Johnson here. There never has been." This was followed by the sound of another voice, but one so quiet we could not make out the words, and then we heard Mr. Wickham again, his voice so harsh that a shiver ran down my spine. "No, and I want you off this place. Don't come round here again," he said, and I thought that whoever heard those words would heed them.

Unmoving, hardly breathing, Sudie stood by my chair. Her air of detachment was gone; her clenched hands told me she was even more caught up in the conversation at the kitchen door than were those of us seated at the table.

When he came back into the room, Mr. Wickham opened his mouth as if to speak, closed it, and then said, "Mildred, perhaps the ladies would like to take their coffee in the living room."

Well! The women, sent from the room, like children! But Mrs. Elam and Lassie Massie, rising from their chairs even before the men had stood, seemed unaware of it. I looked at Josh.

Winking at me, he smiled reassuringly. "Mrs. Arnold brings a clear head and a good mind to any discussion," he said.

He made no move to come around the table and pull out my chair for me. The two of us might have been alone in the room, so lovingly did his eyes rest on me. You decide, Lucy, his expression said, clear as anything. You decide if you want to leave the room.

Mrs. Elam and Lassie Massie stood just outside the door. They, too, waited.

It was nice to choose; it was easy. "Josh, I think I'd like to join the ladies," I said honestly.

In the parlor, Mrs. Elam, looking quite worried, sat on a small rose-colored loveseat, the soft gray of her dress in sharp contrast to the vivid coloring of her hair and the violet blue of her eyes.

"Mrs. Elam, maybe I can help," I offered.

"It's just that lately there's been unrest here," she said softly. "A woman living alone . . . at times, I get very frightened. But these things had best be left to the men."

"But Mrs. Elam—" I began, thinking I'd remind her that with three men and two women in the house, she was not alone.

"Oh, Mrs. Arnold, as a newcomer here, I don't think you'd understand," she said kindly. Turning to Lassie, she requested, "Dear, sing that wonderful song, 'When You Wore a Tulip' for us. That's exactly what we need to pep us up."

While Lassie played *and* sang, I had an opportunity to look closely at Mrs. Elam, to see her white face framed by a crown of luxuriously thick black hair braided across the top of her head. But it was her eyes that one noticed. Not quite blue, but nearer blue than violet, her deep-set eyes tilted up at the outside corners. Watching her, trying not to stare, I decided that she was not quite as beautiful as I had first thought. But there was something more than beauty in the prideful way she moved and in the exquisite clothes she wore and in the penetrating scent of her perfume. What had kept her here all these years, I wondered, in a place like Sweet Shrub.

As soon as we had closed our door that night, I turned to Josh. "What did Mr. Wickham tell you when we left the room? And oh, Josh, I love you for saying what you did!" And I threw my arms around his neck and kissed him even while he laughed at my exuberance. "But who is Mrs. Johnson?" I asked, tracing his lips with my fingertips.

Josh sat down, pulling me into his lap. "Let's just take one thing at a time. First of all, about Mrs. Johnson. Until recently, Mrs. Elam had a laundress named Mary. She thinks her last name may have been Johnson."

"Well? What of it?"

"Lucy, do you know Queenie's last name?"

"No, I don't," I said slowly. "Oh, Josh, isn't that strange? I never thought to wonder what it was."

"Well, that's the way it's always been here too. But Russ Wickham says that lately the Negroes around Sweet Shrub have begun to speak of each other by their surnames instead of by their given names. He finds that threatening. And it does seem . . . curious."

"Mrs. Elam is afraid, but she won't talk about it. She says it should be left to the men."

"Lucy, all her life Mrs. Elam's been protected."

Here it was again. That almost reverent tone in Josh's voice when he spoke of Mildred Elam.

Suddenly, I felt awkward. And I had always been too skinny. "She's very attractive," I said.

"Very," Josh said.

"And she has a good mind."

"Brilliant," Josh said.

I took his arms from around my waist, stood up, and stretched.

"Josh, how old do you think she is?" I asked, trying to sound disinterested and casual.

At this Josh rose from his chair, took my shoulders

between his hands, and with the merriest look I had ever seen, said, "Lucy, no woman, no woman I have ever seen or heard of or read about, not one brings the happiness and the excitement you bring when you enter a room. Don't you know how beautiful you are? How lively?"

And he kissed me, again and again, and soon I was swept up by his kisses, and I gave myself completely to Josh's ardor. And he returned my gift in full measure.

And afterward, in his arms, I said, "I love you, Josh. And right now, I feel so . . . perfect."

"And I'm the happiest man in Sweet Shrub, no, in all of Arkansas," Josh said, "and the first thing I'm going to do for you is . . ."

I waited for him to finish, but the sudden relaxing of his arms from around my shoulders, the slight change in his breathing told me he was asleep.

Too happy to sleep, I lay awake. I knew what Josh was going to say. It was about our house. He wanted to find a house for us right away. Josh had said we'd be going to Helena this weekend because he wanted to meet the partners in the law offices where he'd be reading. But maybe it would be better if I stayed in Sweet Shrub to look for a house. Thinking of our own house, a garden, a croquet court, thinking of beating Josh at croquet, I laughed out loud, and Josh stirred, spoke my name in his sleep. Then I moved closer to him and slept too.

Waking the next morning to the sun's coming through my windows, I found Josh gone and a note on my pillow asking me to come see his school when I woke up.

Feeling happy and hungry, I dressed and went to find Sudie, who was in the kitchen peeling peaches. My mouth watered at the thought of the peach cobbler we'd be having for dinner. Already, she had a pot of beans on the stove and a pan of cornbread ready for the oven.

"Sudie, I slept so good last night. How about you?"

"Yes'm," she said, not looking at me, not answering my question either. She began to peel another peach.

"I wonder if I could have a bowl of peaches for breakfast," I said, knowing that would be an easy breakfast for Sudie, and besides, I loved peaches.

"Yes'm," she said again.

I went into the dining room and in a minute Sudie came with peaches and coffee on a tray. "Sudie, I think I'll eat in the kitchen, keep you company," I said.

Sudie followed me into the kitchen and placed the tray on the kitchen table. "Mrs. Elam, she the only one has a late breakfast. The others, they get they own when they late," she said softly.

Hearing this made me more determined to find a house in Sweet Shrub. "I'll remember. Now tell me, Sudie, where do you live?"

"I stays here," she said sadly. She picked another peach from the pan on the work table and began to peel it.

"Why? Don't you have a home?"

For the first time, Sudie held up her head and looked directly at me. Her big brown eyes were pretty, like coffee in sunshine.

"I *afraid* to walk home," she said.

Mrs. Elam was afraid. Sudie was afraid.

"Sudie, what are you afraid of?" I asked.

Turning her gaze toward the window, she let the peach fall from her hand, ran her finger over the knife's blade. At this angle, her round cheeks, her upturned nose, her full lips reminded me of Annabel.

"Sudie," I said again, "what are you afraid of?"

"Something gonna take me off like it took Mary."

"You mean something happened to Mary?"

"She gone," she said mournfully.

"Sudie, who was that man who came here last night?"

"He Mary's brother. But won't do no good to look for Mary."

Sudie put her finger in her mouth, but not before I had seen the drops of blood on it.

"Sudie, you've cut your—" I began. But all at once Mrs. Elam was there with us, saying, "Sudie, you need to get on with your work," the gentle tone of her voice, the sweetness of her smile, softening the criticism of her words.

"Sudie's all the help I have until I find a new cook and a laundress," Mrs. Elam said, walking with me down the hall.

I decided not to mention Mary, her laundress, but I asked, "What happened to your cook?"

"That's a part of the trouble," she said.

"What trouble? Mrs. Elam, tell me about the trouble."

For a minute, I thought she was going to talk about it, but then she turned away. "I'm not sure what the trouble *is*," she said vaguely, "but you saw those trees. I had to cut them down. Every one of them." She smiled at me, a deliberate smile. "Now, let's do leave all that to the men. Have you ever seen a prettier day?"

For a few minutes we spoke of other things. But all the while Mrs. Elam was telling me that Sweet Shrub had a fine seamstress, though I'd have to go to Helena if I wanted a good milliner, I wondered why those trees had been cut. And I wondered what the trouble was. But I believed Mildred Elam; she was not at all sure.

When I left the house, I saw that Josh's car was in the driveway. Seeing it, knowing he had left it there for me, lightened my heart, made me smile. And stepping out into the bright sunshine of the day, I decided that Josh was right. Mrs. Elam had been protected all her life, too protected.

Now I'd see about Jeremiah as I had promised Queenie. I'd drive to Wickham's Hotel and find him, see how he was getting along. Then I'd go to the schoolhouse. Josh loved peach cobbler and if I stopped by to pick him up, he could come home for dinner.

Driving into town, I saw that Sweet Shrub on a Monday morning was quieter than Bonham. A woman holding a child in each hand hurried across the street in front of my car, and two men wearing overalls walked along the sidewalk, their heads close together in earnest conversation. I wondered if *they* were afraid. My car was the only one on the street, although when I stopped in front of the Wickham Hotel, there were two others there—a plum-colored one and a gray one. Josh would have known what kind they were.

Just as I walked up the hotel steps, here was Mr. Wickham, walking down them.

"Why, good morning, Mrs. Arnold," he said, tipping his hat. "You're out bright and early this morning. Mr. Arnold with you?"

"He's at work this morning. And just as soon as I've found a young friend of ours at the hotel, I'm going to see his school."

"You drove yourself? Most of our ladies prefer to ask their husbands to drive them."

The smile never left his face, but it seemed to me (or was I only imagining it?) that his eyes, when he had seen me, changed. Hardened.

"Doesn't Mrs. Wickham drive?" I asked.

"I drive Mrs. Wickham wherever she needs to go."

"If she knew the pleasure, the freedom it brings, I believe she might enjoy driving herself."

"My wife prefers to stay at home most of the time. But if she needs to go somewhere, I can usually find the time to drive her."

I wondered what Mrs. Wickham would say to that. Mr. Wickham, drawing his head into his shoulders, again started down the steps. But as I turned to open the door of his hotel, he turned back. "Mrs. Arnold, can I help you with something? This is a gentlemen's hotel."

I had to laugh at that. "Mr. Wickham, you sound just a little like my mother," I said. But when Mr. Wickham drew in his neck and compressed his lips so tightly that they almost disappeared, I knew the comparison had been a mistake. "I'm looking for a young man named Jeremiah, one of your employees," I said quickly.

"Oh, that white boy! Talks like a nigger. I told him that. I said, 'Boy, you talk just like a nigger.' "

The words made me flinch. "Mr. Wickham, Jeremiah was raised by a colored woman."

"Children all over, raised by mammies. They don't talk that way. Leastways, when they're almost grown, they don't."

"Would you tell Jeremiah I'm here?" I asked.

"Yes, I'll tell him. Oh, one other thing, Mrs. Arnold." And now his tone was as harsh as it had been when he had spoken to Mary's brother at Mrs. Elam's back door. "You'd better do your shopping before Saturday. Here in Sweet Shrub ladies don't come to town on Saturday."

Wheeling around, he pushed open the doors to the hotel, leaving them furiously swinging behind him. Waiting for Jeremiah, I decided that I would come to town whenever I pleased.

24

THE HOTEL DOORS swung open, and here was Jeremiah, bringing with him the odor of gardening and sunshine. And heart-warming thoughts of Bonham! His smile when he saw me was one of such unabashed delight that I forgot all about my unpleasant conversation with Mr. Wickham.

"Miss Lucy!" Jeremiah said. And seeing him, I felt, for just one second, as if I were back home again with Queenie. And Mama and Aunt Catherine. I told him that.

"Yes'm," he said. "It that way for me too."

"You've grown," I told him. "Just since I last saw you."

"I didn't know it," he said, so solemnly that I laughed.

"Now, Jeremiah, let's find a place to sit down for a minute, and you can tell me all about yourself. I'm going to write Queenie tonight."

"I got to get back on the job," he said. "I tell Mr. Wickham I just be a minute out here with you."

"Tell me right quick, then. How are you? Do you like it here? You look thin. Do you eat enough?"

Jeremiah's smile vanished. He looked down, his thick lashes brushing the curve of his cheeks. "Soon's I get the money for it, I be gone from here."

He turned to go back inside. "Wait a minute, Jeremiah. We've got to talk about this. Don't you want to talk it over with Mr. Arnold? What about tonight, after supper? We can have a good visit then, the three of us."

He shook his head. "I got to work."

"When, then? Jeremiah, what about this weekend?"

He crossed his arms over his chest. "I got some time off Saturday," he said slowly.

"Mr. Arnold will be in Helena on Saturday, but you and I can have a visit. Jeremiah, right after dinner I'll pick you up right here. We can go for a drive, and we'll have a real nice visit."

Jeremiah, no longer smiling, nodded. As he turned to go back inside the hotel, his delicately formed shoulder blades, visible through the thin cotton of his shirt, showed how very thin he had become.

Driving to Josh's school, I wondered what in the world I would say to Queenie about Jeremiah. And when Josh and I got home I found a letter on the hall table from Mama that made me wonder even more. She wrote that, thank goodness, Aunt Catherine was still improving and that Lillian's baby could come any day now. But then she wrote, "Queenie is anxious and unhappy about Jeremiah's *situation* in Sweet Shrub. Can you tell us more about this? Queenie says that if good news doesn't come soon, she'll be on the train herself to see about him."

Josh and I took a walk after supper, and he agreed that it would be best for me to stay in Sweet Shrub over the weekend. "I can catch that early train up to Helena," he said, "and you'll have a car for house hunting."

We talked about Jeremiah too. "I think he's just homesick," I told Josh, remembering how homesick *I* had been when I had first gone out to West Texas to teach.

"When he starts to school, he'll make some friends his own age," Josh said. "He'll be fine then."

"What can I tell Queenie? I promised her a letter right away."

"You'll be seeing Jeremiah on Saturday. Tell her that. And tell her that after next week, I'll see him almost every day. We'll look after Jeremiah for her."

I felt better after that. Queenie liked Josh, and just his saying we'd look after Jeremiah would reassure her more than anything.

Seeing Jeremiah, writing home, caused me to be a little homesick myself. I missed my family, but already here in Sweet Shrub my life was changing. In Bonham I was Mrs. Richards's daughter, Lillian's sister, Maggie's friend. But here I was . . . what? Josh's wife. But I wanted to be more than that. And I knew that if I were a man, I could be more. Then I could be anything.

I looked at Josh. Sitting in his chair, reading, he seemed so contented. Well, I was in the middle of *Jane Eyre.* I decided to have a bath and join him.

Afterward, dressed cozily for bed, I pulled my chair close to the lamp and opened my book. I had not read three pages before I read the words that I knew would change my life. I read them again, and the author, Miss Brontë, spoke across the years to me, telling me what I had always known.

"Josh, you've got to listen to this," I said.

Josh looked up from his reading. "What is it?"

"Listen," I said. "Listen, Josh."

And slowly and carefully I read what Miss Brontë had written so long ago:

> Women are supposed to be very calm generally: but women feel just as men feel; they need exercise for their faculties, and a field for their efforts as much as their brothers do; they suffer from too rigid a constraint, too absolute a stagnation, precisely as men would suffer; and it is narrowed-minded in their more privileged fellow-creatures to say that they ought to confine themselves to making puddings and knitting stockings, to playing on the piano and embroidering bags. It is thoughtless to condemn

them, or laugh at them, if they seek to do more or
learn more than custom has pronounced necessary
for their sex.

Frowning, Josh put his book down and picked up
mine. He read the passage again. "Lucy, is this how you
feel?"

"Oh, it is, but Miss Brontë said it better than I ever
could. I do want to use my faculties. I long to be useful,
as useful as I was in Bonham. And in West Texas. I want
to be more than Josh Arnold's wife!"

Josh looked at the book again and then at me. "What
would you want to do? If you could do anything, what
would it be?" he added.

"I'd teach," I said honestly.

"But you know you can't do that. What about a hardware store? Do you want to work in the hardware store
here in Sweet Shrub?"

"I liked doing that in Bonham. Mama was having such
a hard time, and I *had* to save the family business. But I
love to teach."

"Lucy, I'll put my mind to it. And, somehow, maybe we
can get you back in the schoolroom again."

I went to bed soon, and Josh went outside to smoke his
pipe. Comforted by knowing he understood my desire
(and by the smell of his pipe and the creak of his rocking
chair outside the window), I went to sleep then and slept
all night.

The next morning the Massies left on an overnight
trip to Helena, and Josh told Sudie he planned to be at
the school all day. Only Mrs. Elam, Mr. Sullivan, and I
would be home for dinner.

At noon, right after the first dinner bell, Mr. Sullivan
and I were in the parlor talking about the differences
between Texas and Tennessee.

Although Mr. Sullivan was his usual rumpled self, he obviously had tried to bring about some control over his hair by wetting it and brushing it down so that it lay in a close circle that fell from the crown of his head. But the artificial style of his hair was somewhat offset by the deep dimples on either side of his mouth that appeared and disappeared with charming regularity as we talked.

As I was beginning to wonder if we'd ever be called to dinner, Sudie appeared in the doorway to say that Mrs. Elam would not be down.

"She not feeling well, and she say you go ahead without her," Sudie said, looking at Mr. Sullivan as she spoke.

He ran his hand worriedly through his hair. "Sudie," he said, "fix Mrs. Elam a tray. I'll take it up right now." As Sudie went to the kitchen, he turned to me. "Mrs. Arnold, I hope you can help me persuade Mildred to go back home. Memphis is where she should be. She belongs there. This, all this"—and his vague gesture seemed meant to include all of Sweet Shrub—"all this," he said again, "is too much for a woman of her temperament."

Before I could frame a question, Sudie was returning from the kitchen, and Mr. Sullivan was taking the tray from her hands and carefully climbing the stairs with it. I waited for a while, but Louis Sullivan did not reappear and I ate alone.

That afternoon, I learned why Mrs. Elam would never go home to Memphis. She told me the reason herself.

After dinner I had written Lillian, telling her I hoped the baby had arrived by now and that, if it had, I knew it was the most beautiful child in the world, "except for Annabel," I added. Then I wandered into the parlor and played, as softly as possible so as not to disturb Mrs. Elam, some favorite songs. I played "You Made Me Love

You," one of Josh's favorites, and "Danny Boy." Mama had always loved that song. Then I played "When a Fellow's on the Level with a Girl That's on the Square," thinking it would just suit Lassie's voice. I had just finished "Love's Old Sweet Song" when I felt the presence of someone in the room. I turned and saw that it was Sudie.

"Mrs. Elam, she like the music. She say would you come up? She be pleased to have the company."

I ran up the stairs and tapped on her door.

"Come in, Mrs. Arnold," she called softly.

Mrs. Elam was in bed, propped up by a nest of pillows encased in white linen and edged with lace. She wore a light-blue peignoir. Although her dark hair was piled on top of her head, the blue ribbon carelessly tying it there had allowed several tendrils to escape. A cut glass bowl of rose petals and cinnamon sticks sat on a small table by her bed, filling the room with an aromatic scent.

"Mrs. Elam, I'm sorry you're not feeling well," I said.

"Thank you, Lucinda. May I call you that? And I'm so glad we can finally have this little visit. You see, that first night you watched me come down the stairs, I saw in your face that rarest of human qualities—an understanding heart." She sat up straighter in bed, pushed another pillow behind her back. "Would you open those curtains for me? They've been closed all day, but just your presence has already made a difference, cheered me."

"I know just what you mean. I guess everyone has days like that, when nothing's wrong, but you feel like something is."

"Lucinda, sit down," she said. Gesturing to the chaise longue, she asked, "Would you be comfortable there?"

Nodding, I sat sideways on the lounge, not real comfortable, but *interested.*

She leaned forward, looking earnestly into my eyes. "I need someone to confide in. My dear, could I talk to you?"

"Why, yes," I said, hoping she wouldn't change her mind before she confided.

"One day, years ago, I couldn't have been more than fourteen—I was fourteen, just fourteen, because that was the year my brother went away—I met my true love. Oh, Lucinda, do you have time for this? If not"—and she waved a lace handkerchief toward the door—"we can talk another time."

"Oh, I have time," I said, and the fact was that nothing could have torn me from the room. I wanted to know what had happened to Mary, her laundress. And why she had had the magnolias cut down.

"Well, you know what that's like," she continued. "From that first moment, for the first time in my life I felt . . . complete. Louis was twenty-four (you must have guessed it was Louis), ten years older than I, and he taught me everything. He taught me about art and literature and music, everything that helped to make those next three years so joyous. But he did not teach me how —how to go on living after the scandal."

Nervously polishing the nails of her left hand with the handkerchief, she glanced at me, as if to measure the effect of that last word. I tried not to take any notice of it.

"And all those months I had been so happy. Why, you've never known anyone in your life as happy as I was." Now her voice was lilting, breathless. "I could hardly believe it was me. But after the scandal"—and this time, after saying the word *scandal,* she never hesitated— "I ran to marriage, *ran.* And all those years I was married, twenty-three of them, and living here in Sweet Shrub, I longed for the happiness Louis and I had had together. Sweet Shrub is not so many miles down the

river from Memphis; oh, it's not too far down the river in
miles, but in every other way, it's a great distance. In the
ways of family and society, it's the furthest thing there
is, so that when my first love came here, could come,
that was when I knew what we really were to each
other. Not until he came did I know that he, my first
love, *and* Memphis were what I had so loved. Everything that Memphis was, he was. And more. He loved
me, made me love myself as well, but *in* Memphis. Well,
how can I explain my feelings to you, Lucinda? It was as
if a pair of fish, graceful and spirited, were taken from
the water, and you saw the poor things trying to move,
trying to live in this other element. That's how it was for
us, for our love, out of Memphis. Oh, we knew what we
were to each other, and all of Memphis knew, and then I
ran into my marriage and stayed there, 'made my bed
and lay in it,' in that terrible marriage bed, even though
I thought that I could not go one more day without his
hand in mine. But I did go one more day. And then another. Until the marriage was over. And now I'm here;
have been here, thinking it was only him, my first love, I
needed; but now he's here and I know it's Memphis too.
If he's one half of my soul, then Memphis is that other
half. You see, it's not Mary that troubles me, although I
do wonder where she is and if she's still alive. It's not the
unrest in Sweet Shrub that has made me so unhappy.
Let the men think that if they will. Leave all that to the
men. But, having *him,* how I long for Memphis, long for
it and all that it was to me. We could be happy there, but
I can never go back."

She lay back on her pillow, closed her eyes.

I sat very still, longing for a wisdom I did not have. I
had no idea what to say. Desperately, I tried to unravel
all that she had said. I tried to think how Christobel

would have answered, what Aunt Catherine would have said. Then I thought of Mama.

"Why don't you wash your face, get dressed, and come downstairs," I said briskly. "No sense at all in brooding up here all by yourself. And I just heard Lassie come in."

"Mrs. Massie wears jewelry that is not real," Mrs. Elam said sadly. "And Mr. Wickham . . . in Memphis he would not have been invited into my house."

"I like Lassie Massie," I said.

"Lucinda, you're young. How could I have thought you might understand?" And she turned away.

"I am sorry," I said again, and after a minute, when she did not respond, I left the room.

But that night Mildred Elam came gaily down the stairs, and at supper it was difficult to believe that she had ever been anything but happy. She talked to Mr. Wickham and to Lassie as if they were the people she would have *chosen* as her dinner guests. And at the table, when Louis Sullivan told her he had found a laundress, her face was alive with pleasure.

"Oh, Louis, I don't think I could have gone another minute without one. Wherever did you find her?"

"She's coming out here from Memphis," he said. "She'll be here Monday."

"I just hope that she's not from Chicago," Mr. Wickham said.

"What's wrong with laundresses from Chicago?" Josh asked.

"This unrest we're having here in Sweet Shrub. It started in Chicago, and we don't need anybody else coming in here agitating," Mr. Wickham said.

"Is it a seasonal problem?" Josh said, turning to Mildred Elam. "I expect that with the cotton about ready, everybody will soon be in the fields."

But Mr. Wickham answered. "It's not seasonal, Mr. Arnold. These niggers in Sweet Shrub have decided they're too good to work. Miss Mildred"—and at his use of her given name Mrs. Elam frowned, but he did not notice— "Miss Mildred, tell these folks about our little trip last week when we tried to find a laundress."

"Oh, Mr. Wickham, let's not concern ourselves with that anymore. It's been taken care of by my cousin." Her voice was cool, detached.

"I'll tell it then," Mr. Wickham said, and Mrs. Elam looked right at me, her look saying as clear as anything, "You see? Do you see what I mean about Mr. Wickham?"

"Miss Mildred and I drove to colored town, two Saturdays ago, wasn't it? Yes, it was two Saturdays ago, and we stopped in front of one of the nigger houses (I built every one of those houses), stopped at the first one where we saw somebody, an old woman on the front porch. Just as polite as could be, I said, 'Auntie, Mrs. Elam, here, she's looking for a washwoman. You know of anybody?' And she just sat there, looking at me. And then, without even getting up out of her chair, she said, 'To be right truthful, my husband's working in Chicago, and I'm looking for somebody to do *my* wash.'"

The ending was so unexpected that, at first, I thought it was a joke. Josh looked at me; his eyes twinkled. Then he said to Mr. Wickham, "And that's part of what you mean by unrest, isn't it? That, and having colored people call each other by their surnames."

At this Mrs. Elam leaned forward as if to speak, but Sudie coming to clear the table at just that minute silenced her. And then Sudie's trembling hands as she took the plates from the table and the clatter of the cups against the saucers when she poured our coffee in the now silent room made me realize that Mr. Wickham's story had not been at all humorous.

After the door closed behind Sudie, Mr. Sullivan said,

"Mr. Arnold, it is much more than that. Much more. And that law firm you're reading with, they're part of the problem. That fellow, Bailey, why he's been out here several times, asking questions, agitating the Negroes."

And now he was standing, hurrying to his cousin's side. "Mildred, don't upset yourself about this. You've got enough on your mind without worrying about the help here in Sweet Shrub."

"You're right, of course, Louis. Let's go into the parlor, leave the table to Sudie. Perhaps Mrs. Arnold would play for us. The songs that I heard Mrs. Arnold play this afternoon would cheer a freezing songbird."

I did play, and in a minute, Mrs. Elam began to sing, and then Josh. And we were all singing and so the evening became a pleasant one after all.

But that night, I told Josh what Mrs. Elam had told me in her bedroom, trying to make sense of it. "There was a scandal," I began.

Josh nodded. "In Memphis there usually is. What was the scandal?"

"Mildred Elam and her cousin, Louis Sullivan, met and fell in love when she was fourteen and he was twenty-four. He taught her everything."

Josh raised his eyebrows. "That *would* be scandalous."

"And after the scandal she *ran* into marriage. That's what she said. She *ran* into her marriage."

"And?"

"She made her bed and stayed in it. She didn't think she could, but she did. She stayed for twenty-three years when she didn't think she could stay another day."

Josh shook his head. "Southern women. Lucy, one has to admire that kind of steadfast loyalty."

I wasn't sure I admired it, but I wanted to finish the story. "But then, when her true love could come, she knew he was just half of what she had longed for all those years. The other half was Memphis."

"Memphis!" Josh said, his eyes twinkling. "Are you sure it wasn't Nashville? I could understand a longing for Nashville."

Ignoring Josh's obvious amusement with the story I told, I went on with it. "She said 'Memphis.' And she can't go back to Memphis now, not ever."

"Poor devil," Josh said.

"She is a very sad woman."

"No, it's Louis Sullivan I meant," Josh said. "He must love her very much. But I suspect that, for whatever reason, Mildred Elam no longer returns his affection."

Now I could see it, the fourteen-year-old girl, constantly together with and falling in love with her twenty-four-year-old cousin. And when her husband died, Louis Sullivan had come from Memphis, but by then (Josh was right), Mildred Elam no longer wanted to marry her cousin.

I was thinking about Mildred Elam when I went to sleep, and thinking about her still when I woke up the next morning, surprised at how quickly she and Louis and Sudie and all the others in Sweet Shrub had become a part of my life.

25

"SWEETHEART, WOULD YOU drive out to the colored school this afternoon? Take some books out there?"

Bringing me the car, Josh had come home for dinner, and now he was in a hurry to get back.

"If you can wait just a minute, I'll drop you off, and on the way you can tell me how to get out there. I didn't even know we had a colored school in Sweet Shrub."

Mrs. Elam, just getting up from the table, turned to smile radiantly at Josh. "Used to be our own First Baptist Church," she said. "But after Mr. Wickham came, the town grew off and left the church out there, at Peaceful. So we gave it to the coloreds."

Driving to his school, Josh gave me the directions: "About a mile out of town, take the first turn past the Rosehills' pond and stay on that road until you get to the next crossroads. You'll see the church."

It was farther out than I had thought, but Josh was right. I couldn't have missed it. The church, unpainted, worn, sat on blocks high off the ground. The ground in front was worn smooth, but the land around the church was chest high in yarrow, broom, tansy, asparagus gone wild, and here and there, a few raggedy blackberry bushes.

I turned off the motor and sat a minute, watching the children play. Four of them were jumping rope and as they jumped they chanted:

> *Grab a chicken,*
> *Wring its neck.*

White folks say
That hen won't lay.

When I got out of the car, they stopped jumping and stared. Then the rope started again, and they took up the chant, louder this time, more gleefully:

Catch a pig and
Cut its throat
White folks say
That pig can't smoke.

I got out of the car and, following the worn path, went up the sagging steps of the church. Standing just inside the doorway, I looked down the aisle to the front of the church. On the benches hymnals were scattered about, but I saw nothing that one usually finds in schools—no chalk or chalkboards, no textbooks, no children's artwork on the walls or windows.

I walked down the aisle between the benches to the front of the church. A crisp white linen cloth covered a small table. The front panel hung all the way to the floor and on it was a cross, embroidered with silver threads. An open Bible lay on the table, and beside it sat a porcelain vase, so filled with blackberry vines, broom, and wild oats that the broken handles of the vase barely showed. The sun, coming through the stained glass window high over the table, made the yellow hair and blue eyes of the Lord Jesus Christ into a burst of brightness. The rest of the church was without color—the walls, the floor, the wooden benches—all were dull and unvarnished.

"Honey, yawl want something?"

The voice, mellow and full, came from the cool shadows behind where I stood. I turned and saw a woman sitting on the very last bench in the room. In the shadows, it was impossible to know if she was white or colored.

I walked back to where she sat, eating her dinner from a pail on the bench beside her. I caught the smell of sausage, sweet onions, biscuit.

"My husband, Mr. Arnold, asked me to bring these books," I said. "Some of the backs are off, but the pages are all there," I added.

The woman stood to take the eight books. Silently, she looked at them, taking each one in her hands, turning it over, murmuring, "yes," and "yes" again, and, finally, when they were all on the bench beside her, she said, "Us needs a real school. A real teacher. I ain't no teacher. I keeps the children safe. That's all. Won't let nothing harm these children."

There was defiance in her voice, her eyes, the way she held her head. I decided to take up the last thing, hold it to the light.

"Who would harm the children?" I asked. "Out here, it's so . . . well, it *is* peaceful."

She shrugged her shoulders. "Mary, she gone. Somebody hurt her."

"Who?"

"Can't tell."

Or won't, I thought. Brushing that aside for the moment, I asked, "What do the children do all day? Do they read?"

"When we sing, we reads. And when we reads, we sing," she said.

There was a plentitude about the woman. In her voice, in the generous curve of her mouth, in the fullness of her figure. I wondered if she could read. I wondered what her name was. I thought that whatever she taught, she would teach it well.

"I taught once," I told her. "But since I'm married, of course I won't be teaching again."

"I married," she said, "and I teach. But, I ain't a real teacher." She sighed deeply. "These here children needs a real teacher."

"Tell me about the school. How many children?"

"Sometimes, when it be cold and they not in the field, we got thirty. And somedays I come and ain't none here, and I goes on back home."

"What do you do besides sing?"

"They spells out they names. They counts." She shrugged her shoulders.

All this talk, and still I didn't know her name. "I haven't even told you my name," I said. "I'm Mrs. Lucinda Arnold."

She didn't respond. It was hard to know if it was an oversight or rudeness. After a minute I asked, "What's your name?"

"Ruth," she said softly.

Thinking about Queenie, I said, "And your last name?"

Now a smile hovered about her mouth. "Kitchens. It Ruth Kitchens." Then, smiling broadly, she said, "Too bad you and me can't change places. You married and black you could teach."

I held out my hand, and she took it. Promising more supplies, I told her I'd be back.

I walked outside into the sunshine. The children, never taking their eyes off me, swung the rope higher and higher.

"Teacher, teacher, turn around," they chanted, inviting me to jump. I ran inside the rope. "Teacher, teacher, touch the ground," they said, laughing, but they kept the rhythm, timing the rope, making it hit the ground, stirring up little puffs of dirt with each beat. A new chant.

"Mr. Wickham, turn him round. See his tail, it touch the ground." Now their smiles were gone, and their chant was almost a whisper. "Devil come and devil go, Mary went to work, ain't seen no more."

They dropped the rope and ran. Even the children know something's terribly wrong, I thought, shaken.

In bed that night I told Josh about the school and about Ruth Kitchens. "We've got to help," I told him, moving my head to a more comfortable place on his shoulder. "They need so many things. Most of all, they need a teacher."

"When I come back, we'll put our minds to it," Josh promised. "But right now, I want to think about you," and unbuttoning the first button of my gown, he whispered, "and me."

"Just a minute," I said, slipping my gown up over my hips, turning to slide again into his arms. And then, "Oh, Josh, I love this. Isn't it what we were made for?"

His answer was a deep, sweet night of love.

The next morning, before sunup, I took Josh to the railroad crossing and watched while he flagged down a train. When the train slowed almost to a stop, he kissed me and swung aboard. I watched the train slowly disappear, followed it with my eyes until not even the smoke from its smokestack was visible.

As I turned into Mrs. Elam's drive, the sun was just coming up. Missing Josh, I sat on the front porch and watched the sky take on those first washes of colors, mauves and pale grays and delicate pinks, watched it grow brighter until the eastern sky was a blaze of red.

When the sun was higher, I started to go inside, but then a slight breeze swept across the porch, bringing with it a faint smell of autumn. The weather was changing. I sat down again to enjoy the morning. Even this early, the sun felt warm on my arms. And it was nice to be the first one up.

After a little, I heard the back door close. Sudie, I thought, on her way to the privy. But when I walked around to the back, I saw it was Lassie. She was in the garden, gathering tomatoes.

"Lassie!" I called, surprised at how glad I was to see her. "I'll come help you."

Stooping to pick a bright red tomato almost hidden by its vine, I said, "I didn't know who you were. I thought it was Sudie."

"That poor girl!" Lassie said. "No one could do all this work. It's too much for one person."

"Mrs. Elam's found a new laundress," I told her. Then impulsively I asked, "Lassie, what happened to Mary? Do you know? What do you think happened to her?"

Lassie straightened up. The pockets of her apron were full of tomatoes. She held two more in her right hand.

"About two weeks ago, just a few days before you came, Mary left this house to go home. She never got there. I wish I knew what happened to her. There's some think she's dead."

"Dead? Oh, I hope not that."

"Well, there's others that say she didn't want to work here anymore. But if that's so, why would her people still be looking for her? And they are. Every few days somebody comes here asking about Mary."

"Lassie, I have to know. Why is Sudie so afraid? And why is Mrs. Elam so frightened? After all, a man at her back door asking for Mary by her surname—it sounds silly to be so frightened about that."

"Lucinda, all I know is that Mary tried to quit, but Mr. Wickham wouldn't let her."

"Mr. Wickham!" I said. "Don't you mean Mr. Sullivan?"

"No, it was Mr. Wickham. He told Mary she owed a bill at his store—Mr. Wickham gives credit to Negroes—and he said she couldn't leave until she paid what she owed. He told her if she didn't have the money, she would have to work it out. I heard him tell Mary that."

Lassie's blue eyes, bluer than the sky, grew larger with every word.

"What did Mary say?"

"She said, 'Mr. Wickham, I work day and night. I ain't ever out of debt.'" Lassie was a good mimic. "She said, 'Mr. Wickham, what you do, it ain't right. At your store I has to pay twenty-five cents for a hambone that cost ten cents with cash money. And always owing, I can't keep up and I can't catch up.'"

"And then what happened? What did Mr. Wickham say?"

"He said she was talking mighty smart for a nigger that had to eat."

I thought of how gentle Mr. Wickham's voice was when he talked to Mrs. Elam, how courteous he was at her supper table. But he had another side, a side I had heard at the kitchen door, had glimpsed when I had gone to his hotel to find Jeremiah.

"But why would Mr. Wickham want Mary to work for Mrs. Elam when she owed the money to him? That doesn't make any sense."

"Sometimes Mr. Wickham acts like he owns this house," Lassie said. "I don't think Mrs. Elam likes him, but she's always nice to him, nicer than she is to anybody."

This was something I'd talk to Josh about. Josh would be home the next day, and there were a million things I had to do before he got back. I wanted to find a house for us to live in, our very own house. And this morning, helping Lassie with the tomatoes, I thought how nice a garden would be.

"Lassie, by the time Josh gets home, I have to find a house. And I know just the one I want."

Lassie knew the house and knew its history. "It belongs to Mr. Agee now," she said. "He has the grocery store. You'll meet him. The house used to belong to a Negro preacher. He built it and lived in it for several years. Then everybody said he got too smart, started stirring up trouble, and they ran him out of town. So Mr. Agee got the house for almost nothing."

"After dinner I'll go down to talk to him about it."

"He won't be there. He closes on Saturday afternoon. And on a Saturday, it would be better if you went to his house. He lives just—let me see, one, two—he lives three blocks from here."

"After breakfast, I'll call him up and ask if I can walk over and talk to him about the house."

At the breakfast table, the Massies and I (the only three at breakfast) talked some more about the house.

"I'm not sure I'd want to live out there," Lassie said. "It's too far away from everything and everybody."

"Well, you could come see me and we could fish and go rowing. We'd *have* to have a boat. And we'd have our own garden. I wonder if there's any furniture in the house. Timothy, don't you think that's one of the prettiest houses in Sweet Shrub?"

Timothy smiled. "Lucy, it belonged to a colored. Besides, I like something fancier. More like this," he said, looking around at the brass chandelier, the paneling, the wreaths of roses on the wallpaper in Mrs. Elam's dining room.

"Oh, I like this too," I said, thinking I'd not try to explain all the reasons why I wanted the house out over the lake.

Right after breakfast, I rang up Mr. Agee. His wife answered. "This is Mrs. Arnold," I said.

Quick as anything, she said, "You're Mr. Josh Arnold's wife. I won't say who told me but someone said you drove."

"Yes, I do," I said. I waited a minute. When she didn't comment further about my driving, I said, "Mrs. Agee, I'd like to talk to you about that house on Cypress Lake."

"You better talk to my husband about that. He bought that house for nothing, thinking he could sell it quick."

After dinner I started to walk over to the Agees', but remembering Mrs. Agee's comment, I decided to drive. Before I could knock, Mr. Agee was opening the front door. He had black hair and black eyebrows, and there was a gun in the black holster he wore over his shoulder. The silver badge pinned to his shirt glittered in the sun.

"Mr. Agee, I didn't know you were the sheriff," I said.

"Deputy," he said. "Now, little lady, what can I do for you?"

When I told him what I wanted, he was doubtful. "That's a long way from everybody. Way out there, I'm not sure you'd be comfortable. Besides, it's been lived in by colored."

"Well, we have a car. I could drive in when I wanted something," I said. "And I don't care who's lived in it. It's a nice house."

Mr. Agee looked at the Maxwell parked in the middle of the street. "My wife's been wanting to drive," he said.

"It's the easiest thing in the world."

"Well, she's a mite skittery for it."

"Mr. Agee, how would it be if I just went out to look at the house this afternoon? Would that be all right?"

"No harm in it," he said. "It's not locked. You look all you want to and if Mr. Arnold's interested, we might work something out."

"Thank you, Mr. Agee. I'll let you know right away," I said.

I turned to leave, but, "Mrs. Arnold," he said, "lately there's been a lot of talk here about trouble." The wrinkles that jumped up on his pale forehead when he frowned made him look a lot older. "Tell your husband that I've taken to carrying a gun. Even sleep with it."

"Goodness gracious," I said. "Who would want to hurt you?"

"Maybe nobody, Mrs. Arnold. But the way things are, you can't tell."

"Thank you, Mr. Agee," I said. "I'll tell my husband."

Getting into the car, driving past all those beautiful old houses, I thought how nebulous—people talking about "trouble" and "unrest" and "not being sure"—it all sounded. It was like dust motes in a fall of sunshine. You knew they were there, but you couldn't put your finger on a one of them. But it made me uneasy, all the same.

I'd knew I'd have to hurry to pick up Jeremiah on time. But when I turned the corner onto Main Street, I was so astonished at what I saw that I stopped the car in the middle of the street. The sidewalks, several wagons, even the street, were filled with Negroes. Everywhere I looked the faces were dark. Up the street, down the street. Everywhere. I had never seen so many in one place, and in all that sea of dark faces there was not one white person! I remembered Mr. Wickham's warning not to go downtown on Saturday.

I started the car again, driving slowly, stopping and starting to let men and women and children cross in front of me. The colored people walked alongside the car, in back of it, and in front of it too. When those in front became aware of the car, they moved slowly out of the way so that I could pass, but then there were others walking there, and I'd wait for them to move out of the way.

I was uneasy, almost scared, but I said to myself, "Lucy, don't be silly. Look around. Do you see one sign, one single solitary sign, of unrest?"

I didn't, but it was with a feeling of relief that I saw Mr. Wickham's hotel just ahead. There was no sign of Jeremiah, so I eased the car close to the sidewalk and turned off the motor. Taking a deep breath, I looked around. Everybody was walking along, some hurrying, some not, just as they did in Bonham. The only difference, I told myself, is that all these people are colored.

I got out of the car and stepped up on the sidewalk. As I made my way to the front door of the Wickham Hotel, I saw Jeremiah coming toward me. And how could I not have seen him! The only white face in a sea of darker ones, he was moving at an easy pace, his head held high. He saw me, smiled, and lifting his arm to wave at me, brushed against an old Negro man. I saw him turn toward the man, smile, and put his hand on his shoulder.

The thought struck me that in all that crowd of Negroes, Jeremiah was perfectly at ease. He was one of them, in his own mind as dark as any.

"Hi, Miss Lucy," he called cheerfully.

We walked to my car, and as he started to get in back, I reminded him, "Sit up here with me."

In a few minutes, we were out on the Cypress Lake road. The day was hot and muggy, and it was a relief to be driving in the country, away from Sweet Shrub. I told Jeremiah where we were going. And why. Jeremiah knew the house and knew more about it than Lassie had.

"The white folks say that preacher was stirring up trouble, but it seem to me like he be trying to help us," Jeremiah said.

I looked at Jeremiah, looked back at the road. "Jeremiah, remember, you are white. If someone heard you say *us,* it would sound . . . funny."

"Miss Lucy, it just ain't working. And it ain't *going* to work when here"—he touched his head—"and here"—he put his hand over his heart—"I ain't white."

Hearing the pain in his voice, my throat closed so that I had to swallow. After a minute I said, "But you *know* that what you're doing is best for you. And your mama wants it. Jeremiah, promise that you won't give up. You'll get used to it."

"I been trying, Miss Lucy."

Now I turned onto the trace road that led straight down to the lake and the old house. When we reached the house, I turned off the motor of the car, enjoying the quiet of the country, and then, a minute later, the quiet sounds: a bird calling the same note, raspily insistent, over and over; somewhere, water lapping. I looked and could see it, small surges of water against the house supports that rose from the lake.

We got out of the car and climbed the outside stairs to the long, narrow porch out over the water. In the hot sunshine, the wooden railing and the floor were as dry as a bone and under the bright blue sky the porch seemed bone clean.

I stood by the railing, looking down into the water, hearing a fish or a frog splash. The cypress trees growing out in the lake, each with its own island of shade around it, were huge, but their leaves were surprisingly small, almost fernlike.

"There's a table in here," Jeremiah called from inside the house. "And a cookstove in the kitchen."

I opened the screen door and went inside. This room, like the porch, ran all the way across the front of the house, but it was deeper than the porch. It was bare, but the windows on three sides and the sun shining through them made it seem almost lived-in. I looked around, furnishing it in my mind. A sofa, a small table with a lamp. Maybe a rug and one or two pictures. And big pots of ferns. And Keats in his cage by a window. There would always be the view of the lake.

There were two other rooms upstairs. On the left a kitchen, and on the right a bedroom. I stepped into the kitchen. The cookstove was old but it would do. The table was just two boards on a sawhorse, a picnic table, but Josh had said he wanted our life to be like a picnic. He would like the table.

The bedroom was easy. All we'd need was a bed and a mattress. I could make the curtains, and I had a bedspread. Aunt Catherine had crocheted it.

Now Jeremiah was downstairs calling me to come see the downstairs room. In some ways it was the prettiest of all, snug and cozy, but the view was not as good. It would be our company room. Maybe by Thanksgiving, Mama could come.

Jeremiah and I walked out back. Someone had once had a garden. Remnants of it—half a dozen rosebushes, now gone wild, and fruit trees, three of them—were there still.

"Jeremiah, think what a wonderful garden I could have, just like Aunt Catherine's." I found a stick and began to mark it off. "Here," I said, "I'd have some strawberries. They don't do well in Bonham, but Lassie says they're easy to grow here. And then I'd have a bigger patch, about this big, for melons. I'd have at least two kinds. Then we'd need potatoes, sweet *and* Irish potatoes. Jeremiah, do you know what these trees are?"

"These two, they're peach, I'm 'most sure. But this one, I don't know."

"Maybe it's apricot. Or it could be plum. We'll have to wait and see."

Too excited to leave, I said, "Jeremiah, let's rest a minute before we go back to town."

We went up the steps again, and I sat on a chair without a back that Jeremiah had found in the little room downstairs. Jeremiah sat cross-legged on the floor, close to the porch's edge, his gaze fixed on the cluster of small cabins off to our left. I looked there, too, and saw an old woman working in her garden. A small child, in a bright yellow dress, came from a water pump in the front yard, half dragging, half carrying a bucket of water out to the woman. In another yard an old man holding a long stick poked at something (the week's wash?) in a great iron pot over an open fire. Not far from the fire, two small children, almost babies, tumbled about on the ground.

Jeremiah, glanced over his shoulder, saw that I was watching. "Miss Lucy," he said wistfully, "do you think the Lord has pets?"

"Oh, Jeremiah! No!" I said quickly.

Jeremiah said nothing more, but his gaze remained fixed on the cabins.

I looked again. Except for the children and the old man and the woman, everything was quiet. I wondered if Mary had lived in one of these houses, wondered if her feet had helped to make one of the ribbon paths that circled in and out and around the cabins, binding them together. I thought about Jeremiah's question.

"Jeremiah," I said, "I don't *think* the Lord has pets. But just looking around, sometimes it does seem like it."

Jeremiah's thin shoulders and soft features made me think he was too young to be away from Queenie. He needed his mother.

I leaned forward. "Jeremiah, what bothers you most about being white?" I asked.

"I don't know, Miss Lucy, but I guess it's the white folks' talk. When one of us is in the room, they smile and talk nice. They say, 'Do this. Do that. Hurry up. Get me this. Get me that.' And then, when us leaves, they say, 'Lazy nigger. He move so slow, flies stay on him.' And they laugh."

Oh, I knew it was true. I had heard talk of this kind.

"Jeremiah," I said firmly, "I know what you say is true. But not all white folks are like that."

"Most are," he said stubbornly.

"Well, you promised to try." Then, trying another tack, "How long will it take to save enough money to leave Sweet Shrub?"

"About three . . . maybe four more weeks."

"Well, you've got to try, at least until then. Maybe things will get better. How do the colored treat you?"

"I think they knows. But they not sure. Sometimes they act like they knows and they friendly. Sometimes they act like they suspicious." Jeremiah looked out over the lake again. "Right now, you and Mr. Arnold, you 'bout the only friends I got."

Oh, my. It had been a mistake, bringing Jeremiah here. At least in Bonham, he had Queenie, but not just Queenie. He had all the other colored people as well. He had all of Pig Branch, all those houses where people didn't make remarks about "lazy niggers." But here in Sweet Shrub, there was no sanctuary for Jeremiah, no safe place.

"Jeremiah, if we take this house, if we can get it, would you like to live with us out here? You could have the downstairs room. And you could help me with the garden after school, and I could help you with your homework. Would you do that? With the move and with all there'd be to do, you would be a mighty big help to us."

The smile on his face was his answer.

I drove Jeremiah back to the hotel, and then I drove

right over to Mr. Agee's house. Mrs. Agee was cooking their Sunday dinner, "because," she said proudly, "on a Sunday my cookstove never has a coal of fire in it."

Mr. Agee was fixing his wife's clothesline. His wife suggested I go right out the back door to where he was working.

I took a businesslike approach with him. "Mr. Agee," I said, "that house suits me, and I know Mr. Arnold will like it too. Could you tell me what the rent would be?"

He took a nail out of his mouth and stuck his hammer in his belt. It looked heavy, but not as heavy as the gun in his shoulder holster.

"Mrs. Arnold, I wouldn't know how to talk to a little lady about financial matters. Let's just wait until your husband gets back to settle all that."

"I can't wait until then. By the time Mr. Arnold gets back, I plan to be almost settled."

"Well, it's like this. I'm not exactly sure I'm gonna rent that house. And it will be at least a month, at least until October, before I do know."

"Well, a month isn't such a long time," I said. "We can wait a month. That might be better. We'd have more time to decide on the furniture we'd need."

"The thing is I just might sell that house. A man's interested in it. He said he'd like to have it. But even if he bought it, he'd most likely rent it to you. He sure wouldn't want to live in it."

Well. This was more and more encouraging. Now I felt sure that, one way or another, Josh and I would soon be living out on Cypress Lake.

"Mr. Agee, I'll tell my husband that. Now, exactly what rent were you thinking of?"

"I told my wife that with the way things are, I didn't know why anybody would want to live out there."

Ignoring what he had told his wife, I said, "At Mrs.

Elam's we pay thirty dollars a month for room and board. And we enjoy the whole downstairs and her maid, Sudie, cooks for us. It has some advantages."

"If I don't sell it, would fifteen a month be too much?"

"Not if you could throw in a bed."

"We got one we're not using. But you'd have to furnish the mattress."

I held out my hand. "Mr. Arnold will stop by one day next week," I said. "And, if it's all right with you, I'll go ahead with a little fall gardening. I want to be ready for spring planting."

Mr. Agee nodded, took his hammer out of his belt, and put the nail back in his mouth. I left him there to finish the work on the clothesline.

I went back the way I had come, through the kitchen.

When Mrs. Agee said, "That's a real nice house. Built tight. Not a chink in it!" I knew she'd been a party to the whole discussion. Then she added, "I sure wouldn't want to live out there right now."

Here it was again. Another dust mote, floating in the air.

"Mrs. Agee, it's so beautiful on the lake. And there's room for a wonderful garden. And I like fishing and boating. I'm keeping my fingers crossed that we'll get the house."

She dusted the cake flour off her hands, but the white smudge on her nose remained. Her eyes, behind her small, gold-rimmed glasses, looked pink, but of course they weren't.

Although I expected her to see me out, I was surprised when she came out on the porch, down the steps, and all the way out to the street with me.

"Mrs. Arnold, I think your little machine is the prettiest one I've ever seen. What kind is it?"

"A Maxwell," I said, thinking that with the sun on it, it

was as shiny as patent leather. "But the first motorcar I bought, oh, that was the sportiest little car."

"You mean you know how to drive two kinds?"

"It's like riding a bicycle. If you can drive one kind, you can drive two or three."

"Mrs. Arnold, would you show me how? My husband thinks I'm not suited for it, but I'd like to learn. Oh, Mr. Agee takes me anywhere I want to go, if he has the time. And if he's home when I need to go. Course, being a grocer and all, he does all the grocery shopping."

"I'll be glad to teach you. You could learn in an afternoon."

"Well, I'd like to try it. I'd just like to show my husband I could do it."

"You could surprise him," I said. "One afternoon, you could take my car and drive to town to do your own grocery shopping."

She laughed. "He'd be flabbergasted!"

"And proud of you," I told her.

We made a date for the following week. On Wednesday I'd take Josh to school and that afternoon I'd teach Mrs. Agee how to drive.

It had been a strange day. And there were so many parts of it I wanted to talk over with Josh. All of a sudden, I couldn't wait for him to get home.

26

KEATS'S INDIGNANT SQUAWKS told me he wanted the cover off his cage. "Keats, you'll never sing like a mockingbird," I told him, taking off the cover, "but you are much more beautiful." Keats stood on one foot and looked carefully at the other one, turning his head this way and that. I laughed. "Except for your feet, you're pretty. Keats, don't ever let a woman see your bare feet."

Sunday morning in Sweet Shrub. The weather was ripening; fall was in the air. Lassie had invited me to go to church. And Josh would be home tonight. Thinking of it, I jumped out of bed. Putting on my wrapper, I went upstairs and tapped lightly on the Massies' door, so as not to wake up Mrs. Elam, whose room was just across the hall.

Lassie stuck her head out the door.

"Lassie, you've cut your hair!" I said. Her hair, only the day before in thick coils and braids about her head, was now a mass of short ringlets around her face. It made her blue eyes look rounder. And bigger. "What did Timothy say?"

She giggled. "He said he'd get used to it. I knew it would be all right with Timothy."

I admired Lassie. I had never known a woman so daring! Cutting her hair, just like that!

I was dressed and waiting on the front porch when Timothy came down to tell me that Lassie was still working with her hair. She wanted it to be just right when she made her first appearance in it.

"I like Lassie's hair," I said, ready to go right to another subject if this one did not suit Timothy.

"Oh, that girl! Isn't she something!" Timothy said proudly.

Then Lassie came downstairs in a red dress, and wearing, instead of a hat, a big red bow in her hair. She whirled around, showing off her dress and her lace-trimmed petticoat (You couldn't be around Lassie ten minutes without knowing her petticoats were lace trimmed).

"Like my new dress?" she asked. "Timothy bought it for me in Helena."

"Lassie, you look like a picture in the *Delineator*," I told her.

Going up the church steps, I saw the Agees just ahead of us. Mrs. Agee wore a pink dress, really pretty with her gray hair and her pinkish eyes. When she saw us, she said something to her husband, turned, and came back down the steps to us.

"Mrs. Arnold, I'm so thrilled about learning to drive," she whispered. "I can't wait until Wednesday," she said.

"Lucy, I didn't know you *taught* driving," Lassie said. "I want to learn."

"Now, Lassie, whoa, here now. We don't even have a car," Timothy said.

"But we will. And if I learn now, I'll be all ready to drive ours when we get one," Lassie said.

"Well, I guess it'll be all right," Timothy said. "Just don't hit a cow or nothing."

Then we were inside the church, and Lassie left Timothy and me to take her place with the choir. A lot of people noticed her hair, but they would have noticed her anyway, for when she sang, her voice, full and true, rang out over the others.

After church the Massies introduced me to the Bryans,

and I remembered that he had the machine shop in town. Then a man in a white suit came up and was introduced. His name was Peter Dexter, "And he has the betting parlor," Lassie said.

"Go ahead. Tell her what else I am," Peter laughed. "Tell her that I'm Sweet Shrub's most eligible bachelor."

"Lucy, he's our *only* bachelor," Lassie giggled.

An older couple (they were at least forty) named Quarles walked over. Mr. Quarles said, "We have five young'uns in the school and we'll have another one there pretty soon. You tell your husband if he has trouble with a one of mine to let me know and that young'un will be in twice as much trouble when he gets home."

One of the things I learned the year I taught was that when parents said that, sometimes they meant it and sometimes they didn't. I wondered if Mr. Quarles meant it.

On the way home, Lassie told me more about the town. "It's a funny thing," she said, "but most of the businesses on the south side of Main Street are owned by Methodists and the businesses on the north side are owned by Baptists, except for Miss Roberta Reed at the post office."

"What about her?" I asked.

"She's Catholic," Lassie said. "I don't know what she does on Sundays. I've wondered about it. I'd ask her to go to church with me, but I imagine the Pope would have a fit."

After dinner, I took a little walk, but it was too hot and muggy for exercise. So I came home, made myself a glass of lemonade (on Sundays we have free use of the kitchen), and sat on the front porch to read and to catch the breeze.

Peter Dexter stopped by to pick up Timothy for some fishing. "We might not catch much, the weather being as hot as it is, but then again, something might take a notion to bite. You can't tell," he said.

Lassie had come outside to see her husband off, and before he and Peter were out of sight, Mildred Elam and her cousin drove up to the house. We watched Mr. Sullivan hurry around the car to open the door for her and help her down.

"Lucy, when they're inside, I'll tell you something if you promise not to tell," Lassie said, never taking her eyes off Mrs. Elam and her cousin.

I knew in a minute what it was; Lassie was expecting. But, no, I was wrong.

"Timothy says we're going to buy a car, right away," she said breathlessly. "Then, if there's trouble, we'll have transportation."

"Oh, Lassie, all this talk of trouble," I told her. "We're not going to have any trouble. But I'm glad you're buying a car. Let's celebrate."

"We'll have a glass of sherry," she said.

Remembering Inez and her little glasses of sherry, I said, "Lassie, that stuff's poison."

"No, it isn't," she said. "Come on, Lucy. Let's have a glass. Then I'll sing and you can accompany me. We might work up a program for the church social."

I did want Lassie to try "When a Fellow's on the Level with a Girl That's on the Square." I had learned to play it really well.

"One glass," I said.

And what with the singing and the sherry, I forgot to pick up Josh at the railroad crossing. I forgot all about it and when he came up the porch steps and into the living room, I was so startled that I just sat there, on the piano bench.

"Lucy!" he said, coming over to the piano and pulling me up and into his arms. "Oh, girl, I was worried about you. When you weren't there to meet me, I thought you might have had car trouble." Josh took out his handkerchief and wiped his forehead. "Sweetheart, I've never been so relieved."

"Why, Josh, if I had had car trouble, somebody would have come along and helped me." To take his mind off my not being there to meet him, I said, "Look at Lassie's hair. She cut it herself."

"I copied a picture," Lassie said proudly. "Do you like it?"

"I saw two women in Helena with short hair like yours," Josh said.

Lassie seemed satisfied, but when we were in our own room, he said, "Lucy, if you ever cut your hair, I'll never speak to you again." And he took me in his arms and kissed me until I forgot all about telling him what a silly thing it was to say.

Later, I hurriedly made sandwiches and brought them to our room. I couldn't wait to tell Josh about the house.

"Josh, guess what!" I said. "We can get that house out on Cypress Lake. I'm sure of it. But it might be a month, well, it'll be at least a month, before we can move in."

"That house is out of the question," Josh said. "Just forget about that house."

His voice was stern. He might have been telling a stray dog to get out of the yard.

"Josh Arnold, I want that house," I said. "It's perfect for us and not one bit more expensive than living here."

"Lucy, the lawyers in Helena, Bailey and Hutchison especially, believe that Phillips County has a serious problem. The situation is much worse than I thought."

"The situation!" I said. "What in the world is the *situation*? Josh, I am so tired of hearing about the trouble, when no one seems to know what the trouble is. Now it's the *situation*!"

I was on my feet, shouting across the table at Josh. His voice was steely. "Sit down and I'll tell you. In Phillips County, there are over twenty-six thousand people. And over three-fourths of these people are colored. Now, if there's trouble here, what does that tell you?"

"Why should there be trouble? Why would we have any trouble in Sweet Shrub?"

"For one thing, the coloreds have formed a union, and there's talk they're planning to hold their cotton back this fall. If they do, the Delta farmers are bound to take action."

"Why would they hold back the crop when they need money more than anybody?"

"Bailey's been all over the county talking to the Delta farmers and to their tenants. He says that some of the landowners are downright unscrupulous. They furnish a man with a house and a mule and let him work about twenty acres on the halves. But when the cotton's sold, the sharecropper doesn't get his money for months. And by the time he gets it, he owes so much that it takes all his cash and more to pay his bill. He's always in debt. And the unwritten law up here is that a Negro cannot leave a place as long as he owes money. So in effect, he's an indentured servant."

"Josh, Mr. Wickham does that. Lassie heard Mary tell him that if she worked the rest of her life, she'd never get out of debt."

"Well, I don't know Mary. But Wickham does give credit to the Negroes, and I'd like to know what he charges them. He might well be one of the farmers who are causing all this trouble. Mr. Bailey's been trying to ease the situation, asking every Delta farmer to settle promptly. Now some are saying that Bailey's trying to stir up trouble. Well, you heard Louis Sullivan say that very thing the other night."

Then I told Josh everything Lassie had overheard of the conversation between Mary and Russ Wickham. And about Jeremiah's asking if the Lord had pets. And about Mr. Agee's wearing his gun while he worked on the clothesline.

"Lucy, until all this blows over, I want you to be careful. If I happen to be gone, don't go out by yourself at night."

"Josh Arnold, you sound like you're afraid."

"I'm not afraid, Lucy. You and I don't have anything to be afraid of. Bailey says that all the Negroes want is to be paid when their cotton is sold. And they want an accounting. He says they're afraid to ask for even that much."

"That doesn't sound like much to me," I said, knowing Queenie needed her money every week, sometimes more often than that.

"What sounds reasonable to some sounds uppity to others," Josh said. "But after the cotton picking season's over, things are bound to settle down. And then, my dearest Lucy, we can live anywhere you choose."

"Josh, the colored school needs a real teacher. I'm collecting books for the school (Mildred Elam and Mrs. Agee have both promised to hunt up some), but they need a teacher out there. And the windows need to be replaced. They've got cardboard in them now, but this winter it'll be cold."

"I'm going to bring that up at the next board meeting. Sometimes, well, sometimes people have to be made to do what's right, and in this case, the law says that Phillips County has to hire a colored teacher for the school out at Peaceful."

Josh got up from the table and began to unpack the small bag he had taken with him. I sat on the bed, watching. He took out his shirt and his tie and his underwear. Then he unpacked a newspaper-wrapped package and laid it on the bed, and something about it, maybe because it was so heavy that it made a deep indentation in the mattress, or maybe it was the shape of it, but something made me know what it was.

"Josh Arnold, that's a gun!" I said, and I knew that, despite the reassuring words he had spoken, Josh Arnold was afraid.

In spite of the unrest all around us, the next few days went by peacefully. No one came around asking for Mary, and although it took Sudie almost an hour to walk to her little cabin close to Cypress Lake, she began to go home after she finished her work. The new laundress, Alma, had come from Memphis, and in the daytime I could hear their soft voices as she and Sudie went about their household chores. And once or twice I heard them giggling together, like any young girls might.

That Wednesday I gave Mrs. Agee her first driving lesson.

And the next day I started the garden.

As a surprise for Josh, I planned to get everything ready for spring before I told him. Jeremiah knew everything about gardening, almost as much as Aunt Catherine and Uncle Jerry. "Jeremiah, we can't live out here right now, but if you'll help me, I'll pay you what Mr. Wickham pays."

Jeremiah said he'd be pleased to do it.

The next day, I put Keats in the car and stopped by the hotel for Jeremiah. This time he had waited in front, and we were soon out at Cypress.

"Jeremiah, you'll have to tell me where we ought to begin. By next spring I want a garden Aunt Catherine would be proud of."

Jeremiah looked carefully around. "Clearing needs to

be done, and the ground needs turning. That's first. And the trees need pruning. Miss Lucy, it'll take a right smart a work before we can call it a garden."

"Oh, in no time we'll have the most beautiful garden in Sweet Shrub. Just one thing, Jeremiah. This is our secret, yours and mine. I want to surprise Mr. Arnold with it."

He nodded. "Well, let's get started," he said, looking happier than he had in weeks.

So it was that the three of us, Jeremiah and Keats and I, began to slip out to the lake at every opportunity. Knowing he couldn't fly, we'd find Keats a limb to perch on, and we'd work and plan while Keats watched happily. Over the next two weeks, the garden began to take shape. By the middle of September, we had managed to clear it of rocks and weeds, to prune the trees and to till the portion we had marked off for our vegetable garden.

"Jeremiah, I couldn't have done all this without you," I said one day, enjoying the smell of the freshly turned earth and the easy breeze that stirred now and again, cooling us off.

"Miss Catherine, she taught me about everything. And Uncle Jerry. He know a right smart about a garden too."

Still, there was so much more to be done. Jeremiah said now was the time to plant fruit trees. "Plant them next week," he said. "The moon be full and we plant them by the moon's light."

"I don't know about that, Jeremiah. We can't be slipping out here at midnight. Mr. Arnold would know."

And then Jeremiah, exactly as Josh would have done, threw back his head and laughed.

"Just teasing, Miss Lucy. We plant in late afternoon, and *tell* the trees it's the moonlight."

His twinkling eyes and his shy smile told me he was enjoying the humor. I had never known him to tease before. "Jeremiah, you're pretty funny," I said. "And after the trees, what?"

"A fence around the vegetables, keep out the rabbits," Jeremiah said, going over to the tree where Keats was hanging. "Now, Keats," he said, taking him from the cage to perch on his outstretched arm, "one day you find somebody just like yourself. And you be satisfied then, stop your squawking."

Jeremiah was crazy about Keats, and it worried him that there was no other macaw about. And it worried him that Keats couldn't fly. We had discovered this by accident when the door to the cage had come open. Keats had hopped to the floor and walked to the front door, squawking to be allowed to come out and join us. Now, when we had the time, we'd take him out. Jeremiah enjoyed walking with Keats on his shoulder or his arm.

"Keats thinks he's human," I said. "He doesn't know he's a bird."

Suddenly I was tired, but it was a good feeling. "Let's go home, Jeremiah. We've worked long enough for one day, and it's almost time to pick up Mr. Arnold."

The next day, Saturday, Josh and I slept late and missed breakfast. After a lazy lunch, Josh and Peter Dexter left to go to Cypress to fish a little. "And Peter's on the county school board," Josh said, grinning. "So we'll be talking about a teacher for Peaceful."

His saying that made me happy. Josh has a silver tongue and I wanted the colored school to have a real teacher.

I hoped Josh wouldn't notice the garden at Cypress. I wanted to see the smile on his face, hear his deep laugh when he saw the freshly tilled land, the trees trimmed and others planted, and the three rosebushes Peter Dexter had promised, planted and ready to bloom next spring.

Soon after Josh left, Mr. Sullivan put his cousin on the train to Helena. Accompanied by Mrs. Wickham (I wondered what she was like), Mildred Elam was going to the chautauqua program in Helena.

"The chautauqua comes to Bonham almost every summer," I had told her that morning. "They almost always have a magician," I said, remembering how mad Mama got when the one that came to Bonham made her purse disappear right before her eyes for almost an hour.

That evening after supper, I was in the parlor leafing through Mrs. Elam's sheet music when I heard the sound of the back door closing lightly behind Sudie and Alma, followed, a minute later, by Louis Sullivan's footsteps as he went behind them, locking up. Then he came through the dining room and out into the hall, and I heard the heavy bolt on the front door fall into place.

Silly, I thought. Locking up a house in broad daylight. I stood up, twirled the piano stool a little higher and, as I sat back down again, saw that Mr. Sullivan stood in the doorway.

"May I join you, Mrs. Arnold? I was hoping you would favor me with a selection. Earlier today, I heard you playing one of Mildred's favorites."

Of course I would play, but just at the moment I had something on my mind. "Mr. Sullivan," I said, "why were the magnolias cut down? They must have been so beautiful growing all along the drive."

"They were beautiful. Reaching out across the driveway, their branches so full that the drive was always completely in shade, it made one cool just to look at them. And driving up to the house was like driving through a tunnel of green shadows. But at night it was too dark. You couldn't drive a buggy through without be-

ing crowded out by the darkness. Then after Mary, walking down that same drive, disappeared, Mildred knew that anybody could hide there. A person could make his way from the street all the way to the house without being seen, even in daylight. And one night, right after Mary left, three Negroes did just that, appeared at the back door, asking for "Mrs. Johnson," and Mildred watched them disappear into the magnolias, didn't see them again until they were out the front gate. She said, if three could come, thirty could come. The next day, she had the trees cut down. It's a shame, but it had to be done. But there are those beech trees on the front lawn, more magnificent, really, than the magnolias."

I could see it all. The three men appearing at the back door, asking for Mary or Mrs. Johnson, and Louis Sullivan or Mr. Wickham speaking to them kindly or harshly, depending on who had gone to the door. Mildred Elam might have listened, or she might have watched from her upstairs bedroom as the three, one by one, slipped into the magnolia drive and disappeared.

"Couldn't the gates have been kept locked?"

"A lock won't stay on those gates. We've put at least four there, but a light blow, and they're gone."

Mr. Sullivan took his watch from his watch pocket, and as he did so, I saw the gun he wore.

"Surely that's not needed in the house," I said, dismayed at the idea of another gun.

He glanced down at it, smiled. "Mrs. Arnold, of course, you're right. I had thought to take a little walk when I saw you here in the parlor. Now tell me about that East Texas town you come from. I've never been to Texas."

So I did and I must have been hungry to tell someone, for I told him about the operas we had and about our band concerts on Saturday afternoons and about the wonderful chautauqua shows that came each summer.

"Why, Bonham's the New York City of Texas," I said, bragging a little. "We have more to offer than Dallas."

"You miss it, don't you?"

"Yes, I do. But I'm not homesick, and I thought I might be. A little."

"Poor Mildred. All these years, away from her friends, her family."

He poured himself a glass of brandy and tossed it down. Then he poured himself another one and placed it carefully on the table beside a vase of white roses.

"Mrs. Arnold, have you spoken to Mildred about returning to Memphis? I believe another woman might persuade her. She's quite fond of you."

"Mrs. Elam says she can never go back to Memphis."

"That's such nonsense. She was like that as a child, too, willful and stubborn. Did you know she was just a child, fourteen years old, when we met?"

Afraid I might reveal a confidence, I did not answer. Instead, I said, "You've known her a long time, haven't you?"

"And loved her. In Memphis, we had three years; those years sealed a bond between us."

He took up his brandy glass, drank from it, set it down again. Mama always said liquor loosened a man's tongue, and I believe that it does.

"Strange that she would love me, that a girl so young could love anybody," he said, frowning. "Lucinda, I am, *was,* a man of no great physical charm or grace."

I started to protest, to tell him he was much nicer looking than Mr. Wickham, but he lifted his hand. "No," he said, "it's all right. I have other qualities that serve, and one of these is the ability to love Mildred Elam as she has the right to be loved. In those days, invited to her house by her father, I would sit for hours, just looking at her. She was, *is,* so contradictory. Even her beauty con-

tradicts itself. So fair, but with that dark hair, so strangely exotic. When she was fourteen, fifteen, sixteen, she'd say to me, "Louis, you're not listening to me." And I wasn't. I loved looking at her. I was addicted to it. All her chatter about her friends and her horse and her family lacked any real significance, but her beauty was full-blown. At fourteen, she had a woman's beauty. And when her father told me he was sending her off to Ward-Belmont, I knew I had to have her, we had to have each other, and we ran away together."

Settling back into his chair, his eyes glittering out from the shadows, he looked down at his tightly clasped hands. When he spoke again, his voice was so soft, I had to lean forward to hear. "That night I saw that she was only a child, and the next day I brought her home. But it was too late. Her uncle Haddie had notified the Memphis police and the sheriff's office. By Sunday morning, all of Memphis knew she had eloped with her cousin. And no one believed she had returned before . . . before our love was consummated."

Sighing, he rose and walked to the window. "Two weeks later, she ran away again and married Joseph Elam, a man she didn't know. Never loved."

In that close room, with the rose petals falling on the table by his brandy glass and the smell of roses and brandy, I longed for the high plains of West Texas, and the wild, strong wind.

"I hope it works out," I said. "Maybe it will. Maybe you can persuade her to come to Memphis with you," I said, doubting it.

I liked Mr. Sullivan, liked his kind voice, his unruly hair, admired the strength of his love for Mildred Elam, and something about him reminded me of home. I thought carefully about what it might be. And then I knew what it was! Louis Sullivan had that same vagueness of manner, a dreaminess about his eyes, that Jacqueline Balfour had, although it was more pronounced in Jacqueline. I'd ask Josh if he saw it too.

Slipping out of the room, I tiptoed across the hall and, after a minute, quietly unlocked and opened the front door. It was cooler now, and I walked down the drive to the fence, and then, staying just inside the fence, walked all around Mrs. Elam's property. Coming back to the drive, I noticed that in the big house across the way a single light burned in an upstairs room. But no one else was about.

After my walk I came back inside and silently dropped the lock back into place.

I was in bed and almost asleep, when I heard, or thought I heard, a noise. It came again. A thump! Followed by two or three more. Unidentifiable. I jumped out of bed, and following the sounds, ran to the dining room.

On the long table a black-speckled chicken, its neck freshly wrung, flopped about, spattering blood on the white lace cloth and on the wreaths of roses in the wallpaper. As I screamed, Mr. Sullivan appeared, grabbed at it, missed, and missed again as it flopped off the table to lay beside its own head, and as he picked up the chicken and took it to the kitchen sink, I watched the eyes in the head, which lay beside a chair leg, fade, become opaque. And dead.

"This would just about kill Mildred," Mr. Sullivan said, coming back into the dining room, picking up the head by its beak, taking it to the kitchen.

"Well, it scared me to death!" I said. "And your shirt is bloody."

But as if I hadn't spoken, he said, "I've got to clean this mess up before she comes home."

Still trembling, I stood and began to gather up the tablecloth. "I'll put this to soak," I said, but I was answered only by the *swish* of the dining room door as it closed. And then I heard him hurrying through the upstairs rooms and knew he had a gun in his hand as he searched.

In a few minutes, he hurried through the dining room to the kitchen. "Good Lord, the back door's standing wide open!" he said. "Now, how in thunder . . ."

"I took a walk and left the front door open. Someone might have come in then."

Louis Sullivan and I looked at each other over the blood-spotted cloth. Queenie and Mama had performed the grisly task a hundred times. And I could imagine the furious, silent action of someone wringing the chicken's neck, throwing it on the table, fleeing out the back door.

"But why?" I asked. "Why would anybody do such a thing?"

"It's this Mary thing again. And it won't ever be over. Mildred has got to leave Sweet Shrub. That's all there is to it. Tomorrow, I'm going to tell her that she has to leave."

27

THE NEXT DAY, even the weather was erratic. Early that morning high storm clouds filled with wind and thunder rolled across the southern sky, threatening rain, but these were soon dispersed by a sun-drenched afternoon. Then the smell of rich loam and honeysuckle and wood drying came through the windows into our room. And late that afternoon a cool front came from the north, bringing lightning bugs, and swallows swooping in graceful spirals to feed on them. And that day, Sunday, was marked by a series of events as disparate as the weather.

After the nightmare in the dining room, sleep had been out of the question. Waiting for Josh, I tried to read, but not even Jane Eyre's unhappy flight from Mr. Rochester could hold my attention. It was almost morning when I heard Josh's car, and slipping out the front door, I met him on the front porch and astonished us both by bursting into tears.

"Lucy, what is it? Has something happened at home? Is it your Aunt Catherine?"

"Oh, it was awful," I sobbed. "Seeing a chicken there, dead, but so furiously flopping around on Mrs. Elam's dining table. And blood spattering everywhere. And its head by the chair leg, looking on."

"A chicken!" Josh said incredulously. "On Mildred's table!"

And I told him about the noise I had heard and followed, and about the blood everywhere, and about the slowly fading eyes. "Oh, I've seen Mama and Queenie do it a thousand times (although Mama says it takes her appetite), but to see it there! And in the middle of the night! It was horrible."

"Gol-durn it," Josh said, holding me close. "Somebody is trying to scare this household, or somebody *in* this house."

Sounding tired and discouraged, his arms still around me, he said, "It's too late to go to bed." Then he lifted my chin, looked into my face, and smiled. "I'll tell you what. I'll clean the fish. Just wait until you see the fish we caught! And then I'll fix breakfast."

"Oh, Josh, the dining room. It's still . . . awful."

"Well, I'll take care of that too. By the time you dress, I'll be ready to start breakfast."

Josh was still out back, cleaning fish, and I had just finished dressing when I heard a motor vehicle coming up to the house. It was Miss Reed, delivering a letter. And on Sunday.

"I'm not even supposed to look at the mail today, but I noticed this in the mailbag last night. Look at what your mother wrote on it," she said, holding it so that we could look at it together.

Just below the address Mama had written: *"Please* see that my daughter, Mrs. Josh Arnold, gets this letter immediately! *It is a family matter."*

"I hope it's not bad news," Miss Reed said.

That hadn't occurred to me. I looked at the letter. Except for Mama's message on the front, it looked like any other.

I patted the porch step beside me, inviting her to wait while I opened the letter.

"Miss Reed, my sister has a little boy," I said, and here were the tears again as a flood of love for my sister and her tiny baby swept over me.

Miss Reed smiled and the gold in her teeth caught the sun, made her smile dazzling. "I know just how you feel," she said, her voice thin and childlike, although looking at her big smile and big bosom, what you'd expect was a warm alto. "We have fourteen in our family right now, but most of them I've never seen." She patted my shoulder and stood up, looking at the sky as thunder rumbled across. "Well, I'd better get on back home. It does look like it might pour down just any minute," she said.

I sat on the porch, hugging the thought of our new baby to myself. And longing to see Annabel. I imagined her running out to meet me, taking my hand, proudly showing me her small cousin.

I remembered I hadn't read the rest of Mama's letter.

"Katie's finally grown up," she wrote on the next page. "She's been such a help to us all. Oh, one more thing! Bob will arrive in two weeks to take his little family home. We are trying to get everything ready for his visit."

Bob. I said the word aloud, but it failed to conjure up a face. I said it again. *Bob.* It had been days since I thought about him. And yet, thinking about him now, there was a hard place close to my heart, almost an ache. And it was always there whenever his name or Katie's came to mind, an unpleasant tightening.

Now I thought of Josh, of the fatigue in his voice. "Lucy, for goodness sakes," I told myself, "where is the starch in your backbone?"

And I walked through the dining room (still a mess), and into the kitchen just as Josh came up the back steps with a pan of freshly cleaned fish.

"Josh, let's have those fish for breakfast," I said. "If you'll fry them, I'll clean the dining room. And I've got the best news. Lillian has a healthy baby boy!"

By nine o'clock Josh and Louis Sullivan, saying he had not slept a wink all night either, and I were at breakfast (the Massies sleeping late), when Mr. Wickham's apologetic knock was heard. Seeing us at the table, he stretched his thin lips into a smile, as straight as a ruler across his face. "Having breakfast in the kitchen?" he asked, and then, "Somebody's really done some cleaning in the dining room this morning. Are Mildred's niggers working on Sunday?"

When Louis took him back into the room and told him what had happened, showed him the stains that remained on the wallpaper and the floor, he said, quite softly, "Goddamn mules. The only thing they understand is a blow on the head." Drawing his shoulders up around his head, he went to the back screen door and looked out. "Evidently one's not enough, but when three or four disappear, that'll put the fear of God in them."

He turned, came back to the table and stood, looking down at us. "Everything I have is here, and it's not gonna be spoilt by a handful of mule-headed niggers." As if in reaction to the venomous words he spewed, a jagged line of white slowly appeared around his lips. "Now, I know the law, know what's right. And I didn't come down here to turn everything over to a bunch of thick-headed darkies."

"Mr. Wickham," Josh said, speaking slowly, his voice deeper than I had ever heard it, "they want a prompt settlement when their crop is sold. And an accounting."

"Mr. Arnold, this don't concern you a'tall. We brought you in to teach, and that's all your job is. I got detectives in here from Chicago handling this other."

"Mr. Wickham—" I began, but his soft voice ran roughshod over my words. "Where's Mildred's niggers?" he asked. "They been around here this morning? I'll see what they know about this."

I wanted to strike back at the cruelty hiding behind the gentle voice. But what words would slip through his arrogance? We sat there and watched him.

He got almost to the door, and again turned back. "Oh, one other thing." And now he looked at me. "That boy, that white nigger you're so fond of?" His voice was smooth, each word curling softly into the next. "I told him to get out of Sweet Shrub."

Then Josh was up, his chair flying back, overturning, and he grabbed Wickham's collar, pushed him out the back door, slinging him down the steps to lie sprawled on the ground.

There was nothing in Wickham's face, not even surprise, when he got to his feet. "You may not live long enough to regret what you did," he said.

Without answering, Josh turned and came back into the kitchen. Breathing hard, he went to the sink and washed his hands and dried them. Then he sat down at the table. "Whew!" he said, pushing his chair back and crossing his legs. "Dog-gone it, Lucy, I'm sorry. I hate to lose my temper like that. I wish I didn't have such a temper, but I do," he said cheerfully.

"I'm not sorry you threw him out," I told him.

When we drove off to find Jeremiah, Wickham's car was still there, but I thought it would not be when we returned.

We had only driven two blocks when we saw Jeremiah, walking toward Mrs. Elam's, carrying all he had in a light case.

Josh stopped and, leaning over the backseat, opened the door. "You need a ride?" he asked. When Jeremiah had climbed in, Josh rolled a cigarette, and slowly, deliberately, tapped it down. "Now, Jeremiah, there's lots of fools in the world," he said reasonably, "and you can't waste time worrying about them. When Mrs. Elam comes home tonight, we'll see if she can put you up for a while."

All afternoon, Jeremiah stayed close by. He cleaned Keats's cage and, under Josh's watchful eye, worked his math problems.

"Now, what about your reading?" Josh asked when he had finished.

"Mr. Arnold, I like arithmetic, but we supposed to read about a man by the name of Ulysses, and I don't care for it."

Josh told Jeremiah that Ulysses was a hero and that it was important to think about heroes because, almost certainly, at some point in life, each of us would be called upon to be a hero. And listening to Josh I felt that I, too, could be more, could venture further. Then Josh opened the book and began to read, and as I watched the storm clouds move away and the sun come out, I forgot about Mr. Wickham and knew again that learning was, in a way, as much a part of the excitement of living as love.

After the lessons, Josh said he had to run over to the school to move some desks to the lower grade rooms. Thinking it would be nice to get out, I told Josh I'd drop him and Jeremiah at the school so I could take Polly Agee out for another driving lesson. And Polly had promised to give me two books for the colored school. "But I'm not sure she'll go in the car today," I added. "On Sundays she never has a fire in her stove."

But when I stopped by her house, she jumped right in. "Polly, I wasn't sure you'd come with me," I told her, "since it's Sunday."

"If the Lord hadn't wanted me to have a driving lesson, He wouldn't have put the thought in your head," she said, handing me the books.

It made sense.

That day Polly drove us into the country, past field after field of newly cleared land and cotton ready to pick, or in some cases, picked clean. In the middle of each small field there was a two-roomed cabin with its own fireplace, like those out by Cypress Lake. All around Sweet Shrub land was being cleared and Negro families being moved in to farm the land. No wonder the town was so crowded with colored folks on Saturdays.

"Mr. Wickham owns almost all the land around here," Polly said. "But Mr. Agee and I bought a hundred acres this year. We're hoping to buy another hundred right soon."

The last thing I wanted was to think about Mr. Wickham. "Polly," I said, "you can drive as well as anybody. You don't need more lessons."

"Why, I'd be scairt to death to drive downtown."

"All right," I said. "We'll have another lesson Wednesday. And then you can drive downtown by yourself and surprise your husband."

When we got back to her house, she asked me in for iced tea and cake, and sitting across the table from her, I looked carefully at her eyes. The irises were pale blue and small, but I saw it was the whites, pink-tinged and encircled with pink rims, that made her eyes look pink. With her white hair and pink eyes, she did remind me of a gentle rabbit. I liked her.

That afternoon, Louis went to meet Mildred Elam's train, and when they returned, Josh and Jeremiah and I were on the front porch. We watched as she took Louis's hand, stepped down from the motorcar, and walked lightly up the steps. Seeing her, I thought to myself, Lucy, you've got to take more time with your appearance. She wore bright blue, as bright as any red. Her skirt was tight across her hips that swayed, and the lace at the top of her bodice did not quite hide the soft swell of her breasts. From a coil at the top of her head, dark curls, in vivid contrast to her white face and violet-colored eyes, fell luxuriously around her shoulders.

But her beauty was more than all this. It lay in the sensual silks and laces, the vibrant colors that she wore; in the generosity of her smile, her gestures, her walk; in her perfume, laden with the rich scent of delta flowers. It was something she was born with. Or had learned.

Josh and Jeremiah, as young as he was, watched her get out of the car and come up the steps, their enjoyment visible on their faces. Had I not been sure of Josh's love, I would certainly have been jealous.

Mildred's reaction to the nightmare of the previous night surprised us all. "Just a prank," she said, laughing. "Nothing to be excited about. And I've been thinking, I need new wallpaper in there anyway. Maybe a pale gray, with silver stripes. How does that sound?"

I couldn't believe it. A woman who paled at the thought of someone at her back door asking for "Mrs. Johnson," making light of such an act. But I thought that had she been there, seen it herself, she would have been as shocked as I.

When Josh asked if she could find room for Jeremiah, she said yes right away. "We need more men around," she added, her dimples appearing, her eyes dancing. With a lace handkerchief still in her hand, she cupped Jeremiah's chin in her lace-filled hand. "Jeremiah, go up and look at that attic room. See if it won't do," she told him.

Late that evening, Josh sat in our room, reading *Ulysses,* having interested himself in it again, while I filled a watering can and watered the hanging baskets on the front porch, pinching off the yellow fronds of the fern as I did so.

Cooler weather had come, and it was pleasant to stand

in the twilight of the day, looking across Mildred's property to the road below. Now and then the giant beech trees swayed, sending a rush of leaves to the ground beneath; leaves drained of their color by the fading light. When the lightning bugs appeared, enchanted by the magic of their flickering lights and the graceful spirals and loopings of the barn swallows that came to feed on them, I sat in a rocking chair just outside the parlor windows and watched.

My enjoyment made me unaware of any household activity, so that Mildred's voice, coming through the parlor windows just behind my chair, caught me by surprise.

"Louis, whatever else I am, have been, you must know I cannot, *will* not be without funds," I heard her say.

"But five thousand dollars. Oh, Mildred, to take money from this man. I cannot allow it."

"Then, Cousin Louis, will you pay it?" she said, her voice so harsh that, for a minute, I thought it could not be Mildred's. But it was, and now, again, it was as beguiling as ever, "Dear Louis, of course you cannot, but for a man like Wickham, it's so little, not even a slight inconvenience. He assured me of that."

"Mildred, Wickham was here this morning, asking where 'Mildred's niggers' were, saying he had ordered Jeremiah to leave town. Mildred, you're mistaken to think five thousand dollars is nothing to him. To a man who loves money, it's everything."

"Oh, dear," Mildred said, "if I'd known all this, I'd not have said Jeremiah could stay. But I can explain Jeremiah's being here to Russ."

"And the money you borrowed makes an explanation necessary."

The room was silent. After a minute I looked around the back of the chair and saw that she had turned to go. Now I could leave without embarrassment to anyone. I leaned forward to get up, but Louis spoke again. "Darling, you've got to listen. Josh Arnold threw Wickham out of your house today. And I applaud him for it. You've got to return that money."

"Well, are you all going to make my life impossible? Are you all against me?"

As if to a child, Louis Sullivan spoke quietly, slowly. "Mildred, today Wickham implied that he is responsible for Mary's disappearance. He said, and these are his exact words: 'Evidently one's not enough. But when three or four disappear, that'll put the fear of God in them.' Mildred, you've got to return that money!"

Immediately, I knew that Louis was right. Wickham's words were an admission of guilt. I wondered if he had ordered Mary out of town. Could he have *murdered* her? Tomorrow I'd report it to the sheriff. No, to Mr. Agee, since I knew him better. No longer caring about the two in the parlor, about anyone's embarrassment, I got up and went into the house, where Josh was reading. But he was asleep. I sat on the bed and shook him. "Josh, wake up, wake up!"

He sat up, looked at me, blinked. "What is it? What's the matter?"

When I told him, he said, "Sullivan's right. I'm going to see the sheriff tomorrow. But I don't think he'll do a damn thing about it. Now, Lucy, this is a man's job, and I want you to promise me that you will stay out of it. Accusing a man like Wickham is serious, and I don't want you to be a party to it."

Slipping into my nightgown, splashing water on my face, I decided to talk to Polly Agee about it before I talked to her husband. Listening behind her kitchen door, Polly kept up with things. Without promising anything (Josh was asleep before I could have promised), I got into bed. Sometime during the night, I turned over and felt a gun there, under Josh's pillow. If Josh is this worried about Wickham's threat, I thought to myself, maybe we should go home to Bonham.

When Josh and I went into breakfast the next morning, Mildred was there. She sat at the table's end and poured cream over a small bowl of blackberries. Jeremiah appeared, and smiling at him, she said, "Have some. These late berries—I've never seen them come in this late—are mighty sweet and good." Then laying her spoon beside the bowl, she folded her hands under her chin. "Josh, maybe it would be better if Jeremiah here took his meals in the kitchen with Sudie and Alma. I'd just as soon keep him away from anybody taking a strong dislike to him."

As if Mildred had tossed a handful of pebbles at him, Jeremiah ducked his head at these words. Holding a blackberry in his spoon, he tilted it to the side, letting it fall back into the bowl.

"Until we make other arrangements, I think Jeremiah would prefer having his breakfast with Sudie," I said, putting my hand on his shoulder.

"Sure would," he said, and carrying his bowl so as not to spill the milk, he left the room.

Mildred smiled at Josh as if *he* had answered. "Well, good. Then that's settled." Now she looked at me. "Lucy, I understand your husband has a quick temper."

Josh looked at her. "Louis tell you about that, did he?"

"Josh, you must understand that Russ Wickham has accomplished a great deal since he's been in Sweet Shrub. He's a major supplier of lumber to the northeast, and he's given work to a good many people. But Russ happens to be a very complicated man."

"Does that excuse wrongdoing?" Josh asked.

"I don't know of any wrong he's done," Mildred said.

"His name comes up when it's discussed."

"Mr. Arnold"—and Josh's rueful look showed he had noted Mildred's reversal to the use of his surname—"Russ Wickham is a generous man. My husband's business suffered during his illness, and had it not been for Mr. Wickham's kindness, I could not have stayed in this house."

"As his defender then, what are you asking of me?"

"Your civility," she said, her voice husky with emotion.

"Only a civil man can appreciate that quality. Can Wickham?" Josh said, rising from the table. "You'll have to excuse me, Mrs. Elam. Jeremiah and I can't be late for school this morning."

That night Josh told me he had gone to the sheriff, and, as he thought, the sheriff refused to listen. "Why, that's just Wickham's way," the sheriff had said. "He don't mean a thing by it."

But at last Jeremiah had a friend in Sweet Shrub. Two or three times, I found them side by side, Sudie looking over his shoulder while he worked his sums. And after school, Sudie would ride with us as far as the lake house, and Jeremiah would walk with her the rest of the way home. Or, on the days Josh kept the car, Jeremiah would walk all the way home with her. I was glad. I felt uneasy about them both, but when the two were together, it seemed to me that they were both a little safer.

28

DURING THE NIGHT the rain began, light, steady, the kind Uncle Jerry called a seasoning rain. We had set out the peach trees at just the right time. Next spring they'd bloom, along with the wild plum and the dogwood and the redbud trees. And soon after that, the roses. And all the children would be going to school with the buds of the sweet shrub in their pockets. In the evenings Josh and I would sit out on the porch and watch the reflections of the sunset over the lake. With the garden that would be in bloom and the splashing of fish and frogs, and Keats there too—I grew dizzy thinking of all that spring would bring to the house on the lake.

In a household suddenly become so tense, thoughts of the place on Cypress Lake were a storehouse of comfort. For now Sudie and Alma hurried quietly through their tasks, hurried to make the beds, to sweep, to mop, to cook, and then, as soon as Mildred could find nothing more for them to do, hurried to be out of a house that day and night was kept locked. When they, or anyone, left, one of us was called immediately to drop the lock back into place.

With each day that passed, Josh, while insisting that things would soon be normal in Sweet Shrub, grew more concerned about the war. "Warsaw's bound to fall to the Germans," he announced at supper one evening. "It would be a tremendous boost to the Allies if the United States would come into the war now." At night he'd toss and turn, and sometimes rise and walk outside for an hour or more before returning to bed. At school he worked harder than ever, his concern about the war driving him, as if he could by sheer will hurry his students through the high school education he felt they needed in a country that would soon be at war.

Since his altercation with Josh, Russ Wickham had not returned to the house, and as far as I knew there had been no communication between him and Mildred Elam. Although she and her cousin, as had been their custom, still walked and went for brief drives together, the formality with which they treated each other revealed the tension between them. So, on Monday, I was not surprised when Louis Sullivan left by train "to see about affairs in Memphis," and Mildred, pressing her handkerchief to her face, hurried past me in the hall, whispering, "I don't know. I just don't know what to do." She did not come down for dinner. And that night when she appeared, her gaiety was gone, drained away. Pale, her eyes heavy, she led the way into the parlor; and I thought suddenly, Why, she's almost as old as Mama, astonished by the thought.

Tuesday, I took Josh to school, went by the post office to mail a letter home, and picked up three rose cuttings at Peter Dexter's place. "Lucinda, these are well-rooted. Just put them in the ground, and next spring, you can pick the roses," he told me. He placed them on the floorboard of my car, pushed his hat to the back of his head, and winked. "Lucinda Arnold, the saddest day of my life was when I saw that ring on your finger," he said.

"Peter, you're the biggest flirt in town," I said, knowing that even if I were single, I'd not give him the time of day. But all the same, he lifted my spirits.

That afternoon, I was perched on the front porch railing by Keats, dividing a peach with him, when Russ Wickham drove up to the house, his maroon automobile splashed with mud. Well, Louis is hardly out of the house, and here *he* is, I thought. Although he did not speak, he acknowledged my presence by removing his hat, and in a minute, Sudie opened the door for him. "Mrs. Elam, she say she be right down," I heard her tell him in that light, musical voice of hers as she closed the door behind him.

It was time for Jeremiah to be coming home from school, and I could not bear to see him humiliated again. "Keats, let's go meet Jeremiah, and we'll all go out to the lake," I said, holding out my arm and watching Keats step deliberately onto my arm and into his cage for one more bite of the peach.

Jeremiah was halfway home when I stopped the car and opened the door for him. "Let's go out to the garden. See what the rain's done to it," I told him.

As soon as the car stopped, I smelled the lake smell of mud and water and aquatic plants—lilies and reeds. And moss. As we walked out to the garden, a handful of sparrows tumbled out of a bare-limbed peach tree and, twittering noisily, flew to the next one.

"We gonna need that fence for sure in the spring," Jeremiah said, pointing to a rabbit that froze, then ran, its zigzagging leaps punctuated by its white tail. With a small shovel, I turned over a clod of dirt from which a weed had sprouted and watched a green beetle climb clumsily back into the weed again.

"Jeremiah, I love this garden," I said. "Don't you?"

"Picking the tomatoes, eating the sweet corn, I like it better then."

"Lately, you haven't said a word about leaving town. Don't you think things are a little better now?"

He frowned, and with canny deliberation said, "Not better. Different."

And I followed his eyes to the place where he looked,

and saw the cabin, Sudie's cabin, in the middle of those we could see from the garden.

"Jeremiah, I don't know what will come of all this," I said, trying not to sound like his mother but thinking of this white boy with a colored girl, even though he was Queenie's own son.

Jeremiah mistook my meaning. "Wickham," he said contemptuously, "he tell the coloreds to bring they guns in."

Lately I had noticed that when Jeremiah spoke, sometimes he sounded like he was white and sometimes he sounded colored. I wondered if he was aware of it.

"Well, for goodness sakes. Will they turn their guns in, do you think?"

"No'm. They need they guns for shooting rabbits and squirrels. Killing foxes after they chickens." He shrugged his shoulders. "But some might take a notion to do it," he added.

We watched Keats slowly begin to climb down the trunk of the peach tree where we'd left him and make his way over to stand close to Jeremiah's feet.

"Don't know he's a bird," Jeremiah said sadly, as we watched him unfurl his wings for balance against the wind.

The wind had shifted and risen. White caps filled the lake. The tops of the cypress trees leaned toward us, and the waves, breaking on the supports of the house, splashed over the porch. Suddenly everything seemed in turmoil.

"Jeremiah," I said, "put Keats in his cage. Let's go on back to the house."

For some reason I did not want to drive through town. But taking the back road home, I caught the bittersweet odor of brush burning and trunks of trees smoldering, and then I saw smoke hanging over the town. Wickham, I thought. You can't get away from him.

On Wednesday I took Josh to school. "Lassie's helping her husband," I told him, "and I'm going to give Polly another driving lesson."

As I moved over to the driver's seat, Josh said, "Lucy, you and Polly have a good time. But why don't you do your driving in town until this thing eases off?"

"We will. Polly's going to surprise her husband today."

Before I got to her front door, Polly was halfway down the walk, taking my arm, drawing me into the house.

"Lucinda, I'm so nervous. I don't think I *can* drive today. Oh, if I hadn't promised Mr. Agee, I'd tell you what he told me when he got home last night. But I promised, and I'm not one to break a promise."

"I wouldn't ask you to," I said, wondering what she had heard from behind her kitchen door. "But today's the day. Nervous or not, I want you to drive down and surprise Mr. Agee. I'll be right beside you. I know you can do it."

She did just fine, although her hands trembled a little right at first. When we got to the Agee Grocery Co. she honked, at first tentatively, then she kept her finger on the horn.

The screen door flew open and Mr. Agee rushed out. "Mrs. Agee," he said, "what in the world are you doing out here on the street? Why, you're not driving, are you?"

She nodded her head. "I am."

He looked at me. "Some folks let their wives stay on the road all the time. But Mrs. Agee, I'll not have it. Especially now."

Polly's eyes filled with tears. "She wanted to surprise you," I told him.

"Mrs. Agee, did you tell Mrs. Arnold what I heard last night?"

"No, but I wish I had now," she said, her nose twitching, her mouth quivering.

"Well, tell her. So that the both of you will get off the road. Now, Mrs. Arnold, this will all be in strictest confidence, you understand."

"Well," Mrs. Agee said, and leaned forward to begin.

"No, not here. Every Tom, Dick, and Harry listening in. Leave the car here, and go somewhere private," Mr. Agee said, glancing toward the three men who had come from his grocery store to stand staring at us from the doorway. By their interested expressions, I knew that they had already been given the news that Polly was about to tell me.

We had hardly sat down in Trumper's drugstore when Polly began again. "Well, last night, Mr. Agee and Donald Green went out to the Missionary Baptist Church at Peaceful to try to find out who's been agitating the Negroes." At the end of every sentence, Polly's voice rose, making it a question. "When it got good and dark, real dark, they crawled through a field behind the church," she said, her voice rising with the word "church." I saw that the pulse in her neck was beating as fast as if she had been running. Sighing, she clasped her hands together on the table between us. "Thank goodness, the weeds back there were real high—Mr. Agee almost sneezed three or four times and it would have been terrible if he had, he said it would—but what with it being so dark and the weeds and all, nobody saw them." And now she was whispering so that Mr. Thumper, who was doing his best to listen while he dipped up our ice cream, couldn't hear. "They crawled up under the church— think of the snakes!—and listened and . . . what they heard was too terrible for words!"

"What? What did they hear?"

"Well, the coloreds have made up a list. On it they got twenty-one names." When she got to the word "names," the whisper became a small cry, like it had been pinched off. "On October sixth, every one of those names will be kilt. Just think of it! Twenty-one kilt! Twenty-one marked for death!"

For a minute I couldn't say a word. Then, "Whose names are on the list?"

"They couldn't rightly hear every name, but it's all the farmers, the big farmers in the delta. With just a hundred acres, Mr. Agee doesn't think his name's on the list."

Mr. Thumper came to the table with our ice cream. I had forgotten all about it.

"I tell you one thing," he said, "my name had better not be on the list. But if somebody comes looking for me, that double-barreled shotgun behind the counter is loaded and ready. What we need in here is protection! Somebody ought to call the governor."

Mrs. Agee sniffed at the intrusion. When neither of us answered, Mr. Thumper resumed his vigil at the soda fountain. I struggled to remember what Polly had said before she had told me about the list.

"Wait a minute," I said. "Who is the other man who went out there with your husband?"

"Donald Green," she said. "He's a colored detective, one of them that Mr. Wickham's hired out of Chicago."

"Mr. Green's colored?"

She nodded. "Mr. Agee told the sheriff about the list and the sheriff, he went right off to tell Mr. Wickham. They've already called Helena. Helena's standing by."

My mind wheeled off, seeing all the people in Helena, standing by. At attention. Like soldiers.

Struggling to focus on Polly's words, I asked, "And they couldn't hear any names?"

"Not too plain," she said.

"But they heard everything else?"

"Enough."

"Mrs. Agee, this is horrible. I've got to find Josh and tell him about this. Come on, I'll take you home."

But when I got to the school, Miss Twinkle, the fifth-grade teacher (also music and elocution), said Josh had let school out early. I drove home, and a few minutes later, heard his step on the front porch.

"It doesn't make sense," Josh said slowly. "I wonder what the truth of it is."

We sat on our bed, the door closed, speaking softly. Jeremiah had come home and was in the parlor, helping Sudie with the heavy cleaning. I had no idea where the others were.

"Mrs. Agee said her husband clearly heard the date, October six, mentioned several times. And a lot of talk about the list of marked men."

"But they didn't hear any names," Josh said, rubbing his brow. "I don't put much faith in anything Green says. I understand Wickham only pays those Chicago detectives when they bring him some information."

"Josh, could you talk to Mr. Agee?"

He nodded. "I'll do that. And I called Louis Sullivan as soon as I heard. He'll be in on the morning train. And I want to talk to Paul Yarborough. He's taught here longer than anybody, and he knows the town. And Peter Dexter. And Massie's clear-headed."

"What about me?" I asked. "And why don't you talk to Lassie? She's a good thinker. And what about Mr. Yarborough's wife?"

"Lucy, confound it! This is serious."

"Well, I'm serious. Mrs. Agee has twice as much common sense as her husband."

"Dadblast it, Lucy! I don't have time to argue about which of the ladies is smarter than their husbands. Something like this is like a prairie fire. It can get out of hand, run away from you. I think I'd better get on that early train to Helena in the morning. I want Bailey to come down here and talk to the colored people. He'll have a handle on this. He knows them, understands their problems. And he can talk to the whites too. We've all got to work to cool this thing off."

I started to say that the ladies could cool it off better than the men with their loaded shotguns and pistols under their pillows, but Josh was right. It was no time to argue.

I took Josh to the railroad crossing the next morning, and on the way home I saw that a heavy mist had begun to fall.

About ten o'clock that morning, Mrs. Agee walked over with the news that her husband had been called out to Peaceful, the community of a dozen or so houses near the Missionary Baptist Church. "Ditto Vardy's out there drunk," she said, "just tearing up jack."

Ditto was the closest Sweet Shrub had to Old Man Tyler back in Bonham. Mostly, Tyler just stayed under a car when he was drunk, but I had heard that Ditto, a great huge man, would pick up a fallen limb or a hoe handle, whatever he could find, and walk along with it, hitting things, never a living thing, not even a fly. But he'd hit a car or a shed or, if he couldn't find anything else, the dirt road he walked upon.

Shaking our heads, wondering what Ditto might be hitting now, Polly and I sat at the small table in our room, having a glass of iced tea. Hearing the ring of the telephone, I started to answer, but I heard Sudie's quick, light step and her soft, "This here's Mrs. Elam's," before I could get to the phone. And then I heard the sound of footsteps, running. Sudie was running! Down the hall, through the dining room, and out the kitchen door.

"Whatever in the world?" Mrs. Agee said.

I walked through the hall, past the telephone, its dangling receiver still swinging, and into the empty kitchen. Looking out the back door, I saw Sudie, as graceful as a deer, running away from the house, followed by Alma, who, in spite of her short, square body, was trying desperately to keep up.

I picked up the telephone, but there was no one on the line.

"Something's happened," I told Polly. "I wonder what?"

Jeremiah had come into the hall, his outstretched hands framing the same question. As we stood there, looking at each other as if the answer might be found on one of our faces, the telephone rang again.

It was Peter Dexter. "Did you just call here?" I asked him.

"No." He waited a minute, then said, "But there's some kind of trouble out at Peaceful. Stay where you are. I'm on my way over there now."

I started upstairs to tell Mildred, but she was leaning over the banister. "For goodness sakes. Who's doing all the telephoning? That wasn't Louis, was it?"

"There's been some kind of trouble out at Peaceful. You'd better come down."

"Oh, my good Lord! My husband's out there," Mrs. Agee said softly.

"Polly, your husband's all right. It's just Ditto. No telling *what* he's done now," I said, hugging her.

While Mildred dressed and Polly walked the floor, I

watched for Peter. Then, seeing a figure, distorted by the glass in the front door, bound up on the porch, I said, "Here's Peter now," and hurried to unlock the front door. "He'll tell us what's going on out there."

He stood in the doorway. *Sweating.* Now, why would anybody be sweating on a day as cool as this, I wondered crazily.

Peter opened his mouth, but no words came out. Then he said hoarsely, "Buford Agee's been shot dead."

A thin, high wail told that Polly Agee had heard the cruel words. But Peter Dexter went right on. "And Vardy's been shot too. In the shoulder."

I helped Polly to a chair, knelt by her.

"Where is Buford? Oh, I've got to go to him," she said.

And only then was Peter aware of her presence. He blinked, swallowed. "Mrs. Agee, Green and Ditto Vardy took Mr. Agee to the old Blackman place. Dr. Carter got there as soon as he could, but he couldn't do a thing for him."

"I have to go to him. Lucy, please take me out there."

"Polly, as soon as we can go, we will," I promised.

And now Peter was unlocking the door again, and it was Louis, locking it behind himself, asking, "What's the matter? What's happened here?"

And the telephone was ringing again.

"Buford Agee went out to Peaceful to arrest Ditto Vardy and got shot," Peter said. "He's dead."

"Ditto shot somebody?"

"No, Ditto got shot too. In the shoulder."

And the insistent ringing of the telephone that had gone unanswered all this time was suddenly quiet, and in that moment of unearthly calm I looked at the faces of those gathered in Mildred Elam's entrance hall, and on those faces, which mirrored my own, I saw shocked disbelief. And terror.

29

LOUIS SULLIVAN broke the silence. "I'll call Doc Carter. He can tell us what's happened."

He rang the telephone girl, waited. Rang again. Waited. "She's not answering," he said impatiently. Wheeling, he ran up the stairs, came down with a rifle in his hand. "Let's take a look around," he said to Peter.

They hurried outside, and from the parlor window I saw Peter take a gun from his car. Overnight, Sweet Shrub's turned into an armed camp, I thought. We heard them making their way around the house, Peter calling, "Anything?" and Louis, from the carriage house, "Nothing. Everything's quiet."

Louis stuck his head inside the front door. "We're going over to Dr. Carter's house. Stay inside. Keep the doors locked."

Before he was off the porch, Mildred dropped the lock into place.

"I'm going up to my room. See if I can see anything," Jeremiah said.

His room, the attic room, gave a broad view of Mildred's property and the streets around it. A minute later he was back down. "It's like . . ." he said, shaking his head in wonderment, "it's like everybody's left!"

All that long, dreary afternoon, we waited for news. Mildred wandered from room to room, window to window. I divided my time between Jeremiah and Polly. She lay on my bed, her face burrowed into the pillows, now and then breaking into the most heartrending cries.

Well, Josh would be here soon, I told myself. Comforted by the thought, I went into the kitchen. "Whatever happens, we have to eat," I told Mildred, taking the baked chicken that Alma had left from the oven.

Mildred nodded, and although her hands trembled, she sliced carrots and cut up celery while I rolled out egg noodles for chicken soup.

"Mildred, Mr. Agee's dead and Ditto Vardy's shot. That's bad enough, but maybe that's *all* it is. Maybe that's the end of it."

"Then where *is* everybody?" she asked. "And why is it so quiet?"

As if in response to her question, my heart jumped, began to beat faster.

We had persuaded Polly to sit up and take a little soup when Louis and Peter returned, grim-faced. "It's started," Louis said, "and it's bad."

Peter glanced into the bedroom where Polly sat at the small table. "Let's talk in there," he said, motioning toward the parlor. When we had moved quietly into that room, he spoke in a voice so low I had to strain to hear. "As near as we can figure, what happened was Buford and Green drove up to the crossroads and saw Ditto at the side of the road. They pulled over—they were going to take Ditto in, let him sober up—when somebody shot Ditto. Buford and Green returned the fire. And then Buford went to help Ditto. That was when Buford got hit. In the chest."

Peter pulled a handkerchief from his pocket and wiped his forehead. Putting the handkerchief back, he stood up, walked over to the windows. After a minute, clearing his throat, swallowing, he went on. "Then Ditto, and his shoulder was bleeding quite a bit, had to help

Green get Buford back in the car. Somehow they did and high-tailed it out of there."

Peter sighed, sat down again. Shaking his head, rubbing the back of his neck, "Lord Jesus!" he said.

After a minute Louis took up the story. "Blackman said he knew Buford was a goner when they brought him to his place. He didn't lose that much blood from the hole in his chest. It was his mouth. Blackman said the blood just poured out of his mouth. Dr. Carter didn't even try with Buford. He said he was too far gone."

"What's happening now?" I asked.

"The governor's got all the roads, coming in and out of Sweet Shrub, blocked. He says he doesn't want a bunch of agitators coming in here. And he's called out the army. By this time tomorrow we'll have five hundred U.S. soldiers in here from Camp Pike."

"Josh will be here tonight," I said thankfully.

"No, he won't," Louis said, "Not on the train. They've stopped all passenger service."

Blinking back the tears, I left the room and stood on the front porch looking toward the road. I wondered where Josh was this very minute. If he had heard about the shooting, he'd be frantic. But Josh wasn't here. And I didn't know when he could be. "Lucy, where is the starch in your backbone?" I said to myself. And I dried my eyes and went back inside the house.

Mildred had reheated the soup and was slicing bread for the men. I dipped up a bowl of soup and passed it to Louis.

"Louis, we've got to hurry," Peter was saying. "We've got to be out there in thirty minutes."

"Out where, Louis?" Mildred asked.

"We're meeting at Peaceful. From there, we're gonna make a clean sweep of the whole countryside. But there's not a thing for you ladies to worry about. The whole town will be cordoned off tonight. If there's a gun around, or a nigger holding it, we'll find him." Louis was beginning to sound more like Russ Wickham every minute.

"And somebody will be checking on you all night long. You can rest easy tonight," Peter said.

Louis's mind was still on Peaceful. "We ought to burn that church out there while we're at it," he said. "All in the world it's good for is agitating the niggers."

"A church? You'd burn a church? And it's a school too," I reminded him.

"That poor woman in there is about to die of pure grief. And you're worried about a colored church?" Louis's voice was filled with scorn.

Silently they finished their soup and left, pausing only to say, "Stay inside. Lock the door."

Mildred went from room to room, closing the windows, the curtains, the heavy drapes, closing us inside a house filled with grief and fear. Jeremiah, a shadow that followed every step I took, watched me with a look of such intensity that I said, "What is it, Jeremiah? Tell me."

"It Sudie, Miss Lucy. Where you think Sudie be right now? Hiding under the bed? In that little room at the lake, where we got our tools? She might be there. Now, if Sudie had a boat, she could row herself out on the lake, hide behind one a them big trees."

"Jeremiah, I can't think anyone would hurt Sudie," I said, but when I thought about her, her cabin ransacked, her belongings thrown outside, her cabin burned (if they'd burn a church, they'd burn a cabin), I was not so sure. And where *would* a young girl hide?

I looked out the parlor window. The porch was in shadow, but it was still good daylight. I could see all the way to the road. For the first time, I was glad the magnolias had been cut down.

"Let's step out on the porch," I told Jeremiah. "Get a breath of fresh air."

When Mildred protested, I said, "Mildred, it's all right. I've looked. There's not a soul out there."

Jeremiah went to get Keats. Out on the porch, he opened the cage and Keats, cocking his head this way and that, looked carefully at Jeremiah's outstretched arm, then stepped onto it and, from there, to the porch railing.

Sitting in the rocking chair, I looked out over the tops of the beech trees to the road, which, in the gathering darkness, looked quiet as a church. A lightning bug flickered. It was two or three minutes before I saw it again, just to the right of the porch. I found the evening star, and whispered the words I had loved since I was a child: "Star light, star bright, first star I see tonight, wish I may, wish I might, have the wish I wish tonight."

And looking at the sky and at the single star that hung there, I knew that Josh would come as soon as he could.

"Jeremiah," I said, "make a wish. Wishes you make on the first star come true."

And he did, and for the first time that day, I felt that, somehow, the peace that we had suddenly lost might be recovered. Peace. I said the word again. I had never known a word could sound so sweet.

Then, coming from far away, as far as the lake, we heard something, a popping noise, like firecrackers, sounding harmless. But I knew it was gunfire.

Now a car was turning into our drive, and in the gathering darkness, I thought it was brown, but when it stopped in front of our house, I saw it was Wickham's maroon motorcar.

Taking long strides, skipping the bottom step, he stood

on the porch. "You hear that noise?" he demanded. "That was shooting. Where's Mildred?"

Before he could knock, she was there, opening the door for him, asking, "What was that noise? Was that gunfire?"

In a few minutes he was outside again. "I've got to get back," he said. Then, lowering his head, looking right at Jeremiah, "When this night's over, we'll have no more trouble out of the niggers," he said. He took a deep breath, exhaled with an angry groan. In the porch shadows, his face was black.

Jeremiah raised his arm to take Keats, I can only suppose to get him away from such black rage, and Wickham roared, "What are you gaping at?" He did not touch Jeremiah, clearly he had no intention of hitting Jeremiah, but as he spoke, his arm swung out and brushed Keats. Keats squawked once, flapped his wings. And flew! In a minute he sat on the lowest limb of the beech tree, just over the car. Jeremiah and I looked at each other and, forgetting all about Russ Wickham, we hurried down the steps and stood under the branch upon which the great blue bird sat, calling, "Come on Keats, come on back."

"I'll get a peach," I said and ran to the kitchen. When I got back outside, Keats had begun to climb clumsily down the trunk of the tree, and he would have, too, he would have come home, but at that minute, Wickham started his motorcar. It backfired, and Keats was off again, flying up over the beech trees, veering to the left, and then flying in a straight path toward the lake. Now Jeremiah was running after Keats, and I was calling, "Jeremiah, come back. Oh, come back, Jeremiah." But not for a minute did he pause or look around or break his stride. Then they were both lost from sight.

* * *

All through the night, Mildred and I kept watch. Sometimes one, sometimes both of us would walk through the house, peering out into the blackness, checking the doors, listening. Then she would go back upstairs, and I'd lie down, usually on the sofa in the parlor, but once, I lay on the bed by Polly, who stirred, and "Mr. Agee?" she murmured. And waking up, she remembered. And wept.

From time to time I heard gunfire, and each time, "Jeremiah, Jeremiah, where are you," I said to the darkness outside.

Twice Louis came, once at midnight, and later, around four, each time bringing more terrible news. The first time he said, "The Negroes, they've all run off. And I've never seen men so mad, crazy mad, threatening to burn the cabins to the ground. But the sheriff stopped it, said they belonged to Russ Wickham and if a one of them was burned, he'd have the men who were a party to it in jail." And the second time, "Ed Hoggard's dead," he said, "and a man named Staples is wounded."

"Please find Jeremiah," I begged him. "Don't let anything happen to him."

"What about Sudie?" Mildred asked. "And Alma? If they've run off, I don't know how in the world I'm going to manage!"

Louis said, "There's not a nigger"—glancing at me—"a *Negro* around anywhere. But they're looking, and I almost feel sorry for any they catch tonight."

After Louis left, I lay on the sofa, fell asleep, and at first light awoke to a tremendous sense of unease. Josh? But he would be safe in Helena. Then, dismayed, I realized it was morning. And where on earth was Jeremiah?

In the middle of the morning, I heard the sound of light footsteps on the porch. I hoped, prayed, it was Jeremiah. But, no. A man in uniform, a soldier's uniform, stood at the door.

"Ma'am, we're evacuating all the women and children out of Sweet Shrub. If you and the others. . . . How many are there?"

"Two," I said, wondering how on earth Mildred Elam could get ready to go anywhere without Sudie. Or somebody.

"Just pack enough for a few days. Be ready about noon. Somebody will come for you." Touching the brim of his hat, he turned to go, but then he said, "Oh, miss, don't worry about the house. It'll be well looked after."

Hurrying up the steps to tell Mildred, I heard Polly's voice, tremulously asking, "What is it? Who was that at the door?"

I had forgotten all about Polly. I went back down the stairs. "We have to leave," I told her. "We're being evacuated."

"Leave? But you know I can't leave," she said, sinking into the chair by the hall telephone. "I have to see about arrangements for Buford. I have to bury Buford." And almost as if she were too tired to do even that she began to cry again.

I put my arms around her. "The governor's ordered it," I told her. "We can come back in a day or two."

She shook her head.

"Polly, think. What would Mr. Agee have wanted you to do?"

She looked at me. After a minute, "I'll go," she said.

"Tell you what," I said. "I'll go up and tell Mildred. Then we'll drive to your house and get a few things together, things you'll need."

When I told Mildred we had to leave and why, she was frantic. For a minute, I watched her empty drawers of hats and handbags and underclothes on the bed and sweep armloads of dresses from her wardrobes. And all the while she talked to herself. "Let's see, now, my handkerchiefs, now where in the world are my good lace handkerchiefs?" And to me she said, "Lucy, can you believe this is happening? Why, I can't believe this is happening right here in Sweet Shrub!" And seeing how muddled she was, I spent a precious thirty minutes helping her before going back down to Polly.

Between our house and Polly's, the streets were deserted. I wondered where the soldiers were. But I could imagine the frenzied activity within the silent houses—women hurriedly packing, bathing their children, getting them dressed.

At Polly's house, we hurried past the clothesline Mr. Agee had stretched so her wash wouldn't touch the ground, brushed past his coat hanging on a nail inside the kitchen door, and climbed the steps to their bedroom. Standing in front of the open wardrobe, I saw his clothes. The house overflowed with the life of this man who would not be coming home. Stealing a glance at Polly, I wondered what thoughts were in her mind.

But Polly was caught in a frenzy of activity. Hastily pulling two housedresses and her best dress from hangers, then a gown from the dresser drawer, she packed them. She got her hairbrush and mirror off the dressing table, put them in the case, and closed it. She put on her heavy coat. "I'm ready," she said. Polly's tasks seemed to have steadied her.

Hurrying to the car, I offered, "Polly, would you like to drive? Sometimes it helps to stay busy."

Surprisingly, she got right in the driver's seat. Gripping the wheel tightly, driving very slowly, she said, "I'm glad I know how to drive. It's one thing I won't have to learn now that Buford's . . . now that Buford's gone."

On the way home, I searched the sky, hoping to see a

flash of blue against the dreary gray. If I could find Keats, I thought, I'd find Jeremiah too.

Mildred's cases were on the front porch when we got back, three of them. When Polly stepped down from the car, I slipped behind the wheel. "Go ahead," I told her. "I have to do one more thing. I'll see you at the train."

Already, the car was moving. Polly hesitated a minute, then nodded. "We'll find you," she called, "on the train."

Driving away from the house, I told myself I'd take the back roads to the lake house. That's where Jeremiah would be. And if I hurried, we might both be able to catch the train.

I drove out of town, turned at Thompson's corner, but then, up ahead, I saw two motorcars pulled across the road. And several men, two or three in the uniform of the national guard, stood by the cars. They would stop me, insist that I get on the train.

I turned around and drove until I was out of sight. If this road was closed off, all the roads would be blocked. I'd have to walk. But even skirting the roadblocks, I reckoned I could reach the lake in an hour and a half. At most two.

Leaving the car, I plunged into the tall grass alongside the road. Before I'd taken ten steps, my shoes were covered with mud. Pushing my way through, the grass cut my hands, but I went quietly ahead. And the first roadblock was easy. But I would not have seen the second one had a deep voice not called out, "Jimmy, that you?" and another answered, "Who'd you think it was? After last night there ain't a nigger in a hundert miles a here."

Another roadblock. Looking through the grass, I saw a single car. I turned to make my way deeper into the field of grass and there, close to the trunk of a tree, stood a man. A Negro. Paralyzed with fear, I stood there. He was so still, completely still. He knows I'm going to cry out, I thought. He knows he'll be caught. But to call for help meant I'd not find Jeremiah. Never taking my eyes off him (and after that first look he never raised his eyes from the ground), I slowly made my way around the man, as I had made my way around the roadblock.

After that I went more carefully, staying as close to the road as I dared, so it was late afternoon before I reached the trace road that led to the lake. I stood there in the tall yellow grass a long time, watching the house. It looked deserted. But it would look that way even if Jeremiah was there. Oh, I hoped he was there! I took a deep breath and stepped out of the grass onto the open road that led to the house.

When I got there, "Jeremiah," I called softly. "Jeremiah, it's me, Lucy Arnold."

But Jeremiah wasn't in the downstairs room. Or anywhere. When I knew this, I pulled the broken chair close to the wall, sat down, leaned against the wall to rest. After a while my neck felt stiff. And I was thirsty. I had never been so thirsty. And I needed to go to the bathroom.

A cluster of small bushes at the edge of the lake provided the privacy I needed. Then I took off my shoes and, holding my skirt high with one hand, I stepped into the cold lake, splashed my face, and drank from my cupped hand. Then carrying my shoes, I went back up the stairs to the porch.

Now I was wide awake. Jeremiah would have come here first, I thought, putting my shoes back on. But then where? Of course. Looking for Sudie, for Sudie more than Keats, he would have gone right to her cabin. I walked to the porch railing, looked toward the cabins. In the fading light, they seemed darker, larger.

I've come this far, I thought. Now just a little way

more. Just to Sudie's. Maybe nobody's been out this far yet; maybe they haven't thought to come here.

Outside, I found a path, one so worn that it shone like dull silver in the twilight, and walked toward Sudie's cabin. I walked past the garden, vanquished by an early frost, past the cold iron pot hung over dead ashes and, reaching the cabin, stepped up on the narrow planking outside the cabin door.

I knocked and listened and, knowing all the while the cabin was empty, knocked again. "It's me, Sudie. It's Mrs. Arnold," I said, pushing the door open.

My first thought was that the room was too small for all that it held. Its contents swollen by chaos, by a violence that had overturned the bed; dragged coals, still burning, as evidenced by the charred floor, from the fireplace; shredded mattress and bedding; emptied flour (the precious flour), over the floor; smashed table and chairs—the room was too small, its contents too sparse for the rage that had been visited upon it.

I saw the sleeve of Sudie's coat (was it a week, a month ago, that Mildred Elam had passed it on to her?), and pulled the coat from beneath the torn mattress, picked the remnants of a quilt up off the floor and walked back to the lake house.

Bundled up in Sudie's coat and Sudie's quilt, I heard cars stop and start again on distant roads. A train went through. Once, I heard an owl. Then someone was running! Desperate strides, close by, running into the lake, splashing out again, now along the lake's edge, running, running.

And almost before the idea had come into my mind, the certainty of it was there. It was Jeremiah! I knew it was! And calling his name, I ran to the edge of the porch.

That was when I heard the cars. I ran to the kitchen window and saw them, five or six cars, coming down the narrow road. When they were even with the first cabin, two of them followed the narrow paths through the cluster of cabins and two went ahead, way ahead, and then all of them were circling back toward the house and toward the single car that had driven as far as the garden and stopped. And then I heard the anger that spilled out into the night. "This way, the bastard came this way!" and "Get him! Son of a bitch!" and "Grab the nigger! He's coming that way!"

And footsteps, light footsteps, were splashing through the shallow water, running under the porch. And there was the heavy, jagged breathing of lungs about to burst.

"Jeremiah," I called. "Jeremiah, up here!" But the lights from cars and torches were making a circle of light. Then there were the sounds of struggle, of someone being dragged from under the porch.

After that, silence, a silence so cold my bones and breath were frozen. Then a more deliberate sound, a *thwack, thwack,* and crazily the thought went through my mind that Uncle Jerry was beating rugs. But then I knew what it was, and I was screaming, "No, no, not that! Stop it!" And I ran toward the light that was encircled by men who grunted from the effort of their blows, ran toward the brown and torn figure lying inside the circle. Arms grabbed me, thrust me back; and screaming, "No! No! You're killing him," I ran forward again, and this time I was thrown to the ground and held there, my face pushed into the freshly tilled earth.

The beating went on for a long time. But then a man snarled, "Let's get out of here," and those holding me pushed my face into the dirt with such force that, spitting out dirt, I struggled for breath as they scrambled back to their cars and drove away.

When I could, I walked to the crumpled bloody form on the ground. And when I saw that the dead man was not Jeremiah, I went back upstairs and waited for the first light. Then I walked to the first roadblock and told the soldiers a man had been beaten to death, and asked to be driven home. And in Mildred Elam's silent house, drugged by a warm bath and a soft bed, I fell asleep.

Someone was kissing my hair, my cheek, my lips. I opened my eyes. Josh! It was Josh. I put my arms around him, held him close, and began to cry.

"Oh, Josh, they killed a man. A Negro."

"Who? What man? Who killed him?"

"I don't know. I don't know who they were. But I thought it was Jeremiah."

"You don't know who the men were?"

"I couldn't see. It was dark. And they held my face to the ground."

"Oh, Lucy, they could have hurt you. Sweetheart, where were you? When did this happen? How?"

And so I told Josh all that I knew, and afterward I put my arms around him, held him close, felt his heart beating. But then I asked, "Josh, how did you get here?"

"Lucy, when you weren't on that train, I was just about crazy. I had to know if you were safe," he said, pulling me into his arms again.

"But how?" I said, leaning back so I could see his face. "All the roads are blocked."

"I came on the train," he said.

"But I thought . . . but Louis said . . ." I began.

Another kiss kept me from finishing the sentence.

"Josh, I'm so glad you're here. That you're safe. And now we've got to find Jeremiah. Keats too. But how did you get here? Really."

"Louis is right. Passenger trains are still not running, so Bailey and I—Bailey thought he might be able to prevent some bloodshed—decided to drive, but we couldn't get through the roadblocks. When Bailey turned back, I got out and walked to the railroad tracks. Then, just before the train came, somebody built a fire, a big one, on the tracks. When the train stopped, there I was, beating out the fire, or trying to, with my coat, so the soldiers helped me put out the fire, thanked me, and took me on board."

"You," I said. "You started the . . ."

"I had to get here, Lucy. Why, you're everything in the world to me," he said sternly.

After two more days the roads were open and the passenger trains were running through Sweet Shrub again. But the town was far from normal. Only a few of the women and a handful of children had returned, and those who had relatives nearby or who could afford lodging, would not soon be coming back.

Afraid to leave in case Jeremiah or word of him should come, I stayed at home, but each day Josh went in search of news. And each time he returned, the news was grimmer. Three white men were dead. And the Negroes. After the first nights of terror, all they found—men, women, and children—were rounded up and placed in a stockade. And these would be released only on the recognizance of a white man. But sixty-five had been jailed, charged in the uprising, and eleven others had been found guilty of murder and hanged. But a good many had simply fled, disappeared into the canebrakes, and no one knew what fate these had met.

When Josh came with the news that Russ Wickham's house had been burned to the ground and that his wife had gone to her family in New Jersey, I felt no pity for him.

Once, I went to the stockade, but I did not find Jeremiah. And walking around the outside of the enclosure,

I was glad he was not there. Seeing the colored people, seeing them stand silently, their faces pressed against the enclosure, silently pleading to be recognized, to be set free, their pleading made palpable, pouring out, as it did, on waves of human misery, I was glad Jeremiah wasn't there. Wherever he was, I was glad he wasn't there.

I drove back to Mrs. Elam's house, and before going inside, I stood under the beech tree and looked up at the sky, longed for a glimpse of brilliant blue, but I knew Keats would not be there.

When I opened the front door, Mildred, leaning over the bannister, was calling, "Lucy, come up here. I have something to tell you."

Wearing a brightly colored dress of soft cotton, her hair arranged in severe braids that, strangely, only served to make her face more vulnerable, younger, she had recovered some vestige of her former gaiety.

Her bed was covered with dresses, undergarments, shawls, coats. Moving a stack of hat boxes from the chaise longue, she said, "Lucy, here, sit here." I did, but she remained standing.

Of course, she was leaving. And waiting for her to tell me, I thought how strange that it would take something as horrible and as tragic as an uprising to get her back to Memphis. Well, Louis would be happy.

"Lucy, I know you won't understand this. And how could you? How could anyone? But Russ is taking me away. After all, what are we now but two unhappy people *fated,* oh, yes, I feel it's that, to find some happiness together. With all his money, he's not been happy, and now, his house burned to the ground, his wife fled to New Jersey, maybe he can have the one thing we all want so desperately. Lucy, I can give him happiness. We're going this afternoon. Be glad for me. I can't remember when I could *bear* to think about tomorrow. And now I can. All these worries here in Sweet Shrub— people asking for money and not having any kind of help and the locked doors, all these worries have just been swarming around my head."

"But what about Louis?"

"Oh, Louis will be just fine. Just as soon as he's settled my affairs, he's going home to Memphis. Louis is the lucky one."

That afternoon Josh and I watched them drive away. And later, I told Josh what she'd said.

"Mildred Elam's right about one thing," he chuckled. "Louis *is* the lucky one."

The next day I dropped Josh off at his school. It seemed there was as much work involved in closing a school as in opening one. And Josh was filled with despair that a school, any school, should have to close. "More than anything, what Sweet Shrub needs is its school," he said.

When we reached the school, Josh made no move to get out of the car. "Lucy, all this tragedy, every bit of it, could have been prevented. If we had just had more time. That's all we needed." Then he got out, and leaning inside the open window, he traced my eyes, my nose, my lips with his forefinger. "I don't think you'll find Jeremiah out there. But I know you have to try," he said.

Josh was right. I didn't believe Jeremiah would be there, working in the garden (with Keats perched nearby on a peach tree limb), or sitting on the porch, his eyes fixed on the cluster of small cabins, but driving out, I knew how nice it could be.

I'd stop the car and feel the quiet of the countryside and hear the quiet noises, maybe a bird or water lapping against the lakeshore, and I'd search the sky for a glimpse of this strange blue bird with its bright yellow beak. And if I saw it, I told myself, this great bird of such beauty that it hurt the heart, if I saw it circling, circling, I would see Jeremiah, too, smiling and happy, with his arm outstretched, waiting for the bird to come home.

But it was nothing like that. The day was cold, and a mist, heavy and impenetrable, rose from the lake, shrouding the cypress trees, already enshrouded by their yellow leaves. I stood at the edge of the high porch and peered into the water below. Swollen and thick after all the rain, the green lake gave off a heavy, sweet odor of decomposing plants. A fish floated, belly up, and flies swarmed over a dead frog that lay on the muddy bank.

Oh, and the garden. Seeing its bare-limbed trees and the vegetable patch we had worked in so hard now full of weeds, and the gray sky hanging over it, all hope of glimpsing anything bright was gone.

I got back into my car and drove to the school to find Josh. "Let's go home," I said.

He raised his eyebrows.

"To Bonham."

He nodded. "This week. We'll leave just as soon as we can."

And we did.

PART THREE

WHERE THE HEART IS

30

HELENA. LITTLE ROCK. Texarkana. Paris. The trip home seemed to take forever. Stopping only when we had to stop, sleeping fitfully, the terrible events of those last days were never out of our minds. And again and again I lived through that hate-filled night when the man, who had wanted so desperately to live, had been beaten to death. It hurt my heart to think that someone had waited for him as we had waited for Jeremiah. But on the way home neither one of us talked about it. What was there to say?

And then we were home! Before the car stopped, they came running out of the house to meet us, Mama and Annabel and Aunt Catherine, Annabel leaping into my arms, demanding, "Where you been, Aunt Lucy? Come home right now." And, waving her white apron, Mama was right behind her, hugging me. "Thank God, you're home. We've all been worried to death about you," she said, and raising her voice, calling halfway down the block, "Lillian, Lucy's home. Lord have mercy! She's here!"

The hug she gave Josh was quick, reproachful. "Josh, she's way too thin. You never should have taken her up there. It's a wonder you're not both lying out in some field, scalped. Or worse!"

Hugging Mama, Josh lifted her off the ground. "Carrie, what could be worse than a scalping?"

"Some things," Mama promised darkly.

And Mrs. Walker was there, too, but being careful not

to intrude on a family reunion, she came only as far as our garden. "Lucy, I'm mighty glad you're home," she called. "Your mama's been worried sick."

"Hi, Mrs. Walker," I called back. "Well, I put in a telephone call as soon as I could."

"I know, I know, but that doesn't keep a person from worrying," Mama said.

It was like old times, Aunt Catherine and I smiling at each other over Mama's worries and Josh's teasing. Seeing Aunt Catherine's face, her smile made wider and her eyes larger by the thinness of it, I felt a twinge of sorrow. In every letter, Mama had written that Aunt Catherine was just the same. No better and no worse. But the *substance* of Aunt Catherine seemed to be slowly disappearing, leaving behind only a fragile spirit.

"Where are Katie and Bob?" I asked, careful not to make too much of asking.

"They went to St. Louis. A second honeymoon. But they didn't leave until they knew you were safe, Lucy. And you, too, Josh," Mama added.

Understanding Mama's partiality, Josh smiled and winked at me.

"They'll be home next week," Aunt Catherine said.

"What about Queenie? Is Queenie here?" I wanted to see her, but I dreaded it more than anything.

"She's gone for the day," Aunt Catherine said gently. "But she'll be here in the morning, and she'll want to know about Jeremiah. About those last days."

"Lucy! Lucy!"

I turned and saw Lillian, waving from her porch. "Come down here and see this precious baby. I want you to see him while he's asleep. He's just a little angel."

Lillian. Still as much a part of the family as if she had never left home. I ran down, met her halfway.

"Oh, Lucy, I've missed you so," she said. "And we were

all so scared when we heard about the uprising. Mama just about died. She called up Sam Rayburn and begged him to go up there and bring you home. And it's a wonder he didn't! Mama can get people so riled up when she's worried."

Putting her finger to her lips, she led the way into the nursery. Little Edmund lay on his stomach so that I could see his turned-up nose, the faint brush of eyelash against his cheek, his tiny hand.

"Isn't he beautiful?" Lillian said. "And Lucy, he's smart too. Just like you."

"Thank you, Lillian," I whispered.

At supper that night, we laughed about old times and enjoyed Annabel and took turns holding the baby. But after the dishes were done, we went into the parlor, and Mama said solemnly, "You sit right here by me, Lucy. And now—Annabel, you sit in my lap—we want to hear all about the trouble in Arkansas," she said, patting my knee. "What in the world caused it to happen?" she asked, frowning at Josh as if *he* might have caused it. "And what got into those colored folks up there, anyhow?"

But it was hard to talk about it. And some questions we couldn't answer.

"Josh, who shot Buford Agee? And that Mr. Ditto?" Aunt Catherine asked, when we got to that part.

Josh said we'd probably never know who fired that first shot, but that eleven colored men had been hanged for it. And he said that Sweet Shrub was, in many ways, a lot like Bonham, with its share of people stirring up trouble and not doing right by other people.

And I told about Keats flying off and about Jeremiah running after him. But, not wanting to send Mama into hysterics, I didn't tell her about going out looking for Jeremiah, although I did say a Negro man had been beaten to death. But as Josh and I answered their questions, or tried to, I could tell by the expressions on their faces that the horror we described was as foreign to them as the war in Europe. It was as if Josh and I spoke a language they couldn't understand.

But then, almost as an afterthought, I told them about the chicken on Mildred Elam's table. Aunt Catherine put her hand over her heart, and Edmund got up and walked into our dining room as if he half expected to see it there, and Lillian said it made her ill, really ill, just to think about it. When Mama said maybe we should call the paper, I was sorry I had told the story, angry that it took this, an incident so trivial, to make what had happened real.

But Josh wasn't discouraged. "The thing is," he went on in that slow, thoughtful cadence, "the thing is, it shouldn't have happened. Russ Wickham and men like him are certainly at fault. And yet, in a way, we're all responsible."

"Well, I'm not responsible for what people in Arkansas do. Or don't do," Mama said, bristling.

As if he hadn't been interrupted Josh went right on. "Somehow we've got to make people like Wickham do the right thing. In any town everybody has to be considered, white and colored."

But then he looked at me. "Carrie Belle, this girl's tired. She needs to go to bed." And Mama, in a flurry of turning down our bed and warming it with hot bricks, couldn't get us into bed soon enough.

The next morning I went early to the kitchen, before Queenie came to work. I made a pot of tea and waited. What could I say to her? We had taken Jeremiah off; we had not brought him home. It was a sorrow to bear the rest of my life.

When she came, I hugged her, and sitting across the table from her, I carefully told her everything I knew about Jeremiah. I told her he had planted fruit trees and rosebushes and that he loved Keats. I told her he was proud of the garden and that he liked to work his math problems, and that he and Josh, together, had read about Ulysses. I said that he had asked me if I thought the Lord had pets. I told her he had made a friend in Sweet Shrub, just one, but she was a fine friend to have. I said she was almost as tall as Jeremiah and as slender, but darker, a lovely dusky color. Then I told her about Wickham and about Keats flying off and Jeremiah running after him. And I told her about going out to the lake house to look for Jeremiah and about hearing the running and thinking it was Jeremiah and, then, hearing the sounds of the murder. Last of all, I told her that Jeremiah had kept on being her son in every way. "He was never white," I said.

While I talked, Queenie sat quite still, her face calm. She looked at me once or twice, but most of the time, she gazed out the window. When I had told her all I knew about Jeremiah's brief time in Sweet Shrub, we sat for a while, thinking about him. Then she said, "Jeremiah had some friends alongside that girl. He had you and Mr. Josh."

I felt a deep gratitude for the generosity of those words. "Queenie, I haven't given up. A letter could come. We might hear . . . something."

"We got to hope," she said firmly. "We got to do that."

I started to leave the kitchen, but turned around and came back.

"Queenie, what's your last name?"

"It Brownley," she said. "Mama and Papa name me Elizabeth. Elizabeth Brownley."

"Well, I like it," I told her.

Later, I told Josh about Queenie and about what she had said.

"Queenie's exactly right. We have to hope. And there is a chance that we'll hear from Jeremiah." And in that gentle, thoughtful cadence I had come to love, he went on, "Some folks would just shrivel up and die. But she seems to have quarried a kind of strength from her loss," he said.

"Her full name's Elizabeth Brownley."

"That's a pretty name," Josh said.

Can you settle into any place as fast as you can settle into the town where you grew up? In spite of the fact that the tragedy in Sweet Shrub did not touch my family (and, perhaps, it never would) as it had touched me, their love and solicitude for me were real, and as the days passed I began to feel more like myself. I slept better; my appetite returned. And the terror of Sweet Shrub began to seem like a bad dream. Unless I stopped to think about it.

I quickly fell into old habits—spelling Mama at the hardware store and running down to Lillian's to help with the housework while she nursed the baby—and watched us work.

"Lillian's got to have some help," Mama said. "Little Edmund's a good baby, but she can't do all that work and take care of a baby too. I just hope they don't have any more children. One's about all we can take care of."

Although Mama was concerned about Lillian, her main worry, as far as I was concerned, was white slavers.

"White slavers!" Josh said, incredulously.

"Josh, you and I both know that Lucy's never been prettier now that you've finally brought her home so I can take care of her. And you can laugh if you want to, but the white slavers would love to get Lucy in their clutches."

"Has there been much of that around here?" Josh asked, his eyes twinkling.

But Mama was dead serious. "Personally, I think the white slavers got Olive Ann Lippencott. Everybody says she ran away with the song leader after the Baptist revival, but I'm not sure. I don't think she'd leave that baby. But I tell you, I don't see how her mother sleeps at night."

It was right after supper, and we were in the parlor. Josh was flipping through the new *Liberty* magazine. Mama was turning the collar on one of Edmund's shirts, and Aunt Catherine and I were making a dress for Annabel. She was teaching me how to smock.

Hearing our talk about the new frock and the smocking that was so difficult for me, Josh looked at Annabel. "Annabel, you want a smocked frock?" He laughed and, in high humor, swung her up in his arms.

"Smocked frock. Smocked frock," she chanted, catching up the rhythm, squealing with delight as he danced her across the room.

"Lucy, we need some music," Josh said.

I went over to the piano and played "That Old Girl of Mine." Then I played "Let Me Call You Sweetheart," one of Mama's favorites, and when I got to "Let me hear you whisper that you love me too," Mama stood up and waltzed regally around the room while Aunt Catherine tapped her foot in time to the music.

Then Josh put Annabel down, and bowing to Mama, he asked, "May I have this dance?" and finished the waltz with her. Later that night, he told me, "She misses your father."

I had never thought of it, but I knew he was right.

* * *

Then it was Wednesday, and Bob and Katie were coming home. We looked for them all day and set places on the table for them at dinner. But it was almost time for supper and Mama was beginning to get uneasy when we heard their car, bringing us all to our feet.

Katie stood in the door. Hugging her red muff, with her hair falling from her red woolen cap, she looked like she was about sixteen. I gave her a quick hug, shook hands with Bob, and saying something about finishing the table and heating up the soup, hurried out of the room.

As I put two more soup bowls on the table, opened another jar of peaches, I felt the ache again, close to my heart. I did not want to look at Bob, see his embarrassment. Or indifference. I thought that if I could just throw a cup towel over his head when he came into the dining room and ask him to eat like that, shrouded, the evening would be easier. Wishing I could share the thought with Josh, I went back into the parlor. "Supper's ready," I said.

But with Katie talking on and on, about St. Louis, the clothes she had bought, the plays she had seen, the hotel they had stayed in, supper was easier than I thought. Now Katie leaned forward, pushed her hair up on her head. "Oh, I wish you could have seen the chautauqua program in St. Louis," she said, her voice quivering with excitement. "It was the best one I've ever seen. They had a Red Man, *scare-ee,* a Christian Magician, a College Girl who looked like a star of the silver screen, *and* a Northern Orator."

"A *Northern* Orator," Josh said. "Why, I never heard of such a thing!"

None of us had. Silently, we tried to imagine it.

Josh chuckled. "Must've been a fake," he said.

After supper, the family tried to interest Bob in a number of subjects. The war. "Mama doesn't think we'll get in it," Bob said. The White Star ranch. "Papa says we're not going to run as many cattle on it next year." The Henrietta ranch. "Papa says we haven't had much trouble with the wolves this year."

I glanced at Bob. Sitting in a chair in Mama's parlor, he looked like any man you'd notice and forget. Only his weathered face attested to his ever having been on a horse. I tried to see him again as I had seen him in West Texas, riding across the prairie on his beautiful Surprise.

Josh came to sit by me, pulled his chair close. "Tired?" he whispered. And I knew he was asking, "Do you still care about him? Will some part of you always be his?"

I reached for his hand. Katie chattered on. "Bob, do you remember the name of the restaurant in St. Louis where we ate that first night? Bob? Bob!"

And Bob, answering finally, "What? The restaurant. No, Katie, I don't remember."

Feeling relaxed, easier than I had in a long time, I stood up, stretched. "It's been a long day. I'm going to bed."

As I went upstairs, I heard Josh teasing Mama about getting Bessie shot, and Mama's sharp retort; heard Annabel's "Mama, pick me up. Pick me up!"

Sitting in the window seat, I remembered all those times I had spent with Bob and thought his silence interesting. But I had never known what he thought. I wondered if anybody knew. Catching the faint smell of cigar smoke, I unlatched the screen and stuck my head out the window. "Josh? Where are you?"

I heard him walk across the porch, down the steps, and out into the yard. "What is it, Lucy?"

I couldn't see him, but I knew he stood there, in the darkness, looking up at my window.

"Come to bed," I told him.

Hearing his steps, first on the porch and then coming up the stairs, I slipped off my gown, let it fall to the floor. He opened the door and came toward me. "Sweetheart, let's go to bed," I said, and I opened my arms to him.

This morning a letter came, asking us to return to Sweet Shrub. The school was to be reopened. And Peter Dexter had added a postscript: "Would Lucinda consider teaching for a few weeks? Just until we can find someone? Miss Twinkle will not be coming back. I think it's simply that she's afraid."

Josh was restless. And it had rained all day. Since the middle of the morning the wind had blown, bending the hollyhocks to the ground, tearing the honeysuckle off the fence, and about noon a big limb from the magnolia tree came down.

All day long I had thought about Sweet Shrub, imagined the school children jumping rope while they waited for the bell to ring, the girls in their starched cotton dresses and the boys with haircuts so new that the napes of their necks showed white as the palms of their hands. And coming into the school with the small blooms of the shrub in their pockets and lunch boxes and behind their ears, the school would be filled with a light, lemony scent that would drift out the windows and over the town.

I could see the garden at the lake, everything in bloom. The white plum blossoms, the pale pinks of the peach trees, the brilliant contrast of the red and white roses. And a gleaming flash of blue, circling and circling, and Jeremiah waiting, with his arm outstretched, waiting for Keats. And over the garden and the school and the town, the house on the lake, brooding, warmly brooding, over us all.

Well, some of it could happen! I told myself. I found Josh in the swing on the front porch.

"Let's go back," I told him. "There's a lot to do."

His eyes lit up. "Are you sure?"

When I nodded, he smiled. "Come sit here a minute," he said, patting the seat beside him.

I sat down, gently pushed the swing into motion.

I looked at the magnolia tree, shining from the rain, and at the sky. It was clearing a little. But it was colder too. I shivered and Josh drew me close.

"I'll write to Peter," Josh said. "Tell him to expect us right after Christmas? How's that sound?"

That sounded just fine to me.

AUTHOR'S NOTE

This is a work of fiction. Names, characters, places, and incidents are either the product of my imagination or are used fictitiously. Although Bonham is a small East Texas town with "a rich bounty of natural beauty—roses and honeysuckle, cedars and oaks, elms, too, and still lakes and pretty little streams and everywhere the greens and yellows," all the Bonham characters, as well as those in the imaginary community of Sweet Shrub, are fictitious. The "four days of terror" incident described here was inspired by an incident that occurred in Arkansas just after World War I, but the depiction of and characters described in this incident are entirely fictional.